THE LAST ARTIFACT

A TRILOGY BY GILLIAM NESS

BOOK ONE
THE DARK RIFT

Published by POLYMATH PUBLISHING
Toronto, Canada.

POLYMATH PUBLISHING and the portrayal of the letter "P" within the box are trademarks of Polymath Publishing.

All of the characters and events in this book are fictitious, and any resemblance they might have to actual persons, living or dead, is purely coincidental.

January 2016

This novel is dedicated to the 28% of voters who believe that a secretive, powerful elite is conspiring to rule the world through an authoritarian world government (or New World Order).
It is also dedicated to the 14% of citizens who believe there is at least a small chance of a zombie apocalypse actually happening, as well as the 13% of voters who think that the President of the United States is the anti-Christ, and the 4% of voters who believe that "lizard people" really do control our society.*

*U.S. Public Policy Poling - April 02, 2013
U.S. YouGov Omnibus - May 17, 2013

ACKNOWLEDGEMENTS

First and foremost I would like to thank my dear friend and fellow visionary, Paul Gillespie, for listening to countless hours of my preposterous ruminations (over loads of cheap scotch) and consistently encouraging me to bring this, my very first novel, through to its conclusion. And to my equally dear friends, Lou Martinez and Christopher McEnroe, who poured diligently through duct-taped manuscripts to offer up indispensable criticisms when I needed them the most. Immeasurable thanks to Raika Sheppard, who helped me edit the first drafts.

My thanks once again to Christopher McEnroe, and Paul Gillespie, for helping me to create the awesome video sequences used in this book's trailer, as well as to the talented David Osborne, for his outstanding narration. To my dear friends, Ellen Bateman, and Andrea Corlett, I extend my eternal gratitude for their constant support, as well as to Andrew Vale for his excellent observations, and Jim Latimer for a brilliantly insightful commentary that led to the book's final polishing. I thank them all a million times over.

Finally, in a novel drawing so heavily on primordial wisdom, sublime truth, and humanity's incessant quest for knowledge, I would be remiss if I did not thank the late Eva Pierrakos, whose enlightened lectures on spiritual evolution have been the central source of all the wisdom in this book. Her work truly has been one of the main inspirations that led me to write this trilogy, and wherever she happens to be, I thank her deeply, and with all my heart.

CAST OF CHARACTERS

Dr. Gabriel Parker - Relic hunter and archaeologist. Adoptive son of Professor Agardi Metrovich.

Dr. Natasha Rossi - Artifact historian and theologian. Adoptive daughter of Father Franco Rossi.

Bishop Marcus di Lauro - Head of the Vatican's department of exorcisms and paranormal anomalies. Close family friend to Gabriel and Natasha.

Fra Bartolomeo - Christian brother, and former school teacher. Old friend and assistant to Bishop Marcus di Lauro.

Suora Angelica - Nun, and former school teacher. Old friend and assistant to Bishop Marcus di Lauro.

Professor Agardi Metrovich - Historian, retired relic hunter, and psychiatrist. Adoptive father of Gabriel.

Father Franco Rossi - Priest and Exorcist. Adoptive guardian of Natasha.

Isaac Rodchenko - Brother of Christian Antov. Disowned from the Antov family as an adolescent. Father of the prophesied beast.

Peralta - Gibraltarian smuggler, computer hacker, and engineer. Close friend of Amir and Bahadur.

Amir Mustafa - Trusted assistant of Dr. Gabriel Parker.

Bahadur Mustafa- Former smuggling cartel Captain to Najiallah Nasrallah. Cousin of Amir Mustafa.

Scotty Roberts - Smuggler and close friend of Bahadur and Amir. The brother of Major Richard Roberts.

Major Richard Roberts - Aide-du-Camp to the Governor of Gibraltar. Brother of Scotty Roberts.

Sir William Bentley - Governor of Gibraltar. Mentor of Major Richard Roberts.

Brother Bernardo - Spanish monk in the service of *The Order of St. James the Just*.

Sir David - Captain of the knights of *The Order of Saint James the Just*, and sworn protector of The Two.

Sir Shackleton - AKA: *Melchizedek*. The mysterious dog.

Christian Antov - Recently appointed chairman of the Vanderhoff Group Steering Committee, Anti-Christ, and brother of Isaac Rodchenko.

Doctor Bennington - Psychiatrist to Christian Antov.

Najiallah Nasrallah - Moroccan drug lord and archeology aficionado.

Father Adrianus Vanderwerken - AKA: *The Nautonnier*. Head priest of the shadow organization behind the Vanderhoff Group. Mentor to Isaac Rodchenko.

Prince Vladimir Rodchenko - Vanderhoff Group Steering Committee member. Uncle to Christian Antov.

FRIGHTENING CONSPIRACY THEORIES
- That Appear In This Novel -

The Bilderberg Group Conspiracy —revolves around a real life secret society that was founded in 1954. According to Wikipedia (and numerous other perfectly reputable internet sources) every year 100-120 of the world's most powerful elite (including Presidents and Prime Ministers currently in office) get together in 5 star resorts and hold secret meetings about world governance. Theorists claim that the organization is part of a sinister shadow government that secretly rules the world. In the off chance that it's all true, they are referred to here as the *Vanderhoff Group* (after all, there's no need to piss anybody off, right?).

The New World Order Conspiracy —revolves around a coming fascist world government that, according to many homemade YouTube documentaries, will be split into four unions: The European Union, The American Union, The Asian Union, and the African Union. It will all be headed up by a shadow government under the guise of the United Nations. People (or *Sheeple)* will be governed by martial law and advanced biometric technology in a dystopian environment.

The Zombie Apocalypse Conspiracy —revolves around a secret, genetically engineered virus designed by the government to cull the world's population by turning people into undead cannibals.

The Reptilian Race Conspiracy —revolves around the existence of an elite race of multi-dimensional, demonic, shape-shifting reptilians that currently pose as our leaders. According to a prominent British writer, public speaker and former sports broadcaster, they have every intention of enslaving humanity.

The Evil Pope Conspiracy —revolves around the purported Satanic roots of the Roman Catholic Church, and its history of manipulation of holy scripture so as to further its quest for world dominance, and the enslavement of all souls (by far the most likely of all the theories listed here).

The Bloodline of Christ Conspiracy —revolves around a secret society (with sexy French chicks) whose ancestry can be traced back to a child that Jesus had with Mary Magdalene.

The Galactic Plane Conspiracy —states that climate change is not the result of silly carbon emissions, but rather due to the fact that our entire solar system is moving into the galaxy's super-dense equator. It expounds that this is a cyclical, astronomical event that always culminates in an extinction level cataclysm. Of course NASA knows all about this, but what good could possibly come from telling everyone?

AUTHOR'S NOTE

After the many years of deep contemplation that have brought me to this, my *Opus Magnum Unifying Theory Of All Things Light And Dark*, my best advice to you, my esteemed reader, can only be this: Stockpile Kraft Dinner. You'll be able to trade it for all kinds of stuff when the zombies come, and if everything goes wrong, and the apocalypse never happens, then it'll all get eaten anyway. That crap never goes bad.

—GILLIAM NESS

BOOK ONE
THE DARK RIFT

...And then the final days arrived,
When all the wild imaginings of men came to pass.
When the myths, theories, and legends were made manifest,
And the prophecies and suspicions were fulfilled.

In those final days they trembled and cried:
"How came we to conceive of such monstrous inventions?"
For the gods and demons they had imagined were all realized.
And a great shadow spread across the world.

-The Great Fall of the Angels
(From the Compostela Manuscripts, circa 865A.D.)

The Cantabrian Mountains – 2243 B.C.

A heavy mantle of fog clung to the surface of the small mountain lake, its dark waters emitting a profound stillness. Amid the gurgle of a slow moving paddle, a primitive dugout made its way out into the gloom, its two occupants dwarfed by the looming peaks that encased it on all sides. There was not a soul in sight.

The boy with the paddle completed another stroke, the boat sliding effortlessly forward. Their destination lay just ahead; a tiny island enshrouded in mist.

"It is strange here," said the girl in the boat, "but it does not seem as dangerous as they say."

There was something otherworldly about this place. It was sending waves of excitement through her. Like the boy, she too had turned twelve that day, and to celebrate their birthdays they had decided to investigate the mysterious island, knowing full well that they were forbidden to do so. She studied its dense tangle of trees.

"I want to go ashore."

The boy frowned.

"That was not the plan," he said. "We only came to look."

"We do not have to go into the shrine. We can just find it and see what it looks like."

The boy shot a suspicious glance at the island and then made up his mind.

"Very well," he said. "We go."

They circled the island until they had found a place to land. Above them a veiled sun was already beginning to dip behind the mountains, and the girl felt a sudden twinge of fear. The shadowy trees were dense and ominous.

"It is getting dark too quickly," she said. "We should go back."

"We are here," said the boy. "We will look."

He jumped from the primitive dugout and dragged it up onto the rocks, holding out his hand for the girl to take.

"Very well," she said. "But only for a moment."

The island was unkempt, and the vegetation quite dense. Lush ferns covered most of the ground, and many of the rocks were rounded over with moss. From where they stood, a path could be seen climbing into the foliage. It picked its way through the rocky terrain in a series of natural steps and landings. The two were soon finding it quite easy to navigate their way up.

"My love," said the girl, following behind.

The boy frowned.

"Do not call me that."

She shrugged.

"This was a mistake."

"Why do you say that?" asked the boy.

She peered into the woods. She thought she had seen a shadowy figure moving through the trees.

"I feel we are in danger," she said. "What if the Druid Fathers are not mistaken?"

"The Druid Fathers are old fools," said the boy. "People no longer believe their stories. Come along. Let us see for ourselves."

It was not long before they arrived at a small, circular clearing, not twenty feet in diameter. There was no visible shrine here, only what appeared to be a large flattened boulder located directly at its centre. As they made their way towards it they could see the weathered image of a maze carved into its surface, with a crude figure of a man standing at its entrance. The carving seemed ancient, and was covered in lichen and moss. More disturbing still was what lay at the outer extremities of the clearing: A grouping of fourteen standing stones, each as tall as a man, and forming a perfect circle around them.

"What is this place?" asked the girl.

The boy shook his head and frowned.

"I do not know."

The sound of a large bird taking flight startled the girl. As her eyes followed it up through the tangled boughs she saw how dim the sky had become, and noticed only then the darkness that was growing in the woods. She found herself wishing that she were far away from the island, and more importantly, from this disturbing circle of stones.

"I am frightened," she said, clutching the boy. "Let us go now. I do not like the way this island makes me feel."

"Just a little while longer," he said, taking her hand. "Come along. We are very close."

She followed him reluctantly, deeper and deeper into the thick. It seemed to her that the island was swallowing them alive. After a five minute hike the boy stopped suddenly, his heart pounding with excitement as he pulled her into yet another clearing.

"This must be the place," he said, oblivious to the paralyzing fear that had overtaken her.

"Wait," he muttered, his eyes straining. "What is this?"

He could see the standing stones looming in a circle around them. They had somehow returned to the same place, and something felt terribly wrong. It was too dark. At some point the overcast sky had transformed into a starless void, and only the muted light of a crescent moon leaked through the twisted branches above.

"We have been walking in circles," he stammered.

A shrill pitch of the purest fear was ringing through his body now. He could not understand. The air had become frigidly cold.

"The Druid Fathers were right," he whispered, shaking his head in horror. "By the gods, what have we done?"

A deep and inky void had appeared where the central monolith had been, but just then, something even more unsettling came into view. Shadowy figures were materializing behind the standing stones. They were stumbling forward, their arms hanging limply at their sides, their gazes vacant and cold. The boy's eyes opened wide with fear. These people were dead. Their flesh was crawling with worms, yet they somehow still walked.

"No!" he grunted, unable to move. "This is impossible."

It was only then that it came. It was an invisible force of unimaginable potency. It moved over the two of them with the momentum of an ocean tide, forcing them both to the ground, and driving the sight from their eyes.

CHAPTER 1

Istanbul, Turkey.

Professor Agardi Metrovich staggered out of the examination room and into the hall of the private Istanbul hospital. He was a large, bearded man, dressed in a tweed sports jacket with frayed cuffs. The door closed behind him as he exited, shutting out the chanting priests as they continued with their archaic ritual. Through the walls, the weary Professor could still hear the spitting curses coming from his patient, a sensation of pure evil crawling over his skin like a thousand insects.

As he had expected, he was instantly approached by Isaac Rodchenko, the victim's father. The latter was a patient himself, a decade younger than he, and stricken with paranoid schizophrenia. Over the course of the evening the unearthly cries had driven the poor man into a state of despair.

"Professor Metrovich!" he whispered, his eyes straining with worry. "You must tell me what is happening to my child!"

The Professor could only stare back at him, his own face pale and drawn with fear. After decades of medically overseeing exorcisms, the seasoned Professor had yet to overcome the horror that the rituals consistently provoked in him. He struggled with his emotions, finding comfort in the words of an ancient text he had long ago unearthed in his research.

Fear is an illusion; a ghost without substance. It is easily dispelled.

In many cases, suspected victims were merely suffering from severe psychotic dementia, but on rare occasions such as this, events could not be explained so readily. Demonic possession was an anomaly that defied all rational thought. It was something not of this earth.

"Please, sit down, Mr. Rodchenko," the Professor managed to say, and following his own advice, he collapsed heavily into one of the waiting armchairs. "You must give me a moment to regain my strength."

Isaac Rodchenko sat down at once. He had a healthy complexion for his sixty odd years, along with thick salt and pepper hair and black eyebrows. He wore an elegant charcoal grey suit, and had an air of humble confidence about him, despite his distress. For a long moment Isaac waited obediently, but could contain himself no longer.

"My son has spent thirty-three years in a vegetative state," he said, rubbing his hands together nervously. "How is it possible that he should have awakened from it now, and in this condition? I know you are keeping something from me, Professor. Have pity on a suffering father. Tell me, please!"

The old Professor held Isaac's gaze for a moment, but then let his eyes fall.

How could I possibly tell this man what I suspect to be true?

"Professor Metrovich!" insisted Isaac. "You must tell me at once!"

Metrovich looked up, his tired eyes scanning the distressed face before him. He opened his mouth, as though to speak, but before he could do so an unearthly scream split the silence. It was followed immediately by a call from one of the priests inside.

"Professor! Come quickly!"

In one clumsy motion the Professor rose from his chair and passed into the examination room, a stench of rot and suffering engulfing him as he entered. There, in the half light, he could see two priests hunched over the possessed man, his repulsively obese body contorting in a series of slow and twisting seizures. Having already been severely deformed since birth, the effects of the possession had transformed the victim into something utterly horrific. Metrovich looked to the priests. They stood there in quiet resignation, praying silently over the hideous beast.

"We are losing him, Professor," whispered the ancient Father Franco.

The Professor's eyes found the electrocardiogram and saw that the old priest was not mistaken. The patient had entered into cardiac arrest. In his weakened state, there would be no way of saving him. His joints creaked woodenly as he lurched and twisted, his body becoming suddenly still before moving into a violent death rattle. When it was done, the heart monitor gave off a flat, uninterrupted tone, and crossing himself, Father Franco reached over and muted the alarm.

With the death of the victim, a deep silence had fallen over the room, a residual feeling of the supernatural hanging in the air like a pall. In all his years of overseeing exorcisms, Metrovich had never witnessed a more ghastly case as this, and judging by the expressions on the two priests, he could see that they had not done so either.

Metrovich moved towards the corpse. Ever since they had arrived earlier that evening, he had been plagued by a persistent gut feeling; it warned of something so unlikely that it seemed ludicrous that he should even be considering it.

He took hold of the urine soaked gown that covered the victim's lower torso, but froze instantly in the act. He thought he had felt a slight tremor running through the corpse, and in that instant, a wave of fear rippled through him. He looked more closely. The cadaver was visibly trembling. His eyes darted to the ECG. It was still showing a flat-line.

This is impossible. The body is dead.

Metrovich looked back in time to see the ghastly corpse jerk to life.

"Ahreimanius!" it hissed menacingly, the upper body lurching violently toward him.

All watched in horror as the restraining straps gave way, the thrashing corpse coming dangerously close to the Professor before collapsing back onto the bed. A final quake ran through the body.

Struggling to keep himself composed, the Professor reached forward to resume his task, drawing slowly aside the gown that covered the lower half of its torso. What he saw filled him with horror and disgust. Behind him Father Franco gagged and coughed.

Plainly visible in front of them, grotesque and utterly malformed, were a pair of lacerated genitals, disproportionately large, and belonging to both the male and female sexes. It was at that moment that a shaft of light split the darkness, and Isaac's swaying silhouette appeared in the doorway. He stared blankly at the scene before him.

"You did not tell us that your son was a hermaphrodite, Mr. Rodchenko," said Metrovich softly, his eyes still glued to the victim.

Isaac seemed to wince at the statement.

"Is he dead?"

The Professor turned to face the grieving father, but said nothing, his expression containing a mixture of compassion and confusion. With this latest development, twenty years of skepticism had been suddenly stripped from his mind. The evidence was now irrefutable; the coincidences far too numerous to discount. Through the death of this unfortunate victim, an ancient and obscure prophecy had somehow been made manifest. The impossible had somehow transpired.

"I know this is difficult for you, Mr. Rodchenko," said Metrovich slowly. "Can you remember where your son was conceived?"

The Professor's words struck Isaac like a dull blow. He was too drugged to sense any pain, but the question probed one of the primary causes of his illness. His wife had died while giving birth to their misshapen son, and he had never recovered from the loss of her. Over the years he had progressively lost his mind. He fell to his knees, rocking himself to and fro.

"My wife and I were on a religious pilgrimage in the mountains of northern Spain," he muttered, his eyes squinting ever so slightly as he remembered. "We were on a small lake. We had found a little island…"

Metrovich tore his gaze from Isaac and turned to face Father Franco. The old priest looked back at him, his eyes alight with foreboding.

"God help us all," he said solemnly.
Outside a rumbling chorus of thunder sounded. The storm that had long been approaching had finally arrived.

CHAPTER 2

Florence, Italy.

The thirty-two-year-old Dr. Natasha Rossi sat amid the clutter of her small restoration shop. Before her on a battered workbench lay the ninth century tabernacle she had been working on. It was almost finished. Directly behind it, a large monitor displayed a three-dimensional, infrared scan of the piece. Her computer had just finished rendering it, and she was using it to spot tiny deposits that had been missed during the restoration process. Playing in the background, as usual, was one of her many self-help audiobooks.

...for this reason, traumas in our past relationships can be part of the reason why we keep attracting selfish jerks into our lives. We feel compelled to fix the things that went wrong the last time, and this can happen over and over again until we finally become aware of the cycle...

Natasha applied solvent to a tiny deposit of paraffin lodged in the tabernacle's base, nodding in agreement the whole while. As she listened, she thought bitterly about her disastrous love life, and the seven months she had just wasted on her ex-boyfriend. She had recently discovered that he was married, and she found herself wondering how she could be so adept at finding the tiniest flaws in artifacts when she was so blind to the most blatant flaws in men. Or maybe she was aware of their flaws, and simply thought that their imperfections were something that could be removed if she was meticulous enough, like stripping dirt from an old tabernacle.

"He really was a jerk…" she whispered, blowing a lock of hair out of her eyes as she worked.

It was a dark chestnut colour and fell thick and curly over her shoulders.

"And it *is* true. I really did try to fix him."

Natasha's accent was Italian, but three years at Harvard had tempered it nicely. She ran through her positive affirmations, feeling another wave of depression coming on.

I am strong and powerful. My thoughts and actions create my destiny.

Christmas was approaching, and Natasha was dreading it. There would be all the parties and church functions she would have to attend, and she would be alone the entire time. It seemed to her that she was always alone, even if she happened to be dating someone. The only time Natasha ever felt truly sociable was when she was dancing, but even her love of the ballet had brought her disappointment of late. Natasha's challenging little role in this years' production of *The Nutcracker Suite* had disappeared when the show was cancelled due to poor ticket sales. Months of grueling practice had been lost in the blink of an eye.

Looking out through the panes of her shop front window, Natasha could see the little piazza outside. Its stalls were uncharacteristically quiet for a mid-December afternoon. Christmas in Florence was normally a magical time, but this year had been very different.

After a devastating terrorist attack in Los Angeles, the U.S. economy had suddenly collapsed like a deck of cards. Italy had been thrust into a severe economic depression as a result, along with the majority of the planet. It had left the streets of the Renaissance city bereft of tourists and holiday shoppers alike.

Natasha had been more fortunate than most. Seemingly unaffected by the global crisis, the Vatican had continued business as usual, proceeding with its museum renovations and inundating Natasha's little restoration shop with dozens of artifacts needing to be catalogued and cleaned. It was a tedious job, but one that was constantly reenergized by the small chance that something new might be revealed as the layers of carbon and paraffin were stripped away.

It was this act of revealing, and her strong passion for it, that had inspired Natasha to work in artifact restoration to begin with. Having grown up surrounded by religious relics, it seemed a natural extension to the doctorate she held in theology. With her combined skills, she could not only delve into the mysteries of the spiritual world, but also into those of the material. It was the perfect marriage of knowledge and skill, and one that she had found to be very rewarding over the years.

Natasha laid down her tools and rose from her chair, stretching herself as she did so. Across from her a sixteenth century mirror reminded her of how many hours she had been working.

"I look horrible," she whispered, the tips of her fingers automatically arranging her bangs to cover the pale, dime-sized scar at the centre of her forehead.

It had been there for as long as she could remember; the remnant of abuses she had suffered in an orphanage as an infant. There were other burn marks on her body as well. Plastic surgery in her late teens had made the scars almost imperceptible, but they still haunted Natasha nonetheless. They were ghosts of an evil that had touched her before her earliest memories. They made her feel malformed and inadequate, despite her rational knowledge that they were practically invisible. Although everyone had always insisted that Natasha was a beauty, she had always felt a little like a fraud. She thought her soft brown eyes were far too big for her face, and that her body was far too skinny.

Continuing with her stretching, Natasha approached the windows in time to see a mass of heavy cloud swallow the sun. The bright afternoon was transforming into an ominous grey, and within moments, heavy drops of rain began to spatter the cobblestones outside. Following a particularly violent barrage of thunder and lightning, Natasha turned to find that her computer had shut down, along with all the lights in the room. Outside, the storm exploded into a deluge.

"I forgot to save that scan..." she said gloomily, and then her eyes darted to the front door.

A powerful gust of wind had just blown it open, bringing with it a spray of torrential rain. Natasha wasted no time. Priceless artifacts were getting wet. She arrived at the breach in seconds, reaching up to take hold of the outer door and slamming it down with a crash. The workshop plunged into darkness. It was only then that a distinct and irregular banging could be heard coming from the back room.

"What is that?"

A wave of fear ran through her. Natasha was not one to be easily frightened, but she could not deny the eerie feeling that accompanied the sounds she was hearing. She dispelled her fears and made her way into the darkness. The banging would have to be seen to.

For almost one hundred years, the back area of the workshop had been used as a storeroom; a place that Natasha rarely ventured into. It was cluttered with thousands of religious artifacts, and bric-a-brac of every kind, its few naked bulbs never providing enough light to dispel the fears she had held for the place since she was a child. Even still, she now found herself venturing into its depths, groping through cobwebs with nothing but a flashlight to illuminate her way.

"Hello? Is anybody there?"

A crack of thunder sounded as if in response.

Natasha bit her lip and made her way into the maze of cluttered shelves, stepping around obstacles with grace despite her fear. She swallowed slowly. She could feel the little hairs on her arms and neck standing on end. It was as if something had invaded her workshop; something paranormal; something demonic. She reminded herself how ludicrous this sounded, but she frowned in confusion nonetheless. All Natasha's instincts were telling her to flee, yet there was something else drawing her forward despite her fear.

It was not long before Natasha found the source of the banging, and she breathed a sigh of relief. The same gust of wind that had blown open the front door had opened the back door as well. She could see it swinging to and fro in the dim light of a gas lamp outside, banging the old door frame at irregular intervals. Its rusted latch had obviously given way under the jolt of wind.

Natasha looked down suddenly and swallowed hard. There was a tattered street dog crouching in the shadows of an antique cabinet, its eyes glowing coldly in the reflected light. It stood as if ready to pounce and Natasha felt her body going limp with fear.

It must have come in when the door blew open.

Natasha knew the way of animals. She knew that if she were to escape this situation unharmed, she would have to conquer her fears and emit a feeling of tranquility. She moved to sit down as slowly as she could, but stopped herself halfway. The dog was not growling at her, but rather at something else; something behind her.

Natasha jerked her head around, the dog lunging forward as she did so, but there was nothing there. Looking back at the dog, she saw that it was pacing around nervously, the hair on its back still on end. Animals could see things that humans could not, she knew this, but what had it seen? Her mobile phone rang suddenly just then, the shrill tone of it startling the dog. With a loud bark he bolted, rushing through the back door and vanishing into the storm.

"Pronto?" she said, bringing the phone to her ear.

She was hurrying to the door now, wanting nothing but to close it. Outside a sheet of lightning lit up the sky.

"Is this Natasha Rossi?" said a crackling voice on the other end of the line.

It spoke in English, but bore a heavy Spanish accent.

"Yes."

"Miss Rossi, this is Sergeant Alberto Martinez of the Spanish Civil Guard. I am afraid I have some very distressing news, señorita."

"Yes, I am listening," said Natasha, a sick feeling growing in her stomach.

She closed the door and locked it shut. Darkness engulfed her.

"I am so sorry, señorita. A private plane chartered yesterday by Professor Agardi Metrovich and Father Franco Rossi has crashed in the mountains southwest of Santander. All including the pilot have been killed. Father Franco was your legal guardian, no?"

"What have you done with him?"

"We managed to land a paramedic to see if there were any survivors, señorita, but there were none. Their plane is very high in the mountains, and it is in a very dangerous position to access due to the high winds. We have been unable to retrieve their bodies. This might not be possible until the coming spring, señorita."

"I see," said Natasha, lost in a daze. "Thank you, Sergeant."

Natasha sank to the floor, the musty storeroom plunging into blackness as the light from her mobile phone went out. Father Franco had cared for her since she was a little girl, and if those at the church orphanage in Rome had been her family, Father Franco had been her father. Now he was gone, and her heart burst open with grief.

Natasha's thoughts went to Father Franco's lifelong friend, the Bishop Marcus Di Lauro. He lived close to the orphanage in Rome, and had been like an uncle to Natasha all her life. He and Father Franco had been inseparable since they were young students.

How can I tell him what has happened? He is too old. The shock will kill him.

Suddenly, from within the inky hollows that surrounded her, the sinister presence that Natasha had felt only moments before, returned. It seeped over her like fetid flood water.

"Oh, God," she moaned. "Make it go away."

But the evil remained. In her sorrow she almost welcomed it.

CHAPTER 3

Boston, Massachusetts.

Dr. Gabriel Parker tilted the bottle and watched as the golden liquid tumbled over the ice in his glass. It was shimmering in the halogen light of his bedside lamp. He threw himself back onto the oversized pillows, bringing the glass to his lips and inhaling deeply before downing its contents in one gulp.

Gabriel looked up to see a beautiful young blonde working her way into a pair of tight jeans at the foot of his bed, and then watched expressionlessly as she strapped a lacy bra over her perfect breasts. A second later she was back on the bed, straddling him, and giving him a deep and sensual kiss.

"Yum," she said, pulling away and savouring the whiskey on her lips. "You taste like a man."

Gabriel's hands explored her curves, travelling over her body and down to her buttocks.

"I taste like whiskey," he said, giving her bottom a squeeze.

The girl kissed him again. When she pulled away Gabriel noticed she was pouting.

"What's wrong now?" he asked, stretching over to refill his glass.

"What's wrong with you, Gabriel?" she said, her eyes downcast and sultry.

Her fingers were tracing over a dime-sized scar at the centre of his chest. It had always fascinated her. Gabriel took a gulp of scotch and then lifted her chin to have a look at her.

"Nothing's wrong," he said. "I'm just tired."

She raised an eyebrow.

"You've never been tired before…"

The girl ran her fingers through his shaggy brown hair, and then traced them over the stubble on his chin. He had a strong jaw; perfectly at home with his rugged features. Hidden behind the stubble on his throat she found the other scar, and then pushing aside a thick lock of hair, she traced her thumb over the one on his forehead.

"Are you getting tired of me?" she asked.

Gabriel put down his glass and sat up.

"Listen, Mica—"

"Mica's my working name," said the girl, pouting. "You know that. I'm Mary."

"Mary— " began Gabriel, but she cut him off.

"You still haven't told me about these scars," she said, kissing the one on his forehead.

Gabriel felt the usual pang of discomfort at the mention of the scars, and it annoyed him as always. He was thirty-two years old. Should he not have got over this nonsense by now? A recurring scene played itself out in Gabriel's mind.

"Hey, Ashtray!" cried one of the bullies who surrounded him. *"Has daddy been using you to butt out his smokes?"*

"Ashtray did it to himself!" said another. *"Faggets love pain!"*

The group of boys exploded into laughter.

"Ashtray's gay! Ashtray's gay!"

"Earth calling Gabriel…" said Mary, looking down at him intently. "The scars…?"

Gabriel drained his glass and then feigned severity.

"Electrode torture marks from the Iraqi prison."

She slapped him playfully.

"You're never going to tell me, are you!"

Gabriel reached over and poured some more scotch into his glass. Time, and his general hairiness, had made the scars almost imperceptible, but it had not been like that when he was a boy. Back then they had stood out starkly; like bumpy red cigar burns. Gabriel told himself that the mysterious scars had made him strong, but the truth was they had only made him proud. As a boy, the pain of the constant taunting had turned into apathy, which in turn became arrogance; a defensive trait that still plagued him to this day.

"Tell me," whispered the girl, nibbling at his ear. "You know how much I love you."

Gabriel forced himself to be patient. He hated hearing this kind of thing. It was not necessary.

"You don't love me, Mary," he said. "I'm a regular customer who treats you well."

Mary smiled naughtily, her pretty hands finding his crotch.

"You treat me *very* well."

Gabriel gave her a gentle shove that sent her tumbling to the other side of the bed with a squeal. He got up and pulled on a pair of baggy brown pants and a sleeveless undershirt, securing his belt as he made his way to a nearby table. Gabriel had a flat stomach and strong arms, his legs, back and shoulders shaped by a lifetime of deep sea diving. He took hold of the battered leather duffel bag that lay on the table before him, opening it slowly and double checking the things he had packed inside.

He was not having a great day, or a great month for that matter. Something in Gabriel ached with emptiness, and he knew it was not entirely due to the recent death of his father. Gabriel was feeling a general weariness with the world, as though everything were losing its meaning. He could not understand what was causing it. Nothing had changed. He had been happily living like this for a decade now; lecturing at the university, researching and locating sunken ships and lost treasures, entertaining beautiful women in every port, and getting together with his friends and colleagues on a regular basis. Life was full and exciting. Even still, Gabriel could see that something was not right. He would be turning thirty-three soon. Something was changing in him, even if he could not say what it was.

"Where are you going this time, Gabriel Parker?" asked Mary, her voice sounding timid as she came up behind him. "Take me with you. I hate Boston."

Gabriel turned around and looked at her, forcing himself to smile. It was not difficult. The girl was riveting. Her blonde hair was falling like satin over her perfect, suntanned shoulders, making the silky strands almost glow in contrast. Gabriel took her by a belt loop and pulled her to him, giving her an assertive kiss. When he was done he opened her hand and gave her a roll of banknotes, carefully closing her fingers around it.

"You don't have to pay me this time, Gabriel," she said quietly. "We haven't done anything."

He walked her to the front door, producing his phone as he did so. It was buzzing. His electronic boarding pass had just come in.

"I'm sorry to kick you out," he said, opening the door for her, "but I've got a plane to catch."

CHAPTER 4

Rome, Italy.

To anyone else, the distant knocking would have been impossible to hear, but even in his eighty-third year of life, Fra Bartolomeo's hearing had remained as acute as it had been when he was a boy.

"A blessing and curse you have given to me, Father," he prayed aloud.

His accent was thickly Italian, but years spent in the service of a British-born Bishop had made English his habitual tongue.

"Where is Suora when one needs her?"

The old Christian brother gave a long sigh of resignation. He was in the kitchen's pantry, attempting to extricate a box of tea biscuits from the back of a cluttered shelf. The distant knocking was persistent, and he knew that it was coming from a rarely used service door located at the back of the rectory.

"Nobody ever knows which door to use."

He made his way along ancient hallways belonging to what had once been a small monastery, centuries before. Located in the centre of Rome, it was now the private residence of the retired Bishop Marcus Di Lauro, a man whom despite his advanced age was still very active in church matters, especially those pertaining to the paranormal.

Fra Bartolomeo accelerated his pace, arriving at the door just as the knocking stopped. Opening it, he saw a delivery man walking away.

"Si, pronto!" he exclaimed, scratching the back of his head where a little bit of silver hair still grew. "Can I be of assistance?"

"I have a delivery for the Bishop," said the courier, turning around.

"I will take it to him, my son."

The old, white-bearded Bishop Marcus was at his desk when he heard the quiet knock on his door. He took one last look at the framed photograph he had been studying, and then turned to place it back on the credenza behind him. It was an image of himself standing before Mont St. Michel, in the company of his two dearest friends: Father Franco Rossi, and Professor Agardi Metrovich; both recently lost.

"I am an old man now," he whispered, producing a well used handkerchief from his pocket.

"I will see you both very soon, my friends."

He vacated his nose in a series of short, staccato salvos, and then cleared his throat.

"Come in," he said in perfect British tenor.

Fra Bartolomeo appeared at the door. As always he wore threadbare corduroy pants, a flannel shirt, and a tattered woolen cardigan, each article a different shade of the same muted grey. He held out a small parcel in both hands.

"A package has arrived for you, your Excellency."

"Thank you, Fra," said the Bishop, smiling kindly. "Come in, come in. What say you to having our Cognac a little early today?"

When their drinks were done, and the old Brother was off on his business again, Bishop Marcus leaned forward and picked up the package.

"Father Franco," he said quietly. "What could you possibly have sent me?"

In the package the old Bishop found the battered leather-bound journal he had so often seen the Professor with. He picked up the accompanying letter and scrutinized it through a brass rimmed magnifying glass. It was from Father Franco, and written on the day of his death. He held it under his desk lamp and proceeded to read.

Istanbul, November 29.

My dear friend,

The exorcism was a complete failure, the victim dying just hours into the ritual. We were shocked to discover that he was intersexed; a hermaphrodite. Impossible as it seems, last night's possession reflects the myth perfectly. The Professor is now convinced that the Cube of Compostela still exists. He claims that it is residing in the archives of the Museum of Antiquities in Tangiers.

As I write, we are awaiting a chartered plane that will be taking us to the place of the hermaphrodite's conception. It is an island on a small lake in the mountains south of Santander. We fear that this is the island mentioned in the prophecy. There is a deep dread in me.

The Professor believes the time has come to unite Gabriel and Natasha. He does insist, however, that the two of them be united before the Cube is recovered. He has asked that I send you his Cube diary so that you might study it with them. As you know, everything he has learned concerning the artifact is contained within it. Enclosed you will find the name of the Professor's contact at the Vatican museum. He will assist you in obtaining the Cube.

Your faithful friend, F.R.

The old Bishop laid the letter out on his desk and fell back into his chair, releasing a long, drawn-out sigh.

"I feel you are here with me, my old friend."

He reached forward and took hold of the journal. On its tattered cover were the remains of what had once been a gold embossed stamp.

The Cube of Compostela
Reality or Myth?

Bishop Marcus hesitated a moment, and then taking a deep breath, proceeded to immerse himself in the mysterious lifetime obsession of his dear friend and colleague, the late Professor Agardi Metrovich.

CHAPTER 5

The Atlas Mountains, Morocco.

Gabriel grumbled under his breath. He was dragging himself through a copse of dry bushes that was serving as his only means of cover. He knew that the lack of a moon, coupled with the dark fatigues he was wearing, would make him invisible to the armed guards, and he was glad of the fact. Right at this moment they would be scanning the castle's perimeter, including the place where he now found himself.

Gabriel pulled down his cap. Invisibility was a good thing, and he thanked the dark night. If he were spotted, here in the shrubs, casing out the villa of one of the most powerful drug lords in North Africa, he would most certainly be skinned alive.

Completing the last leg of his approach, Gabriel arrived at his final position. He was high on a rocky perch now, hiding safely behind the cover of a dense grouping of shrubs. Below him, a panoramic vista of the Atlas Mountains spread out in all directions, lit from above by a star studded sky that seemed to hover only inches above his head.

Sandwiched as he was between that infinite glowing cosmos, and an earth that seemed to almost embrace him as he lay upon it, Gabriel felt a sense of safety that he had never before experienced. It seemed ludicrous to him. This was by far the most dangerous expedition of his career, yet instead of feeling anxious or worried, he was perfectly at peace. He whispered into his radio.

"I've reached the entry point."

"Well done, Boss," came the muted reply.

It was his trusted assistant Amir who spoke, his Moroccan accent giving life to a peculiar fusion of British and American English. Amir was high in a tree, gazing at the castle through a pair of binoculars, and chewing, as always, on a hot cinnamon toothpick. His build was agile and muscular, his groomed dreadlocks shoulder length and adorned with a few dark beads. He brought the radio to his mouth and whispered into it.

"They still haven't left the conference room, Boss."

"What's been going on in there?" asked Gabriel. "I thought I heard a gunshot."

"You did. Nasrallah shot one his guys in the stomach. The poor bloke's still in the room. They sat him right next to Nasrallah."

Gabriel shook his head in amazement.

"Let me know when they leave that room. As soon as it's empty, I'm going in as planned. Over and out."

Gabriel settled in for what he knew could be a very long wait. Apart from illustrating Najiallah Nasrallah's cruelty, the shooting was an indisputable sign that trouble was afoot in the castle, and where there was trouble, routines would almost certainly be upset.

Gabriel knew that it could be hours before the smugglers vacated the conference room and settled into their nightly pastime. It was a ritual that would take place in what Gabriel had dubbed *The Opium Den;* a room filled with rugs and cushions, where the men would lie nightly in drug-induced stupors. Across the gorge he could see the room's uninhabited window, a tiny black dot in a massive stone wall.

Almost two weeks had passed since Gabriel had left his home in Boston, and if anything, the feelings of world weariness he had begun to experience there were only getting worse. Adhering to his new habit, he locked away the painful emotions, focusing instead on the many tasks at hand.

Over the past nine days he and Amir had photographed, filmed and recorded every event that took place in the castle, going to great lengths to gain every scrap of information possible. At one point they had even entered onto the grounds in the guise of electrical repairmen, using the opportunity to map the areas of the castle pertinent to their mission.

Gabriel considered how the unexpected crisis in the castle might affect their plans, but he knew that ultimately it did not matter. It was too late to abandon the mission. Amir had laid explosive charges all over the castle grounds. Removing them would be impossible to do without being detected, and leaving them behind to be discovered at daybreak would make returning impossible. There was no turning back. All Gabriel could do was wait and hope for the best.

For more than ten years Amir had been a close and trusted friend of Gabriel's. They had originally met in the port of Tangiers when Amir, then just a boy of fourteen, had approached Gabriel as his ferry had landed. Amir had been wearing a tie-dyed Bob Marley shirt, his messy head resembling a tangled brown mop. He had offered to be Gabriel's guide, and even though Gabriel had told him to go away over a dozen times, he had followed him all the way to the marketplace, singing *Everything's Gonna Be Alright* while jogging happily at his side.

"I will show to you the medina!" he had said in broken English as he bounced around. "I know best places to shop!"

To this day, Gabriel could not be sure if it was the long climb to the old Arab quarter that had finally broken his will, or if he had indeed taken a liking to the kid. In the end he had given in. It was the best thing he could have ever done.

"Very well," Gabriel had said, "but you won't get a dime out of me. You'll have plenty with all the kickbacks from everything I buy. Now, where can I get a decent drink around here anyway?"

"Kickbacks? No kickbacks!" the young Amir had said, a twinkle in his eye. "I work for free! I take you for drink! Very illegal. Best place!"

The medina's narrow streets had bustled around Gabriel in a dizzy tangle of crowded shops and bellowing merchants, and before long, Amir had led him into a secluded courtyard café. No sooner had Gabriel sat down than he was brought a forbidden bottle of Johnny Walker Black, coincidentally his favourite scotch. It had been the start of a great friendship.

Gabriel studied the castle through a pair of infrared binoculars, all the while thinking back on their long friendship. How many artifacts had they retrieved together? How many times had they narrowly escaped with their lives? The reggae-loving Arab was truly fearless, and had saved his life on more than one occasion, despite all the hashish he smoked. What was more, Amir had been a favourite of Gabriel's adoptive father, Professor Metrovich, and that in itself was a very difficult standing for anyone to have achieved. The Professor had been very selective with those he consorted with.

Gabriel put away the binoculars and reached sadly into his pack, unfolding a loose sheet of paper covered in his father's scribbled handwriting. He had found it stuffed into a notebook in the old man's desk; a letter to his colleague, Father Franco, that he had obviously forgotten to mail. Gabriel's mind went over the mysterious events for the hundredth time. The Professor had been on an assignment in Turkey with the priest. For some unknown reason they had chartered a plane to Santander. Two days later Gabriel had received a phone call from the Spanish Civil Guard, informing him of their deaths. That was all there was. He was still reeling from the news.

It was thanks to his father that Gabriel had the unique career he had. Just as Professor Metrovich had been in his younger years, Gabriel too, was a treasure hunter, and a very good one at that. His father had taught him everything there was to know about locating and retrieving lost artifacts, especially those found in sunken ships. Being on the board of directors for the Vatican Museum, the Professor had also ensured that Gabriel's pieces would be purchased with no questions asked. In this way, Gabriel had become a very wealthy man. Even still, he would have given it all up if it had meant getting his father back again.

The Professor had been everything to Gabriel. He had rescued him from an orphanage when he was an infant, and had over the years taught him what it meant to be a man. Under his constant support and tutelage, Gabriel had grown up to become a noted archaeologist. As a child he had practically lived on the Harvard campus where his father worked, spending his nights on the restored, turn-of-the-century schooner that was their home. Growing up, Gabriel's life had revolved around sailing, diving, travelling, and above all else, studying. He had read more books than the most diligent of scholars, and had visited more countries than he could keep track of. To Gabriel, acquiring knowledge was an effortless pastime, like eating or drinking. Travelling, treasure hunting, diving, and sailing were just the things he did in the time that was left over. It had always been that way.

Under the stealthy red light of a military flashlight, Gabriel scanned the letter until he found the part he was looking for. He had studied it countless times, but seeing it here, on the top of that ridge, high in the Atlas Mountains, renewed his sense of purpose, and gave him the stamina he needed to go through with the task at hand. In the letter before him, scribbled in the Professor's barely legible hand, was a short paragraph concerning something that Gabriel was totally unfamiliar with. It spoke of a legendary artifact known as the Cube of Compostela; an artifact Gabriel had never heard of before.

I've been turning over some rocks here in Istanbul and have made an important discovery. The long lost Cube might still exist. I have narrowed its location to one of three places. If it is found, the legend will be validated, and there will no longer remain any doubts concerning the mystery surrounding the births of Gabriel and Natasha, and their birthright to the inheritance of the Cube.

Below these notes, was a crude drawing of the cube that had been referred to. It appeared to be a medieval quadriform, measuring fifteen centimeters on each of its sides. In essence, it was a simple box. Jotted down next to it was a name.

"Gutierrez de la Cruz."
Priest/Cartographer.
835 - 901 A.D."

Below that, three more lines had been written. Two had been scribbled over and were illegible, but the last line was easily read:

The Museum of Antiquities, Tangiers, Morocco.

Gabriel folded the letter carefully, and put it away. That was all there had been to go on, but given his passion for relics, and the knowledge that his father was not one to speculate on anything other than facts, it was enough to start him on a quest to find the Cube. Even still, there were so many questions left unanswered.

What was this Cube? It appeared to be an important artifact, but if this were the case, in all his years of study, would he not have heard mention of it? And who was Natasha, and why was this artifact *their* birthright? Was it possible that he might have a sister? If only the Professor were still alive.

All of his life Gabriel had seen his father working in an old battered diary, but he had never been permitted to look inside it. His gut told him that the answers to any question he might have concerning the artifact would be found in that book, but where was it? Gabriel had turned the boat upside-down, but had found nothing. He was perplexed. His desire to learn more about the Cube had taken on an almost obsessive quality.

Within a few days of finding the scribbled letter in his father's desk, Gabriel had boarded a plane to Tangiers. At the Museum of Antiquities, he had learned that the Cube had been stored in the archives for as long as the museum had existed, but had never been displayed to the public.

"It was a beautifully illuminated quadriform," the curator had told him, "but not particularly impressive when compared to other illuminated artifacts from the same period. For that reason I was very surprised when the museum was broken into last year, and only that piece was stolen."

Not knowing where to begin his search, Gabriel's thoughts had naturally gone to his assistant. Amir had grown up in the streets of Tangiers. If anyone could find out who had stolen the artifact, it would be him.

It was not very long before Amir and Gabriel were sitting in a busy café, sipping mint tea and talking to an informant that Amir had arranged to meet with. He was a giant of a man, with a fleshy scar that bisected the entire left side of his brown face. His massive head was shaven clean, and a patchwork of scars and bumps covered it as though it were a piece of battered luggage. On his neck was the symbol of a moth; an artless image brought into relief by the crude branding of a primitive hand. Gabriel was impressed. Despite his rough appearance, there seemed to be a profound dignity to the ugly giant. There was a quiet wisdom in his eyes.

"Najiallah Nasrallah," he had said, his voice as deep as a diamond mine.

He spat in disgust.

"He is a dog, living in the palace of a king."

Gabriel could still remember the informant's face in every detail, and the way he had scowled when he had spoken that name. Amir had put a roll of banknotes into the enormous hand, and exchanged a knowing look with the man. Moments later the dark giant had vanished into the milling crowds.

"Nasrallah's a powerful drug lord, Boss," Amir had said, squinting up through his dreadlocks. "He's said to have a taste for archaeology. I should've known it was him. He employs a lot of people in this town, but everybody hates him."

"Where can we find him?"

Amir had slugged back the last of his tea and was holding out the glass, admiring the bright green leaves that filled it.

"He lives in a Moorish castle," he had said, sitting back in his chair. "It's high in the mountains, north of Tetouan. It's impenetrable, Boss."

"Impenetrable," muttered Gabriel under his breath.

He was looking through his binoculars, and had just seen the lights go on in the opium den.

"Impenetrable until the Moors decided to hook-up to the electrical grid."

Just then his radio vibrated.

"You're clear to go, Boss. They all left the conference room. Be careful."

"Alright," said Gabriel into his radio. "Here goes nothing."

Gabriel lifted his body as though he were doing a slow push up. He took a deep breath.

Everybody else gets lawyers to arrange their inheritance. Why does it always have to be so difficult for me?

Reaching up with one arm, Gabriel hooked an insulated zip line trolley onto the power line that hung directly above him. He could see it disappearing into the darkness, stretching across the gaping gorge that separated him from the castle. Somewhere in the distance, the cable would end at a narrow sill where it connected to the castle's main power supply. He would have to fall ten feet to a rooftop below, or be electrocuted instantly.

Suddenly a flash of light spread out behind the castle, followed almost immediately by the buffeting sound of an explosion. Amir's distractions had been detonated, and for an instant the castle looked like it belonged in Disney Land. A huge star-burst spread out behind one of the turrets, followed by another and yet another. The wheels were in motion. There was no going back now.

"I sure hope the brakes work on this thing," said Gabriel, leaping from the cliff face and sliding out into the starry night.

CHAPTER 6

Soho, New York City.

Christian Antov lay on the floor, curled into a semi-fetal ball at the foot of a dark and immense unfinished painting. He was a middle-aged man, thin and pale, and wore only tailored, medium grey suites; always with a white shirt and a neutral coloured tie. Around him his expansive Soho studio stretched out like a war zone, the lofty ceilings and exposed brick walls of upper-scale Manhattan real-estate doing nothing to mask the sordidness of the scene that surrounded him.

As usual it had been a late night of debauchery, the scattered debris of empty bottles and cigarette butts leaving no doubt that there had been a large gathering there the night before. Christian opened an eye, only to take note of the handful of guests who had remained to spend the night. They littered the floor like scattered corpses in a lost battle, framed, as it were, by a backdrop of the vast and morbid paintings that comprised the bulk of his work.

"Get the hell out," he said weakly. "Get the hell out of my studio."

Groaning in pain, Christian propped himself on an elbow until he had managed to sit up and face the fifteen foot canvas that hung before him.

"Get the hell out of my studio!" he bellowed at the painting. "Get out, you ungrateful pieces of shit!"

Christian's head screamed out in pain. Behind him he could hear groans and muttering, followed by the quick patter of feet. His guests were well familiar with his unpredictable temper, and they made no delay in their exodus. Seconds later Christian heard the door slam shut behind them, and he cursed aloud, letting his head fall into his hands. His brain was still reeling from the drink, and his body trembled from the excessive cocaine he had consumed. He swallowed hard, making an effort to control his loose bowels. At least he was alone now. All he needed was a cigarette and a drink.

He turned to search for an abandoned butt on the floor and groaned from the effort. It was then that he saw them: Two men at the door. They were wearing black suits.

"I told you to get the hell out!" screamed Christian in fury. "GET OUT!"

There was a long pause.

"Now, this is no way to treat your guests," said one of them at last. "And it is certainly not the way you were raised to behave."

They were too far away for Christian to discern their faces, but he immediately recognized their familiar Dutch accents. A feeling of hatred filled him as the last of his strength ebbed slowly away.

"What do you want?" he said listlessly, falling back onto the canvas behind him.

He picked a trampled cigarette off the floor and lit it, inhaling deeply.

"What the fuck do you want from me?"

He could see the men approaching. They were immaculately dressed, and they picked their way through the carnage of the party as though it were human waste.

"You will be grieved to know that your father is very near death, Christian," said one of the men. "He has sent us to collect you. He wants to see you."

Christian laughed coldly.

"He can die and rot for all I care."

"Get up, Christian," said the other man firmly. "The jet is waiting."

CHAPTER 7

The Atlas Mountains, Morocco.

"Amir!"

Gabriel's whisper sounded more like a scream. He was speaking into his radio, the sound of the fireworks outside still echoing through the castle.

"Can you hear me?"

"Yes, but I can't see you."

"I'm still in the conference room," he said. "The Cube's not in the safe."

Amir threw down his toothpick.

"You gotta get out of there, Boss. They're already starting to comb the place. You don't have much time."

"I'm not leaving without the Cube," said Gabriel, still searching through the safe. "Where are they concentrating their search?"

"Perimeters, for now," said Amir, his normally smooth tenor beginning to roughen a little at the edges. "Guards are all over the grounds. They even got dogs. It won't be long before they start searching the castle."

"And where's Nasrallah?"

"I don't know," he said, frustrated. "Inside somewhere. Boss. Truly. You gotta get out now. You're in a lot of danger. Your escape route could be cut off at any moment."

"I'm not leaving without the Cube."

Gabriel pocketed his radio and scanned the room. It was without a doubt the castle's most important chamber, its twenty-foot ceilings held aloft by four massive columns. On the room's northern wall ran a long arcade of elegant sandstone arches. They opened onto an expansive terrace. At some point the arcade had been glassed in, and it was through these windows that Amir had been spying on the meeting only moments before. In the centre of the room sat the large wooden conference table where the criminals had gathered.

Coagulating under one of the chairs was a large pool of blood, its contents having been tracked about the room, painting the stone floor as though it were an abstract canvas. Gabriel stood before the empty safe he had only just blasted open, its twisted door lying on the floor at his feet. Next to it, he could see a set of footprints that stood apart from the other boot prints in the room. He knew in an instant that they were made by the dress shoes that Nasrallah wore.

Gabriel followed the prints out of the room. Whereas all the other traffic had gone in the same direction, namely to the opium den, Nasrallah had taken a different path. Gabriel could see his footprints leading down a long stone corridor and he followed them to a spiraling flight of descending steps.

Moving as silently as possible, he made his way down, arriving at a small antechamber containing a heavy wooden door. He could hear two guards calling out in Arabic somewhere above him. He pressed himself against the wall and remained there motionless. Behind the door there was only silence. Once the guards had moved away Gabriel tried the handle and found that it was unlocked.

"Here goes nothing," he muttered.

He slowly opened the door.

With nothing but the dim light from the stairwell to illuminate the room, it was difficult to see what lay within. Gabriel entered regardless, closing the door behind him as quietly as possible. He made use of a large deadbolt to lock it shut. If the guards decided to come that way they would have one more obstacle to get through before finding him. With the door closed, the room plunged into darkness, but Gabriel had come prepared. In the green hue of his infrared goggles he saw that he was in a storeroom of sorts, the chamber littered with cluttered tables and shelves, all laden with scales, cardboard boxes and plastic bags.

"The packaging department," he muttered to himself, "but no drugs anywhere. Weird."

There were three doors in this room. Two were shut and one slightly ajar. From the open door came a cooler reading than the others, leading Gabriel to consider that the room might be a connecting chamber, and the one Nasrallah had taken. He approached it with great stealth. In a chamber such as this, even the slightest shuffle would be amplified twenty times over. Gabriel eyed the door, listening intently for any sounds behind it.

"Let's see if you took door number three," he muttered under his breath, pushing the door open.

Producing a black light scanner, Gabriel switched off his night vision and was immediately able to see the glowing residue of blood from Nasrallah's shoes. It shone brightly back at him, leaving a track of prints heading off into the chamber. Gabriel entered silently, activating his night vision once again. He was in what looked to be the castle's original kitchen, the giant hearth before him still blackened by the soot of ancient fires. To his left, beneath a row of crudely hewn sinks, he noticed a drainage trough emptying into a narrow pit.

Gabriel cocked an eyebrow and pushed back his shaggy hair. A faint glow was radiating from an open doorway just ahead of him. He removed his goggles and approached it cautiously, pressing himself against the wall and peeking in. Within was a medium-sized room, its worktables cluttered with computers and an assortment of scientific apparatus. What had once been an ancient pantry had now been converted into a laboratory of sorts. The tiled floors and walls provided the perfect hermetic environment.

He stepped silently forward, a particular table catching his attention immediately. It sat apart from the others, and was the only one not covered in clutter. Above it hung a single halogen fixture, its dimmed light illuminating a very out of context piece of equipment.

What would a drug lord be wanting with a portable X-ray machine?

Gabriel made his way to the table and was almost disappointed by what he found. There, resting on a tray of lead was the treasure he had been seeking, but it was by no means what he had been expecting. Under the halogen light he saw it for what it was: A typical quadriform cube, measuring some fifteen centimeters in width, and constructed from what appeared to be velum or wood.

My God, is this what all the fuss is about?

Gabriel had seen countless treasures; priceless works of art boasting outstanding materials and craftsmanship. Disappointingly, the piece before him seemed rather unremarkable; a mediocre artifact at best. Typical of such quadriforms, each of its six sides were decorated with illuminations, but in this case, the illustrations consisted of six, crudely rendered apples, their peels removed, but curiously left coiled around them. Gabriel was perplexed.

What kind of medieval subject matter is a peeled apple?

He bent closer to the relic, noticing only then the elegance of the framework that encased it. Constructed in time-blackened silver, it comprised an exoskeleton of intertwining branches, each section encrusted with what appeared to be heavily soiled rubies and emeralds. It was not, however, until Gabriel had carefully picked up the artifact that he was at last made aware of its uniqueness. Whereas most of the quadriforms he had encountered had been hollow and used strictly for decorative purposes, this artifact was surprisingly heavy for its size.

Now I can see why he was trying to x-ray it. There's got to be something inside.

The artifact was definitely not what Gabriel had been expecting to take hold of. In it he felt an inexplicable quality; something that defied any kind of rational description. As he turned it over in his hands he would have easily lost track of time were it not for the vibration of his radio calling him back to reality.

"I found it," he whispered into the receiver, snapping out of his trance. "Amir. I've got the Cube."

"Boss. You gotta listen very carefully."

It was the first time Gabriel had ever sensed fear in Amir's voice. By its varying volume, Gabriel could tell that Amir was running as he spoke.

"I had to give up my lookout point. There are guards everywhere. I just saw Nasrallah. He came out screaming. They know you're inside!"

Gabriel heard a violent pounding. The guards had arrived at the door he had bolted shut. He looked up, startled.

"Shit."

He could hear Amir's urgent whisper through the radio.

"Get to the escape route right away! You might still be able to make it there in time. Call me the minute you get through and I'll set off the charges. I'll meet you at the river rendezvous point."

"Amir," said Gabriel, his voice calm and steady. "I'll never make it out that way now. I'm deep in the castle. I want you to blow the escape route right away. Hopefully it'll confuse them a bit, and give me time to get out of here."

"What? Are you crazy? That's the only way out. You know that! You gotta run!"

"Amir!" said Gabriel, a little too loudly. "There's no time to argue. Blow it NOW! That's an order. I'll meet you at the river. Just look out for me. I don't know where I'll be. Now do it!"

Gabriel turned off his radio. He could have no more distractions. He produced a plastic food container from his pack and placed the Cube in it, sealing it tightly. He had got this far. He had retrieved the Cube; *his* Cube. He would get out of this place. He knew he could do it.

The pounding was getting louder. More guards had arrived at the door. He had a few minutes at most. He sprinted back to the room he had just been in and approached the dark pit that the wash basins emptied into. He produced a flashlight from his belt and shone the beam into its depths. The channel angled its way down and looked to be unobstructed.

"The Moors were geniuses," he said to himself, trying to think straight. "Geniuses are practical people. Practical people always dump their shit into the closest body of water they can find."

He peered into the drain.

"If this goes anywhere, it goes to the river. It just has to."

Behind him, the banging had turned into a violent pounding. The soldiers had found something to ram the door with. They would be on him in seconds. Gabriel tightened the straps of his pack. In the beam of his flashlight he watched a six-inch millipede scurry into the pit. He passed a hand over his two-day beard, battling his fear of the crawling insects.

Suddenly, the castle shook underfoot, jarring him to attention. Amir had just blown up his former escape route. Any other option he might have had for escape was gone now. Cursing under his breath, he lowered himself into the tight passage head first. At six-foot-two Gabriel was not a small man, but the channel was just big enough to wiggle through.

"Good thing I'm not claustrophobic," he muttered, lying to himself.

CHAPTER 8

Los Picos De Europa, Northern Spain.

Only when the last throbbing beats of the rescue helicopter had faded away did Isaac Rodchenko at last regain consciousness. Before him, precariously perched on a cliff's edge, and set high in the midst of a sweeping mountainscape, lay the wreckage of the chartered floatplane. Trapped in it were the lifeless bodies of Father Franco Rossi and Professor Agardi Metrovich –as well as the plane's pilot– all inaccessible to the Spanish Civil Guard's retrieval team, due to the high winds.

After many failed attempts, the team had at last been able to hover long enough to lower a paramedic down to confirm that there were no survivors. The man had picked quickly through the wreckage, finding the bodies of the dead, but failing to locate Isaac Rodchenko. Having secretly stowed himself away on the plane, Isaac had not appeared on the plane's manifest, and as he had been thrown clear of the impact zone, he had gone completely unnoticed. As it was, he lay pinned beneath a section of fuselage, battered and delirious, yet miraculously still alive.

Earlier that day, and much to the surprise of the Professor and Father Franco, Isaac had listened attentively to their strange request, and had granted them permission to conduct a special burial ceremony for his son on the island where he had been conceived. Given his faltering mental health, it had been agreed that Isaac would not attend this ceremony, but unbeknownst to the Professor and the priest,

Isaac had secretly boarded the floatplane and hidden himself in the cargo area, where the coffin had been stowed.

The sun was low in the sky when Isaac began to slip once again into unconsciousness. His face was badly bruised, his dark grey suit torn in places but amazingly free of blood. Overhead a rushing mass of cloud sped past like a giant floating landmass, lulling him into a delirious half sleep.

Below the crash site, the jagged mountains of *Los Picos de Europa* stretched out like a mouthful of teeth, each peak a mountain unto itself. It was here in this wild place, far from the world of men, and surrounded by death on all sides, that Isaac witnessed something that defied all the laws of physical nature. To his utter horror, he could feel the corpse of his son jerking and twitching at his feet.

"Dear Father in heaven," he prayed, his eyes wide with fear, "deliver me from this evil. Bring peace to the body of my child."

Isaac tried in vain to move his foot away from what he knew to be an abomination, all the while battling with his guilt for wanting to do so. This was his beloved son; his own flesh and blood. But like a frozen stone, the malformed cadaver seemed to be drawing the life from his body. Through the sole of his shoe he could feel its malignance. This was no longer his poor and helpless son. It had transformed into something utterly evil. He looked down to see the body twitch and jerk with the force of a recently severed limb. His son was dead; he had watched him die. What lay at his feet was no longer his child. It was a beast; a cold corpse that somehow still lived.

.

CHAPTER 9

Rome, Italy.

The rain was coming down in torrents as Gabriel's cab pulled up to the old stone church. It was 6:30 a.m. and Rome was just waking up. In the distance he could hear the siren of an ambulance cutting through the humid air, the wet cobblestones at his feet reflecting the erratic flashes of headlights as a growing number of rush hour cars rumbled past.

"Grazie," he said, handing the driver a fifty euro note.

With a nod of thanks, the cab driver passed him his luggage; a single leather pack, travel worn and battered.

Navigating his way through an obstacle course of puddles, Gabriel made his way into the shelter of the monastery's arcade, much like a child playing hopscotch. Before him a towering wooden door barred his way.

He shook the rain from his equally battered leather flight jacket, sounding a great iron knocker that hung at the centre of the portico. Within moments a little door had opened within the larger door, and Gabriel had to duck low to get through. An old Christian Brother waited on the other side, and he shut the postern behind Gabriel after he had entered, the clank of the deadbolt echoing through the empty chapel.

"Good morning, my son," said the old Brother, embracing him heartily. "The Bishop is presently at his toilet. He will be meeting you for breakfast very soon."

Gabriel released him, but kept hold of his shoulders.

"Thanks, Fra," he said warmly.

He was always amazed by the strength in the old man's body.

"It's good to see you."

"And it is always good to see you, my dear boy. I see that you have not yet discarded that decaying pack of yours."

Gabriel held up the leather duffel bag. The old Brother was right. If it were not for the meticulous reparations he had made to it, the thing would have fallen apart then and there. As it was, it was fully serviceable.

"It's hard to part with an old friend," he said, and he thought it funny that within such an old and battle scarred pack could be one of the most important artifacts he had ever come across.

They made their way along the aisle of a dark chapel, passing a large bank of burning candles that flickered in their little red cups. They sent up plumes of vapor that mingled with the incense that burned. Gabriel breathed deeply. He loved the smell of an old church, and although an unbeliever himself, he had always basked in the profound sense of peace that seemed to accompany that smell.

Up in the rafters, the sound of the pounding rain could be heard on the chapel's roof. It echoed through the space, giving life to the stone statues that looked down at him from their niches above. It was a familiar feeling to Gabriel, being under their gaze; something that had always comforted him as a boy. His eyes scanned their familiar faces.

A man made fantasy to explain the inexplicable.

He had never been able to understand how anyone could dedicate their entire lives to a myth, but at the same time, he respected their so-called faith. It was to him a testament of the power of the human mind, be it sane or delusional.

Fra Bartolomeo made a quick turn into a small alcove, and within moments they had passed through a concealed door that led into a narrow passageway. With the arched ceiling only inches above his head, Gabriel found himself having to duck at regular intervals in order to avoid the naked light bulbs that stretched out before him. He could see a long line of them ahead, emerging from a conduit that ran the entire length of the tunnel.

Where did this tunnel come from? I thought I knew every inch of this monastery.

"Please pardon my detour," said the Brother over his shoulder. "This way we can avoid getting wet from the rain in the cloisters. His Excellency's chambers are just up ahead."

Gabriel had to rush to keep up with the old man's pace.

"That's quite alright, Fra," he replied cheerfully. "I've only just been in much tighter quarters."

Gabriel shuddered at the memory of his harrowing escape. Not a day had passed since he had made his way through the Moorish sewer pipe. It had been a hell he would soon make every effort to forget. For two hours he had squeezed his way through the entrails of the castle, caked in raw sewage, starved of oxygen, and beleaguered by rats and insects of every kind.

On two separate occasions he had been forced to cut through iron bars using the mini acetylene torch he had thankfully packed among his equipment, the choking fumes nearly making him lose consciousness. With the stench of sewage still trapped in his olfactory, Gabriel followed the old Brother, reliving the final moments of his trying ordeal.

Deep under the Moorish castle, when he had, at long last, reached the end of the tunnel, he found that the passage plunged into a reservoir of sewage water. In his pack was a breathing apparatus containing just ten minutes of oxygen. It was meant to have been used to cover the short distance underwater that had been part of his original escape route. On this occasion, however, he had no idea how long he would be required to stay submerged. With no other options available to him, Gabriel donned the mask and proceeded downward into the fetid water.

"It won't be long now," said the Brother, but Gabriel was too lost in thought to reply.

Nine minutes had already passed when he came upon a second set of iron bars. He knew that he only had a minute of air left and was unsure as to how much acetylene gas remained in his torch. Gabriel did not waste time finding out. In the murky light of his flashlight he could see that two of the three bars had already rotted in their mounts. He shook them and they fell away easily. The middle bar however, was anchored quite firmly. In a moment his torch was blazing, cutting through the old iron effortlessly. Even still, Gabriel wondered how much tunnel remained on the other side. His air had run out sometime ago now, and he had only been able to half fill his lungs. Suddenly the bar broke loose and he was through, feeling the surrounding water drop in temperature almost immediately.

With burning lungs Gabriel pushed his way upward, moving freely for the first time in two hours. After what seemed an eternity he reached the surface at last, sucking in the night air hungrily. Somehow he had done it. He was out, and he was still alive.

"Boss, is that you?" came the whispered call.

A large inflatable river raft appeared suddenly, and a strong hand grasped Gabriel's shoulder strap and pulled him out of the water.

"Amir," said Gabriel as they landed on the river's edge, "if you had shaved this morning I'd probably be kissing you right now."

Amir stuffed the raft under a grouping of bushes and covered it with twigs and dried leaves.

"Not smelling like that you wouldn't," he said, pushing aside his dreadlocks to get a better look at him. "Where the hell have you been anyway?"

Gabriel smiled and shook his head in disbelief.
"That was far too close."
"I thought it was quite far," said the Brother, and Gabriel remembered how sharp the old man's hearing had always been.

Arriving at the end of the tunnel they approached a small wooden door that swung out effortlessly. Ducking low, Gabriel emerged into a large stone room. It was warm, and the furniture was plush and velvety.

"Wait here, Gabriel," said Fra. "The Bishop will come down soon."

Gabriel made his way into the waiting room as Fra disappeared back into the tunnel. He had always loved this room, but he had never entered it as he had just done today.

"Who would have thought," he muttered, looking back at the section of bookshelf as it swung closed. "A secret passage I didn't know about."

He walked into the carpeted room. Above him the vaulted ceiling rose solidly, with four gothic arches curving up to meet at a circular stone bearing the cross of St. George. Around him hung an assortment of detailed tapestries depicting great historical scenes. He approached his favourite one. It was a large work depicting the famous *Burning of Savonarola* in the Piazza della Signoria of Florence.

In the centre of the composition the puritanical priest could be seen chained to a great iron cross, with two of his supporters crucified to his left and right. At their feet, great flames licked upward. Savonarola had been a priest vehemently opposed to the Renaissance movement, and was infamous for his rampant destruction of what he considered to be immoral works of art, and heretical writings. Below the scene, on the tapestry's ornate border, was an inscription quoting the executioner who had supposedly lit the flames.

The one who wanted to burn me is now himself put to the flames.

"I see you are reliving one of the greatest victories of the Florentine artist," came a familiar voice from behind.

"Marcus!" said Gabriel turning. "Have I got something to show you!"

"Well," said the old man smiling. "I certainly hope it can wait until after breakfast."

The two embraced as they always did. A great love existed between them, and although the retired Bishop had no blood relation to Gabriel, he had been a lifelong friend of his father, and as a result, had always been like an uncle to him. Throughout his life, Gabriel had spent so much time in the old monastery that it was like a second home to him. He was familiar with the entire grounds, the bedroom he had always stayed in as a boy having had a set of doors that opened directly onto the main cloisters. Many a night he had sneaked out to explore the countless mysteries the old building had to offer.

Walking side by side, the two slowly made their way to the *breakfast room*, as the old Bishop liked to call it. In truth it was a small overgrown greenhouse that opened into the monastery's private gardens. They arrived to find a little table set for two, complete with a linen tablecloth and full silverware. It sat in amongst copious plants, and beside it, a mossy fountain gurgled, silenced almost entirely by the rain that pounded the panes of glass high above. All around them finches chirped and fluttered.

"Your father and I breakfasted here quite often, as did you, my son," said the old Bishop, sitting down slowly. "I can remember you as a boy, taking your sausages into the ferns, and feeding your crumpets to the birds on the sly."

Gabriel remembered too, and for a moment, a deep sadness took him. He missed the big man dearly.

"Marcus, I've got something I want to show you."

"Tut tut!" interrupted the Bishop. "I know, my son. We have much to speak of, but first, we old men must have our nourishment. You forget the hour at which you come. I would normally still be sleeping."

"I'm sorry. I came here straight from the airport. I didn't think."

"Not to worry," said the old Bishop with a reassuring smile, and just then, Fra Bartolomeo arrived with a large silver tray.

"Ah yes!" said the Bishop, rubbing his old hands together. "God bless you, my friend, and thanks be to God. We have been graced with one more meal. Let us enjoy it. It could very well be my last!"

"If you continue to say such things I will take this away and bring you lent rations," scolded the Brother lovingly.

"God forbid such cruelty!" came the immediate reply.

Even the most perfect stranger felt a warm affection for the old Bishop. It would have been impossible not to, and Gabriel smiled, knowing the Bishop's encompassing love for the gastronomical delights. Looking down at his plate, Gabriel welcomed the hot food. As always, it had been lovingly prepared by Suora Angelica, a very competent Italian nun whom Gabriel had also known since his childhood. It was the regular breakfast fare. Poached eggs, bacon, sausages, potatoes, fried fish, baked beans, fresh croissants and coffee in a French bodum. The perfect continental breakfast, and the eighty-five year old Bishop showed Gabriel that he still had quite an appetite. By the time he had finished his meal, Gabriel was dizzy with sleepiness.

"Let us now retire to the library," said the Bishop, noting Gabriel's fatigue. "There we can discuss your Compostela Cube."

"But how did you know?" said Gabriel, rubbing his eyes sleepily.

"I'm not as dumb as I look!" said the old Bishop with a wink.

He scrubbed at his beard with a napkin, loosing a fragment of egg that had clung there the whole while.

"That is to say, I am much smarter than I appear!"

When they arrived at the library, Gabriel could barely keep his eyes open. The food was settling into his stomach, and his body was beginning to respond.

"Take off your shoes and lie yourself down on that sofa, my boy," said the Bishop from the threshold. "I'll be right back. We've got a lot to talk about, you and I."

Finding himself alone in the room, Gabriel decided to take the Bishop up on his suggestion. Wearily he kicked off his shoes and stretched himself out on the soft leather sofa. Beside him, thin orange flames flickered lazily behind the glass doors of a cast iron stove, the familiarity of the room instilling a feeling of peace and security in him. As his eyes wandered around the paneled library, roaming dizzily from bookshelf to bookshelf, Gabriel began to feel a deep slumber take him.

"I'll just close my eyes for a second until he gets back."

CHAPTER 10

Amsterdam, North Holland.

It was night when the private jet landed in Amsterdam. Christian had slept the entire way. He emerged from the executive cabin to find his two escorts standing on either side of the door, their arms crossed over their chests officially.

"I trust you had a good flight, Christian?" asked one of the men.

Christian walked past them as if they did not exist. He was a prisoner. He always had been. Bending to look out the window, he felt a distinct pang of hatred surface somewhere in the back of his head. This was his hometown, and he did not know what he hated more, the city or his father. The mere thought of the man filled Christian with bitterness and scorn.

The plane came slowly to a stop beside a waiting limousine, and Christian, familiar with the mechanism, opened the hatch in time to see the motorized staircase pull into place. Before it had come to a stop he had already stepped onto it, making his way off the plane and into the car before his two escorts had time to follow.

"Take me to my family residence," he ordered, closing the car door as the two men hurried down the steps toward him.

"Now!" he barked.

The car sped off instantly, leaving the two men behind on the tarmac. Christian lowered his window, feeling a flow of cool, Dutch air wash over him. It was a familiar smell that he deeply despised. It was too fresh, too clean, and it smacked of the forward-moving mentality characteristic of the Netherlands. He lit a cigarette and passed a hand through his greasy hair.

The Antov family estate was located in the outskirts of Amsterdam, its manicured grounds, majestic stone walls and shining copper rooftops sending an instant message of power and affluence. How long these buildings had housed his ancestors, Christian did not know, but if he was sure of one thing, it was that his family was much older than the stately Napoleonic residence; much older indeed.

"Take me to the west entrance," he ordered, "and call ahead to have a bath prepared for me. I want a bottle of red wine and Eggs Florentine waiting for me when I'm done."

"Very good, sir."

The car rolled down the long drive that led into the grounds, its wheels rumbling over the uneven cobblestones. Christian lit another cigarette.

Maybe I'll get lucky and he'll be dead when I arrive.

* * * * * *

"Your father has only just awoken," said the desiccated old butler. "Your timing could not be better, Master Christian. Please follow me."

Christian passed through the large oak doors to find his father lying within a great bed in his darkened chambers, a battery of nurses surrounding him on all sides. A bearded doctor was bending over him, his patient's limp wrist held in his probing hands. The doctor looked up in time to see Christian enter the room. He shook his head gravely, and for a moment a feeling of relief sparked in Christian's heart.

Is he already dead?

His hopes were soon dashed when he saw a brittle arm dart upward, its bony hand clenching the doctor's shirt and pulling him in with uncanny strength. Christian watched the doctor's face as his ear drew close to his patient's mouth, noting the change in his demeanor as the words were said.

"Everyone out," whispered the doctor to his medical staff. "The Baron wants a word with his son."

Christian remained motionless at the threshold, a knot tightening in the centre of his chest. In a matter of seconds the entourage had flowed past him, closing the doors behind them and leaving him alone with the man he most hated in the entire world. An instant later a deep fear was welling up in Christian, conjuring the specters of childhood abuse, and reminding him of his despicable and worthless status.

The room was dimly lit now, the majority of the light having vanished when the doors had been closed. It was a massive chamber, the distant walls and towering ceilings dissolving into the gloom on all sides. The only thing visible was the four post bed; a dais like structure encased in hanging textiles and ornate cushions the colour of dried blood.

Christian stood there silently, frozen with a fear that had been nurtured in him since infancy. He could hear the scratching hiss of his father's breath, and his knees felt on the verge of giving way. It was all Christian could do to remain on his feet. Real or imagined, his father's customary psychic assault was working its way into his brain, and it was doing so with an unprecedented intensity.

All power is based in fear. Fear must be maintained at all costs.

These were his father's words; words that had been drilled into Christian for as long as he could remember, and they now filled his head with the power of a swelling ocean. He had always felt his father's malicious presence, but never before had he experienced it with such clarity. What had always been vague and hidden was now suddenly visible.

"Come," came the hiss, and like a lamb being led to slaughter, Christian obeyed, his hatred giving way to a silent plea for mercy.

"Father," he whispered, arriving at the bedside.

The sight he witnessed was ghastly, and he fought back a desperate urge to flee. It had been more than three years since he had last seen the man, and the transformation that had taken place in that time was nothing short of demonic. There before him, lying amidst the finest silks in the world, was the grey and wasted form of what could only be described as a lizard; a reptilian corpse that somehow still lived.

"You need not fear me any longer, my son," said the beast of a man in a dry whisper, "for now that you have learned fear, it is you who shall be feared. You will know power the likes of which no other man has ever known."

Christian remained silent at first, the implications of such a promise filling him with dizziness. It was only after a few seconds had passed that a full comprehension of his true identity struck him. He was no longer a misfit. He was an Antov, and this would soon be his estate.

Christian swayed on his feet. Along with this sudden realization came an unobstructed awareness of his father's repugnant presence in him. In that moment he realized that it had always been this way. Since his early childhood, Christian's father had infested his body and mind. The problem was that Christian had never known any other way of being, and as such, the violation had always been undetectable. A reactionary rage flooded into Christian, erupting in a murderous fire.

"Get out of me, you filthy piece of shit!"

Christian heard the words escape from his lips like venom; words he would never before have dared to utter. He spat on his father's face.

To Christian's utter surprise he saw a dry smile appear on the beast that lay below him, the last of its tentacles withdrawing from his psyche as it began to die.

"Nautonnier!" cried his father suddenly, expending the last of his strength.

Christian bent forward despite himself, a look of disgust contorting his features as he strained to hear the words that followed.

"It is done, Nautonnier," his father whispered. "The boy is ready."

From out of the shadows Christian saw the figure of a brittle man emerge. His head was covered in a hood, but hints of the ancient face within could be seen in the lamplight.

"Behold, Christian," the man hissed, removing a serpentine ring from his father's finger and giving it to Christian. "Your father is dead. You are master now. Use your power wisely."

CHAPTER 11

Rome, Italy.

Gabriel awoke suddenly, the only light in the room coming from the wood-burning stove that glowed warmly in the corner. The same person who had covered him in a blanket must have also turned out the lights.

"What time is it?" he whispered, looking down at his watch.

The dial glowed a bright blue in the darkness. 11:23pm. Gabriel sat up stiffly and made the calculations in his head. It took him quite a while. He was still half asleep.

"Let's see. I got here at around six-thirty this morning. Finished breakfast by eight..."

He stopped short with a sudden realization.

"I've been asleep for more than fifteen hours."

Rubbing his face back to life, Gabriel found his way to the end table and switched on a lamp. There was a note resting directly beside it. It was written in the calligraphic script of the Bishop, a little shaky, but still assertive and elegant.

I hope this note finds you well rested, my son. You have been through quite an ordeal. Please feel free to make yourself comfortable in the guest room. I will see you for breakfast at eight-thirty sharp.
M.D.L.

Gabriel put the note down sleepily. Had he read it more carefully, he would have understood that it was not his regular room that he was being told to use, but rather the guest room; a suite next to the chapel that had always been used for more prominent visitors.

Entering into the hallway Gabriel found it to be much colder than he had expected, and as he made his way along the dimly lit corridor he was suddenly taken by a desperate urge to urinate. With his bladder ready to burst, Gabriel rushed frantically along the corridor until he arrived at the door of his usual room. Here he would find a toilet, and with no time to spare.

He moved the latch slowly, not wanting to wake the sharp-eared Fra Bartolomeo in his chambers next door. There was no time to even reach for the light switch. He knew that just to the right, past the armoire, was the door to the bathroom. He entered into it without hesitation, finding the toilet and relieving himself in a single, perfectly executed motion. The relief that fell over him was encompassing, and he sighed fully and deeply.

"Twenty-four hours without a leak," he muttered, reveling with satisfaction at the deep rumbling sound of his stream.

He threw back his head, smiling proudly at the musical quality of an accompanying note of flatulence. Feeling invigorated, Gabriel moved to the sink and proceeded to rinse his hands. It was there where he noticed that something was not quite right. Reflected on the tiles he could clearly see a dim light where there should have been no light at all. It was coming in from the bedroom outside, a fact that puzzled him greatly, considering there had been no lights on when he had entered. A feeling of dread suddenly washed over him.

"Shit," he muttered, the last of his grogginess vanishing.

He recalled the Bishop's note.

The Guest Room. Shit!

Turning slowly, Gabriel made his way to the bathroom door. It was ajar. Through it he saw that a lamp in the room

BOOK ONE : THE DARK RIFT

had indeed been lit. Whoever was outside was clearly awake. He stood there without moving. Listening.

"Hello?" he said at last. "I think I might have just used your restroom."

A young woman's voice replied almost immediately.

"Yes, I believe you did."

Her voice was calm and timid, her accent clearly Italian, but schooled in American English.

Gabriel was at a loss.

This is not good. There's a girl out there and I just barged into her room, pissed in her toilet, and blew a massive fart to boot. Marcus is going to kill me.

He tried to think of what to do next, but no solution presented itself. She was clearly in her bed, so he could not just walk out, but he could not remain where he was either. His mind seemed to stall. There was an awkwardly long silence.

"Will you be staying long?" asked the young woman, clearly annoyed.

It took a moment before Gabriel could respond.

"No. I'm quite done."

There was another long pause.

"You can pass through," she said. "I am covered."

Gabriel made his way out into the bedroom and froze. Wrapped in the blankets of his bed, the bed he had slept in since he was a boy, was the most stunning woman he had ever laid eyes on. The soft light of the bedside lamp made her look angelic, and her startled eyes were almost childlike. Thick chestnut hair fell over her shoulders in heavy ringlets. Gabriel swallowed hard.

"My name is Natasha," she said carefully.

Gabriel was silent for a moment.

"I'm Gabriel."

Her stern expression made him want to smile, but something told him to be careful. His eyes twinkled despite his best efforts.

"I'm sorry," he said as sincerely as he could. "It's just that I normally stay in this room. Bishop Marcus is like an uncle to me. I was half asleep."

"I did not know that Uncle Marcus had a nephew," she said, sitting up and eyeing him distrustfully. "And you would think I would know, considering that he is like an uncle to *me*."

Gabriel was too unpolished for Natasha's tastes. He had a messy, travel worn look about him that made her want to throw him in a bath. She sat up a little further still.

"And for your information," she added, "this is the room where *I* normally stay."

Gabriel's mouth hung open. He was about to speak when a soft knock sounded at the door. A second later Fra Bartolomeo poked his head into the room.

"Natasha," he whispered. "What is going on here? I thought I heard the voice of a man."

He looked around.

"Gabriel!" he cried. "What are you doing in this young lady's room? Have you lost your senses? This is completely unacceptable!"

"No, Fra. It was a mis—"

Gabriel's words were cut short as the old Brother burst into the room. Reaching up he took hold of Gabriel's collar and escorted him out with practiced agility. Fra Bartolomeo had long been a school master before his retirement.

"Please, Fra," pleaded Gabriel as he was removed from the room. "I thought this was *my* bedroom."

CHAPTER 12

The Atlas Mountains, Morocco.

"You have betrayed me, and now you are lying to me!"

It was Najiallah Nasrallah who spoke, his voice was as greasy as his shoulder length hair, and his accent impossible to trace. He wore a shiny black suit under a blood spattered apron, his gaudy silk shirt the colour of dried mustard. A huge, muscle-bound man slumped before him under the trembling fluorescent light; naked and battered, and strapped to a barber's chair. They were in the middle of a windowless chamber, deep in a Moorish dungeon.

"No, Master," said the giant of a man, his deep voice broken but still dignified. "There was talk in the streets. An American was asking about the relic. His name is Gabriel Parker. There were many leaks after the robbery. The informer could have been anyone."

"Do not lie to me!" snapped Nasrallah, venomously poking a cattle prod into the prisoner's ribs.

A deep and resounding scream ensued, and much to Nasrallah's annoyance, the tortured man slipped into unconsciousness. Nasrallah turned to face a middle-aged doctor who stood nearby. His lab coat was heavily bloodstained, his gaunt face pale and haggard.

"Why did the drugs not prevent this from happening?" hissed Nasrallah through grey and crooked teeth.

The doctor scrambled up to the victim to take his pulse.

"I gave him a massive dose, sir, but he is still only human. If you continue this he will die."

With the prisoner's tortured head now tilting to the side, it was easy to see the large scar that bisected his face. In charge of two hashish production operations in Tangiers, and a smuggling ring in Algeria, he was Nasrallah's top Captain; the only one left alive who had been involved in the Cube's robbery from the Museum of Antiquities. Nasrallah scowled with hatred.

You have betrayed me, Bahadur. You are a slithering worm.

Within hours of Gabriel's escape, Nasrallah had ordered his helicopter to Morocco to collect the giant, and bring him back. His family had also been taken, and they were currently being held in another cell within earshot of his screams.

"Son of a whore," said Nasrallah in disgust, stripping off his apron and turning to leave. "He had a hand in this. I am sure of it. I should have killed him with all the others."

Nasrallah stopped at the door, his mobile phone ringing. He held it to his ear.

"Yes?" he said, his expression changing as he listened. "But Father Vanderwerken, how can this be? No sir, I do not doubt you. If you say it is, the Cube must be in Rome. Yes. Most certainly. Yes, sir. Thank you, sir. Kindly relay all your data and I will send a team out immediately. Yes, sir. At your service."

Pocketing his phone, Nasrallah turned to face the doctor, his mouth twisting with hatred.

"Clean him up and make him well enough to work! I've got plans for him yet."

CHAPTER 13

Rome, Italy.

Gabriel sat in a plush leather armchair, scanning the guestroom he had just been escorted to. He was completely awake now, and he looked around with a refreshed alertness that was more in keeping with early morning than the time on his watch. His eyes fell on his leather duffel bag. He could see it resting on a rosewood table at the foot of his bed.

"Couldn't hurt to have a look," he muttered, rising from his seat. "Anything to take my mind off that girl."

Even before Natasha had introduced herself, Gabriel had known in an instant that she was the woman mentioned in his father's notes. According to the Professor, the Cube was as much hers as it was his. He rubbed the stubble on his face.

She said Marcus was like an uncle to her...

It made no sense. Surely somebody would have said something about her. The thing that bothered Gabriel the most was the way she had made him stop in his tracks.

"I don't know who that girl is," he grumbled, opening the duffel bag, "but she's got high-maintenance written all over her face. Another prissy little Princess."

Gabriel shook off his misgivings and produced the container that housed the mysterious Cube. As he had noted before, it was surprisingly heavy, having a density that reminded him of an uncooked roast. Stopping suddenly, Gabriel turned away from the artifact to face the window. A noise from outside had caught his attention. It had sounded like something had fallen with a crash. He remained motionless.

Most likely a tree bough downed by the storm.

In truth, the rain had yet to let up. Roman winters tended to be very rainy, but this season had been particularly cold and damp. Outside, the downpour pummeled the wooden shutters, and Gabriel was glad of the fire that burned low in the hearth. It was a foul night, and the room was really quite comfortable. He moved to the desk and placed the artifact down carefully.

It was such an odd thing, this Cube, quite unlike anything he had ever seen before. When closely scrutinized it was easy to see that the thing was not at all what it appeared to be on the surface. Its density was of course the first give away, but surpassing this was the lack of attention that had been given to the actual illuminations that adorned it. Compared to the detailed work that had gone into the carving of its external framework, the illustrations themselves seemed overly crude in contrast; each side containing the same image of a single apple with its peel removed and arranged in a coil around it.

Gabriel noticed something peculiar. Having studied similar quadriforms of the same epoch, he knew that their frameworks were always attached last, thus preventing any of the vellum from peeling off the artifact's surface over time. In this case however, that precaution had not been observed. Gabriel could clearly see that the edges of the vellum were peeling up, even if ever so slightly.

"Wait a minute here," he muttered, gently passing his finger over an upturned edge. "Is it possible that there could be something behind this illustration?"

Gabriel groaned as the full realization dawned on him. These were not merely illustrations of peeled apples; they were instructions. Producing his pocket knife, he tested a loose edge to find that the old vellum offered little resistance to being peeled back. He stopped himself.

What the hell am I doing? I'm about to mutilate a twelve-hundred year old artifact.

Even still, something drove Gabriel onward, and he was soon uncovering a golden sub-layer, one that was so well preserved that in his excitement he forgot to breathe. One side at a time, he carefully pulled away the outer layers, revealing a shining artifact beneath.

Adorned in intricately worked parchments of deep ruby reds and glowing emerald greens, it was a gold encrusted work of medieval art the likes of which he had never before seen. Reminiscent not only of the Islamic and Christian works found in the cathedral of St. Sophia Hagia, the piece also reflected an uncanny similarity to the mystical arts of India, as well as the sublime elegance of those masterful works originating from the Far East.

"This is unbelievable," he whispered, turning it slowly under the light.

The truth of the matter was that he had quite simply never laid eyes on such a masterpiece. It was beyond a doubt, the finest example of medieval craftsmanship in existence, and there could be no doubt as to its authenticity. It was only upon arriving at this conclusion that Gabriel noticed something that dumbfounded him.

"Wait a minute," he said aloud. "This can't be right."

Reaching for his pack, he retrieved an examination kit, producing a large magnifying glass. After a moment's inspection, there could be no mistake. On each of the six sides were miniature texts belonging to six distinct world religions.

"Buddhism," whispered Gabriel, turning the Cube under the magnifying glass, "Judaism, Islamism, Taoism," his eyes were wide with amazement, "Hinduism, Christianity. This is impossible."

The likelihood of there existing a ninth century artifact that housed texts belonging to the six major world religions was unheard of. In this artifact was evidence of a cultural contact that, according to the history books, would not occur for another four hundred years. Gabriel placed the Cube back on the desk and reclined in his chair, trying to digest what the existence of such a piece could signify. Who had made it? Why had they made it? Who in the ninth century would have had such detailed knowledge of the six major belief systems, not to mention knowledge of their languages? And what would have inspired them to want to unify them in such a manner?

"This is certainly very unusual," he muttered, taking his eyes from the Cube to look around the room. "What the hell is going on? Why is all this happening? Why did my father say that the Cube was my birthright? What the hell was that supposed to mean?"

All the while that Gabriel studied the Cube, and hours passed without him knowing, there resided in his heart a strange and disturbing familiarity for the object, one that he could not begin to explain. It was as though he had dreamed of the Cube, or seen it as a child. An elusive recollection of the artifact seemed to be hovering just out of reach, like a word on the tip of his tongue. Perhaps he had simply slept too much. Sensing that he had had enough, Gabriel packed away the strange artifact and headed for the bathroom.

It's almost two-thirty in the morning. I could use a shower and a shave.

CHAPTER 14

Natasha jerked herself into a seated position. A scuffling sound had just awoken her. It was coming from outside.

What is that? Is it the rain?

She left her bed silently, approaching a louvered set of doors that lead into the cloisters outside. Through the downpour she could see a wet dog sitting patiently in the shadows. Its fur was glimmering in the lamplight. He pawed at the door again and Natasha gasped in surprise, her intuition peaking.

"You again," she said, biting her lip. "But how can it be?"

Natasha's rational mind was sounding its objections. Florence was almost three hundred kilometers away from Rome. There was no possible way that the dog could have found her here. Even still, something in her was absolutely sure that the dog outside was the same one she had seen in her storeroom. She took a deep breath and opened the door.

CHAPTER 15

"Gabriel!" came the distressed call. "Get out of there and get dressed immediately. There is no time to waste!"

Gabriel shut off the water and poked his head out of the shower. Through the steam he could see Fra Bartolomeo standing at the door of the bathroom. In one hand he held a two-way radio, in the other, the battered old duffel bag that Gabriel had left lying on the bed.

"What's going on?"

The old Brother held out a hand to silence him, bringing the radio to his mouth.

"It is true, your Excellency. There are men outside."

"Are the telephones still down?" came the Bishop's voice on the other end.

"Yes, and there is no mobile coverage either."

"Collect Gabriel, Natasha, and Suora Angelica. Meet me in my quarters immediately. I want all of you prepared to move. Bring some warm clothes and any food supplies you can find. Make haste!"

"What's going on, Fra?" asked Gabriel, donning a bathrobe.

"There is no time to explain," said the old Brother, turning to leave. "I will wake Suora and get some supplies. Meet us at the Bishop's study."

The old Brother handed Gabriel his pack.

"*E per tutti i santi*, Gabriel," he said. "Do not take your eyes off this. It is the Cube they have come for!"

Gabriel stayed looking at the door after Fra had gone.

What the hell is going on?

It did not take him long to get dressed. Begrudgingly he packed away his razor, rubbing at the three day growth on his face.

"I'll get that shave if it kills me."

Making his way through the old, familiar corridors, Gabriel found it very difficult to believe that there was an enemy lurking outside. It was just the storm. It had to be. Even still, he was glad that Fra had left all the lights off. If there truly were men waiting for the right time to invade the monastery, it would be best to keep them thinking that everyone was asleep.

"They could never have got on to me so fast," he muttered to himself. "It's impossible."

He made his way briskly toward the Bishop's apartments, a thought occurring to him suddenly.

"Amir," he gasped aloud, his brow furrowing.

Had they captured him? Was that how they were able to locate him here in Rome? Could they at this very moment be torturing his friend? Gabriel stopped abruptly despite his urgency, an anger alighting in him.

If they've got him...

He shook it off and started walking. He was just being paranoid. He had seen Amir installed in his Gibraltar flat not thirty-six hours before, safely out of Morocco and in one of the securest ports in the Mediterranean. He brought his thoughts back to the matter at hand and just then arrived at the Bishop's quarters. He burst into the room, forgetting to knock.

Natasha was sitting on the corner of the Bishop's desk, and Gabriel felt his heart skip a beat despite himself. She was dressed in a pair of faded blue jeans, a cream-coloured cotton blouse, and a dark knit jacket that had an eclectic, military edge to it. Her boots were soft black leather; low healed and laced, and matched her little leather backpack perfectly. It sat next to her on the desk, a lit up iPad sitting on top of it. Oddly enough, there was a chocolate-brown hunting dog lying at Natasha's feet. Behind the desk sat the Bishop, smiling happily, as though there were no danger at hand.

"Well, well," said the Bishop. "It would appear that the long awaited reunion has at last come to pass. I would introduce you if I had not already been informed of your accidental meeting earlier this morning."

The Bishop gave Gabriel a stern look.

"You could have read my note a little more carefully, my son."

Gabriel nodded and shrugged. He looked over at Natasha but said nothing. The Bishop stood up and walked around the desk toward Gabriel.

"Do you have the Cube?" he asked in earnest, his untrimmed eyebrows gathering into a single, silvery mass.

Gabriel nodded.

"Would you like to see it?"

"No, no. Now is not the time, my son. I must pack a few things."

With that the old Bishop turned, instantly shaking off his seriousness. His eyes were alight with an almost youthful glow. In all the excitement, his eighty-five years of life seemed to have dissolved away. Even the old man's posture had changed, and as he walked across the room, his gait seemed like that of a man twenty years younger.

He arrived at an antique armoire and removed a small pack from one of its shelves, whistling quietly as he filled it with some things. Gabriel looked over at Natasha only to find that she was looking directly at him, her eyes suspicious.

"I didn't see him in your room," he said, acting like he had not noticed her glaring eyes.

He nodded towards the dog.

"That is because he was not there when you came in," said Natasha, sliding off the desk gracefully.

She knelt down next to the animal and began scratching its proud neck affectionately.

"It is a strange story," she said to the dog. "We met in my workshop in Florence about two weeks ago, and I was sure he was going to attack me. Instead he ran away, and I thought I would never see him again. A few hours ago he came to my door. I still cannot believe it."

Gabriel frowned and then moved around the desk to sit in the Bishop's chair. His body still ached from his ordeal in the sewage tunnel.

Why does her accent have to be so damn sexy?

He closed his eyes, opening them a minute later to find that she had taken up her place on the Bishop's desk again. Gabriel frowned. She was looking directly at him; scrutinizing him again. He tilted the chair onto its back legs and closed his eyes.

"Shackleton is the reason why we are all up in the middle of the night," he heard her say.

Gabriel kept his eyes shut.

"Shackleton?"

"That is what I have named him," said Natasha. "He is quite the traveller."

"So it would seem."

Natasha examined Gabriel from head to toe.

"He led me to a little window in the washroom."

She nudged his balanced chair with her foot.

"I am sure you know the window I am talking about?"

Gabriel opened an eye and then closed it again. Natasha kept talking.

"Shackleton got up on his hind legs and looked through the panes," she said, biting her lip as she remembered. "He was grumbling. When I went to see what he was looking at, I saw two dark figures squatting beside the fountain outside. Some of them were armed with rifles, so I woke up Fra. He says that they are surrounding the monastery."

Gabriel opened his eyes and leaned forward.

"You're being serious."

Natasha nodded, and Gabriel could finally see the fear in her eyes. He rose to his feet, and just then Fra Bartolomeo entered the room. He was accompanied by a tiny old nun dressed in a pale blue skirt with a matching blouse and cardigan. She appeared to be laughing and crying simultaneously.

"Suora!" exclaimed Natasha, rushing to her and falling into her arms. "Do not be frightened. Bishop Marcus knows what to do."

Gabriel nodded in agreement. It felt odd that Natasha should be so familiar with Suora, and he felt a kind of childish jealousy at seeing the two embrace.

"Ciao, Bellissima," he said, giving the little nun a hug. "Don't cry. Everything's going to be fine."

"Ah, my child," she said quietly, her accent as thick as Fra's. "I am an old woman awaiting death. What could I be frightened of? I am not crying for fear. I am crying because I am happier now than I have ever been. I never thought I would live to see the two of you united. It seemed to me it would never happen. Thanks be to our blessed Virgin Mary!"

Gabriel and Natasha looked at each other suspiciously. They stood on either side of the nun, each of them holding on to one of her hands. Suora Angelica had been like a mother to them both; the only mother they had ever known. Crying with delight, the old nun brought Gabriel and Natasha's hands together, intertwining their fingers as she spoke.

"The love between you will see no bounds," she said.

Natasha exchanged an uncomfortable glance with Gabriel before pulling her hand away. In the meantime, the Bishop had finished packing, and was in the process of throwing a dark cloak over his black vestments.

"The time has come, my dear family," he said, slinging his pack over a boney shoulder. "We must flee this place immediately. Follow me!"

CHAPTER 16

By the time the Bishop had led them to the church's sacristy, Nasrallah's men were already making their move. With great stealth they gained entry into the monastery and fanned out in every direction, their dark forms moving without a sound. Their orders were simple. Retrieve the Cube and kill everyone in the building. There could be no survivors; nobody to relate what they had seen. For this reason, every square inch of the monastery would have to be searched.

* * * * * *

In the shadows of the chapel's sacristy, the Bishop used an old iron key to open the gate that stood before them, revealing a narrow flight of steps leading down into the darkness.

"We will be taking a secret underground passage that leads to what was once a convent, a very long time ago," said the Bishop, his voice barely audible. "The tunnel travels for approximately one kilometer. I cannot be sure if the way is still passable. I have never personally explored it, but it is our only chance of escaping this place undetected. If nothing else, it will offer us a place to hide."

Natasha looked perplexed. A tunnel connecting a monastery to a nunnery defeated the purpose of each institution entirely. She looked at Gabriel. He was in the act of digging through his duffel bag.

"We'll be needing these," he whispered, handing both Natasha and the Bishop a flashlight.

He continued to dig around, quickly producing a compass and yet another flashlight which he kept for himself. Suddenly Fra Bartolomeo approached, gathering the group together with his arms.

"They are inside the building," he whispered urgently.

All heads scanned the surrounding shadows. Even Shackleton was looking.

"Follow me," mouthed the old Bishop. "Now!"

He led them down into a chamber that was located directly beneath the sacristy. Gabriel locked the gate behind them, working the key as silently as possible. He was the last to arrive below, and saw them standing in the middle of a round room. Its shallow domed ceiling was so low that he was forced to bend over as he descended into it. Gabriel knew that this was a burial place; a grotto containing the tombs of Christian martyrs from the second century.

The old Bishop approached a round marble altar in the middle of the chamber. Around them, within evenly spaced niches, lay seven sarcophagi. The Bishop embraced the dais and strained against it.

"We must slide this aside," he whispered. "The entrance to the tunnel lies beneath it."

Gabriel and Natasha jumped to his aid, and within moments the stone altar began to move. Fra Bartolomeo crossed himself, thanking God that the ancient hinges had somehow remained silent. Only a damp gust of wind had escaped from the tunnel mouth, the thick air smelling of musty earth. It seemed terribly cold. Suddenly from above, filtering down the marble steps, came the soft patter of dozens of feet. All looked up. Nasrallah's men were just outside.

"We have no time to lose," whispered the Bishop. "I will go first."

The Bishop descended a short ladder into the tunnel. Its walls were of raw earth, with the only support coming from crude timbers erected at odd intervals. The others followed immediately, including Shackleton, who surprised everyone by descending the ladder as adeptly as a circus animal. Gabriel came last in order to struggle with the closing of the altar above. Much to his surprise, it swung into its closed position almost effortlessly.

Somebody went to great lengths constructing this hinge mechanism. It was built for stealth.

* * * * * *

The giant Bahadur stood dizzily beside the marble sacristy. In the dim light his countenance was almost horrific; the fleshy scar that bisected his face accentuated by the blood and bruises that covered his entire head. Clinging to his battered throat, the tattooed moth seemed almost alive, changing in shape as he continuously swallowed the blood that was still oozing from his broken sinuses.

Bahadur had been given little rest before being dispatched on his assignment, and his huge body still trembled from its wounds, his head reeling from the painkillers he had been given. Around him he could see his men searching the small church. They had spread out into four lines and were combing the space, methodically checking every pew, every niche.

"My family will soon be safe at home," he muttered deeply, his elocution at odds with his brutish appearance. "We shall do this quickly. There is no other way."

Bahadur jerked his massive head to the left. He seemed to have heard or felt something coming from below. It resembled a soft rumbling sound, but he could not be sure. Moving with all the stealth he could muster, he made his way around the sacristy, his pistol at the ready. It was not long before he found the gate and saw the narrow passage leading down into the darkness. Finding it to be locked, he hissed at one of his men, motioning him to come.

"Open this gate," he mouthed, and within moments the soldier had picked the lock with an expert hand.

The chamber was empty, and Bahadur, weary with fatigue, approached the central dais and leaned on it heavily. He had heard something. He was sure of it. Taking one final look around, he pushed himself off the altar.

"There is nothing here," he said to his men. "Help the others. Search the rectory."

* * * * * *

Gabriel stood frozen at the top of the ladder, his left hand outstretched to the others in a plea for absolute silence. Above him he could hear the guards speaking amongst themselves. They seemed to be moving off.

"They've gone," he whispered back, wedging a spare battery into the hinge mechanism to prevent it from being opened from above. "We're safe for now. Let's get moving."

They proceeded into the tunnel, walking silently for some time. It was Natasha who at last broke the silence.

"Why was this tunnel made, Uncle Marcus," she asked. "I thought that monasteries and nunneries were built to *separate* men from women."

"Right you are, my child," said the Bishop, smiling. "But even under the most severe barriers, Mother Nature has a way of bringing together what was meant to be together."

"A secret tunnel," said Natasha, amazed.

"A tunnel of love," added Gabriel from behind.

The Bishop's smile vanished suddenly as he shone his flashlight on the earthen walls.

"Yes, a tunnel of love," he said, "but also one of tragedy."

Under the roaming beam of light, all were able to see that the walls of the tunnel were lined with burial niches, or *loculi*, as they were called, and within each were the skeletal remains of infants.

"Behold the products of their love," said the Bishop sadly. "The pregnancy of a nun could well be hidden under her habit, but once born, the child would be brought here and left to die."

Natasha cringed in horror. In the distance she could see the tunnel looming in the darkness, rows upon rows of loculi open, and in full view.

"But why not just cover them?" she asked.

"Penitence loves guilt," said Gabriel. "The corpses must have been a great way to remind them of their sins."

"Come," said the Bishop. "Let us not linger here."

The group moved forward into the gloom, with Shackleton leading the way. Apart from the many burial niches and twisted wooden support structures, the tunnel offered very little to see. It worked its way forward, crudely veering around or beneath boulders, but always keeping to its general heading. Gabriel followed with his compass, imagining what it must have been like for those who had dug the passage, and the decades of repressed sexual urges that had driven them to do it.

Ten minutes into their journey they approached their first major obstacle and both the Bishop and Suora Angelica took the opportunity to rest. They sat down on some large rocks that had caved in from above, and Fra Bartolomeo was soon to follow. Their flight had been exhausting, and in the limited light offered by their flashlights, the obstacle looked impassable.

Gabriel lit a flare and the tunnel burst to life. Within their shadowy loculi, the sepia coloured remains of the infants glowed ominously, the flickering shadows bringing them to life. Whereas the addition of light would have normally made any place seem less oppressive, it was having the opposite effect here. Behind them, at the fringe of the flare's reach, a curtain of impenetrable blackness loomed oppressively. Natasha concentrated on the obstacle in front of her, trying to forget the fact that they were in an enormous tomb, filled with the remains of hundreds of dead babies.

"We might be able to dig a way through up there," she said, pointing to an area just below a collapsed wooden support.

Gabriel shook his head.

"It's no good," he said. "The dirt's too loose. It would only cave in on us."

"So what do we do?"

Gabriel looked into Natasha's eyes, lost in thought. She held his gaze for a moment and then looked away.

I do not trust this man.

It was only then that she saw motion at the bottom of the caved in section. In all the time that they had been looking for a way over the obstacle, Shackleton had found a way under it. Natasha's face lit up with delight.

"You are really pulling your weight this morning, Shackleton!"

The dog came out of the shadows and nudged Natasha's leg, turning around with a wagging tail only to disappear back where he had come from. Natasha followed, shining her flashlight into the gap.

"It seems to go right through," she said, looking back at the others.

"Now who would have thought that at my age I would be having such an adventure!" said Suora, shaking her head in disbelief.

The old nun was on her hands and knees, halfway through the passage and laughing merrily. Gabriel watched Natasha as she helped Suora along with lighthearted words of encouragement. He scratched the back of his head pensively. Maybe he had been a little hard on the girl. There was a sweetness about her that seemed so sincere, and she was a lot like Suora too; able to laugh when anyone else would be scowling.

Gabriel felt a sudden twinge of sadness run through him. He pushed it away instinctively. He would never have admitted it, but the reason for his sadness was really quite simple. Natasha seemed unattainable to him, just like all the women he truly desired.

In so many ways Gabriel was self-assured and confident, but when it came to women, he was inherently crippled, despite his apparent charm. There was a voice in him that simply said no to ever being fulfilled in a relationship; a voice whose legitimacy he had never thought to question. Gabriel was not one for introspection. Instead he clung to the same rationalizations as always.

She's not for you, buddy. Nice girls only want assholes.

Gabriel had fallen for beautiful women like Natasha before, and he had been burned every time. The way he saw it, they were either game-playing flakes, wanting nothing more than to be desired by men, or hopeless martyrs, self-ordained to fix abusive degenerates. In either case, he was convinced that only heartless jerks knew how to deal with women like Natasha. She was not for him. The truth of the matter was that Gabriel had long ago given up on ever finding true love. He had taken a more pragmatic road to sexual fulfillment, and it was too late to go back now. All this being said, he felt more empty than ever. He struggled to reassure himself.

A call girl will never screw you around if you pay her well.

Natasha was on all fours before the opening now, helping the old nun through the last stretch. She turned suddenly and caught Gabriel staring at her, mistaking his serious expression for something sexual.

He is so typical. Why are all men the same?

The truth was that Gabriel was not so mistaken about Natasha. Through her troubled history with men she had only managed to pair up with the selfish and abusive type, and yes, she had always tried to fix them. The reason for this was quite obvious to her. She could not abide 'nice guys'. They seemed to her like whimpering puppies ready to follow her anywhere.

Natasha was attracted to confident men with a backbone; men who could make their own decisions, and not be in need of her constant approval. Unfortunately these kind of men always turned out to be selfish boys in the end; their manly airs nothing more than manifestations of egoism and insecurity. Just like Gabriel, Natasha too was jaded, or at least beginning to become so. She could feel her childhood hopes of finding true love ebbing away a little more each day. As sad and empty as it made her feel, she was realizing that real men did not really exist. They were simply a childhood fantasy; make believe Princes from fairy tale fictions.

Natasha turned back to Suora and tried to push Gabriel from her thoughts. It happened immediately when she saw the absurd predicament the old nun was in.

"You are doing great, Suora!" she said, laughing. "Be careful with your head!"

It took the better part of twenty minutes for the party to traverse the obstacle; more than enough time for Gabriel and Natasha to forget about their ruminations and get back to the task at hand. Being the last one through, Bishop Marcus decided that they should take a short rest now, reasoning that they had all made quite an effort that morning, and that a break was well deserved.

"Fra Bartolomeo," he said with a twinkle in his eye. "Might you have had the chance to bring along a few things to snack on? Even your Lent rations would seem a feast in this place."

"I did manage to put together a few items in our haste," said the old Brother.

He removed his pack and proceeded to place the contents on a table-like boulder. Around it a pair of large rocks had fallen, giving the elders a place to sit. Gabriel and Natasha found perches close by, and soon all were resting.

"I see you found the roast pork," said Suora, shaking a finger at Fra.

He had spread a tablecloth out and was unwrapping the slab of meat, placing it next to a crusty loaf of bread.

"I know every one of your hiding spots, my darling," he said. "And you'll not hide the crackling from me either!" and pulling out another wrapped parcel, he added, "Nor the gravy!"

Natasha clapped her hands in delight, her mouth watering.

"The pantry," said the Brother proudly to all, "is the domain of the clergy!"

And with a magician's bow, he produced a bowl of roasted potatoes.

"Dinner for breakfast!" he said, and all gave a cheer.

"And what is dinner," said the Bishop, producing two bottles from his pack, "without water and wine."

After a short prayer of thanks, the five of them dined happily under the light of Gabriel's flare without a worry in the world.

"If faith is good for one thing, my canine friend," whispered Gabriel to a chewing Shackleton, "it's for the delusional sense of safety it offers. Anyone else would be trembling with fear, but these guys think they're on some kind of a holiday picnic."

Their meal ended when the flare began to burn itself out. Fra and Suora busied themselves packing away the remaining food.

"That was exquisite!" said the old Bishop, rising to his feet and adjusting his vestments. "Excellent foresight, dear Brother."

Fra bowed to the Bishop and then handed Shackleton another chunk of roast before packing it away. The dog took it gently, looking at him thankfully.

"You are certainly the most charming animal I have ever met," said Fra to Shackleton, patting the dog's back awkwardly.

Natasha had just given him a potato, and she bent down and kissed his head.

"Shackleton has saved us twice today," she said, ruffling his ears. "He is the best dog in town!"

The dog buried his muzzle in her lap and grumbled contentedly.

"Alright guys," said Gabriel. "I hate to break it up, but we really should be moving."

The tunnel continued on unchanged, and once the distressed areas had been left behind, it seemed no different to what they had already passed through. Inky blackness, eerie graves, and the unsettling skeletal remains of countless infants. Gabriel calculated that they had already travelled more than a kilometer, and consulting his compass, saw that they were still headed in the same direction. Their pace was slow, but they were making headway. If they did not encounter any more obstacles, the chances were good that they would soon be arriving at the convent.

This being said, all hopes were soon dashed by yet another cave-in, only unlike the previous collapse, this one was most definitely impassable. Whereas the other had been comprised of boulders and loose rubble, the cave-in before them was formed entirely from earth and sand. There was simply no way through.

"It would appear that we have arrived at an impasse," said the Bishop. "We will hide in the tunnel for as long as our food lasts, and then return to the rectory. Let us pray that the soldiers have gone by then."

"There's another option," said Gabriel, aiming his flashlight in the direction they had come.

Everyone turned to look.

"Not a hundred meters back I saw what looked like a tunnel leading off in another direction."

"You did?" asked Natasha curtly. "Why didn't you tell us?"

Gabriel took note of her tone.

"Because I didn't think there was a need, Sergeant."

He looked over at the Bishop.

"I thought we'd be arriving at the convent at any moment."

"Well, my son," said the Bishop, "it would seem there is a need now, would you not say?"

"Most definitely," said Gabriel. "Let's go back and take a look."

The opening was small, low, and crudely cut into the tunnel wall, almost as though the excavators had encountered it by accident. From within there came a draft of slightly warmer air. Gabriel crouched down and entered.

"I'll just take a quick look," he said over his shoulder. "Be right back."

The others stood by the opening, Natasha squatting before it and gazing in. In a moment Gabriel had disappeared past a curve in the passage, the light of his flashlight fading away soon afterwards. All waited expectantly, but Natasha was the most impatient of all. As the minutes passed, she seemed to grow more and more anxious.

"What if he gets lost, Uncle?" she said, biting her lip. "It has already been ten minutes and there is no sign of him."

"Have faith, Natasha," he said reassuringly. "Gabriel will be fine."

Natasha checked herself at once.

"Why do you say that?" she asked sharply. "I do not care what happens to that man. I am only thinking of the three of you."

She rose to her feet and stepped away from the opening. Something was drawing her to Gabriel despite all her efforts. He was a player, and she wanted nothing to do with him. In the end her concern proved impossible to resist and she made her way back to the opening.

"I am going to take a quick look," she said, entering. "I will be back in a moment."

No sooner had she gone in than Gabriel appeared. There was not much room in the tight passage and his face was only inches away from hers. He was smiling dryly.

"Miss me?"

Natasha looked daggers at him.

"What took you so long?"

"I wanted to make sure it was what I thought it was."

"Well? Was it?"

"Yes, and much more. Back up and I'll tell you outside."

The three seniors were greatly relieved to see the two emerge from the dark passage. Gabriel looked delighted.

"OK. I think we can get out this way, but it could take a while."

"What is it, my son?" asked the Bishop. "Where does it lead?"

"To the catacombs," said Gabriel. "While those monks were digging their tunnel of love, they happened to bump into one of the largest necropolises in Europe."

"Good heavens!"exclaimed the old Bishop, his eyes alight with sudden excitement. "*The Catacombs of San Callisto*!"

CHAPTER 17

Amsterdam, North Holland.

Christian Antov walked briskly through the lobby of an opulent five star hotel. Around him were some of the most powerful people in the world, each of them members of a private organization that would soon be holding its yearly weekend conference. He stopped at the reception desk, only to be immediately greeted by his new personal assistant. She was the youngest daughter of one of his father's associates, and she made no attempt to mask her innocent worship of him.

"Hello, Mr. Antov," she said flirtatiously. "Can I help you with anything?"

Christian did nothing to return her smile, but instead looked down at the generous cleavage she seemed to be proffering. Cynthia had been a little girl when he had last seen her three years before, but she had since blossomed into a beautiful young woman.

"How old are you, Cynthia?"

"Seventeen and a half."

Christian paused, looking straight into her eyes.

"Email me a list of the guests who will be arriving today."

Christian moved off before the girl could respond, the hint of a cold smile on his lips. He would revisit her invitation in six months. For now he would use her for other purposes.

All things considered, Christian was quite proud of how rapidly he was adapting to his new responsibilities. It was a drastic departure from his decadent life as a New York City artist, but he was enjoying the power tremendously. It had only been two days since he had taken over his father's position as Chief Head of the Vanderhoff Group Steering Committee, but oddly enough he felt completely at home in the new surroundings; as though he had been born for the position.

Making his way through the lobby, Christian thought back on the previous day, still trying to digest all that he had learned from his uncle, Prince Vladimir Rodchenko. They had met outside the Vanderhoff Group Headquarters earlier that afternoon. It was a palatial residence in the centre of Amsterdam. The old Prince had escorted Christian into the building, leading him through an opulent hall and up a sweeping staircase to his new offices. On the way Christian had been greeted by many staff members, each one offering their respectful condolences with regards to his father.

"Today I will be telling you many things you do not know, Christian," his uncle Vladimir had said. "Things that will help you understand who you are, and why you were raised as you were."

Vladimir Rodchenko was the brother of Christian's late mother; a woman whom Christian could only vaguely remember. He was a brittle and impervious man, with a temper that could suddenly lash out like a whip, and then vanish just as quickly. Being the only relative that he had ever been permitted to meet, Christian was not sure whom he hated more, the Prince or his father.

"This is your new office," the Prince had said flatly, leading Christian into a luxurious apartment. "Everything here was your father's. It now belongs to you. All of its contents, along with the position your father held, are a part of your inheritance. It might seem strange to you, Christian, but you have been training for this job all of your life."

After the Prince had left, Christian had settled into a big leather armchair that resided behind an equally sumptuous desk. In the simple act of leafing through an appointment book, Christian had learned more about his father than he had done in the entirety of his life. His father's affairs had never been discussed at home, and up until that very day, Christian would have been at a loss to explain exactly what it was that his father did for a living. Simply put, his father had never told him. Nobody had, until now.

Christian made his way into the hotel lounge.

"Orange juice and champagne," he said to the bartender, sitting down at his private table and lighting another cigarette.

On his notebook computer he could see that the guest list had already arrived.

"Very prompt, Cynthia," he muttered, scanning the email.

He was soon lost in thought, smiling bitterly at what had always been kept from him. A scene played out from his childhood. He was in his bedroom, its minimal furnishings cold and sterile. With all forms of amusement strictly forbidden to him, not a single toy was visible.

"Your father is a businessman."

It was his nanny speaking. She was laying out his clothing.

"That is all you need to know," she said dryly. "The rest is none of your business. You will not be disrespectful."

Having lost his mother as a child, the Austrian nanny had become Christian's only means of connection to his mysterious father, and indeed to the entirety of his family. She had been a cold and militant woman, following explicit orders to under no circumstances reveal anything to the boy concerning his relatives. On one occasion Christian had been told that his father worked with his uncles, but he had never been permitted to meet any of them. Prince Vladimir had been the only one; no grandparents, no aunts, no cousins. As a child, Christian had always been kept apart.

A barely audible alarm sounded from Christian's phone, bringing him back into the present, and reminding him of the Steering Committee meeting he had to attend. He cleared his mind and made ready to be the new chairman. How they expected him to do this he did not know, but he would play along. As the Prince had told him earlier that day, the machine was built and functioning. All that was needed was a steady hand at the wheel.

"All power is based in fear," muttered Christian, rising from the table. "Fear must be maintained at all costs."

The words were of course his father's, but Christian had long ago adopted them as his own, absently hearing them echo in his head more often than not.

As he walked, Christian found himself thinking of his new position, and all the responsibilities it entailed. There would be no person above him, and it seemed natural to him that it should be so. His father, it turned out, had been a leader of leaders, and all his life, Christian had been groomed to be the same. In his possession were the controlling shares of the Vanderhoff Group, arguably the most powerful organization in the world.

Smiling with self-satisfaction, Christian strode arrogantly to his first official meeting as the Chief Head of the Steering Committee. The Vanderhoff Group, he had learned, was named after the hotel where its first meetings had originally been held. What had initially started out as a handful of American, British and German businessmen working to smooth trade relations, had since grown into a group of more than one hundred members, each of which dominated arenas in global business, media, and politics.

The group itself was an unofficial organization, regularly hosting annual conferences in five-star resorts in Europe and North America. This year, the conference would be held here, in the same hotel where it had all begun; a hotel that had long ago been purchased by the founding member of the Vanderhoff Group, Christian's very own grandfather.

Officially speaking, Christian's new responsibilities did not extend beyond the role of host and organizer. Unofficially, however, he was the chief administrator of a deeply enmeshed geopolitical agenda, one whose nefarious roots dated back centuries. Plainly said, his father's Vanderhoff Group was a secret society, one whose primary objective was to centralize economic and political power with the sole aim of forming a single world government, corporately run by their own offices under a mask of a free democracy.

Leaving the lobby, Christian made his way along plushly carpeted hallways until he had arrived at his private boardroom. He entered to find it populated by men, who in their own individual positions of power and social standing, comprised the steering committee. There were twelve of them in total, each one a blood relation, and they sat around a large wooden table engaged in a variety of isolated conversations. Noticing that he had not yet been seen, Christian took the opportunity to scan the faces of the twelve old men who filled the room, amazed at how every one of them bore the same bitter and hardened expression.

"Good morning, gentleman," he said confidently, walking to his place at the head of the table. "I believe we will be discussing items relevant to a new North American currency in this meeting."

CHAPTER 18

Los Picos de Europa, Northern Spain.

The section of wing that trapped Isaac Rodchenko was merciful. By collecting the splashing droplets of a nearby spring, it was channeling a meager stream of water close enough to his face to hold death at bay. For many days now Isaac lay trapped in the airplane wreckage. He was high atop a frigid mountain in the wildest regions of northern Spain, battling a new and invisible enemy.

From the corpse of his son had come an unspeakable blight. The same demons that had possessed his child, were now accosting him. Wave upon wave their relentless attacks came. In his weakened state he feared that it was only a matter of time before they entered into him.

Even in his struggle with mental illness Isaac Rodchenko had remained a staunch Roman Catholic, and he now clung to its doctrine like a drowning man to a piece of flotsam.

"Dear Father in heaven," he whispered fervently, "I accept this punishment. I know that it is my past sins that have caused you to unleash these demons upon me. Had I not abandoned Christian and Alina, none of this would have happened. What I did was unforgivable."

Isaac went over the tragic events of his childhood and adolescence. At the age of twelve, his father had cast him from the Antov family, and sent him to live at Vatican City. He had remained there ever since, taking his mother's surname, and disinheriting himself entirely from his wicked father. At the Vatican, a venerable priest by the name of

Father Adrianus Vanderwerken had encouraged him to forget his past and start anew.

"God has wonderful plans for you, my son," he had often said when sadness haunted Isaac.

In not returning home, Isaac knew very well that he had abandoned his little brother Christian and baby sister Alina to a hell at the hands of their abusive father. It was the guilt and regret stemming from this decision that had over the years become the root of Isaac's mental illness. Despite Father Adrianus' smooth tongued assurances that he had done nothing wrong, a dark specter of guilt had remained buried in Isaac's heart; one that would soon be growing in intensity as the numbing effects of his medication began to wear off.

Exposed to the elements and slowly dying, Isaac Rodchenko continued his hopeless battle against the demonic forces that accosted him. Unspeakable things had been happening of late. The corpse of his son was somehow reviving, its occasional twitches escalating into prolonged seizures that filled Isaac with horror. Even now as it lay there motionless, Isaac could hear its icy whispers. The corpse was urging him to surrender; to let the demons take control.

CHAPTER 19

Rome, Italy.

"The most venerable and most renowned of all Rome!" exclaimed Bishop Marcus as he led the way through the dark tunnels.

He was quoting what Pope John XXIII had said of the catacombs of San Callisto in the early nineteen-sixties.

"When we were boys, Father Franco and I would sneak into the restricted areas of these catacombs!" he said brightly. "They might very well have been what inspired me to become a priest."

Natasha was amazed. How could dark and tangled passages possibly be a source of religious inspiration? Even still, she had never seen her uncle so enthusiastic about anything before. It was as if the spark that had been rekindled in the old man earlier that morning had now blossomed into a beautiful flame.

"These Catacombs are a resting place for almost half a million Christians," he said. "As well as sixteen popes and many, many martyrs. The necropolis covers almost ninety acres!"

"That is quite daunting, Uncle," said Natasha. "Will we be able to find a way out?"

She was walking beside him now, trying her best to see the beauty he saw in the arched and crumbling passages.

"Find a way out? Oh, most definitely, my child!" he chimed. "We are presently on the lowest of five levels; an area off limits to the general public, but one that I explored at great length with my schoolmates."

Gabriel fell to the back of the group. Entertaining as the old Bishop's enthusiastic discourse was, he had become much more concerned with Suora. She was walking in front of him now, slightly behind Fra, and seemed to be hunched over more than usual. Ever since they had entered into the catacombs her breathing had become more and more laboured, and Gabriel could see that she was having trouble keeping up with the group's already slow pace. Even Shackleton seemed to sense something. Instead of his normal place at the head of the group, he was lingering at the back, near the old nun, and looking up at her every now and again with those gentle amber eyes.

"How's about a break, Suora?" asked Gabriel, trying to make it sound offhand.

"I am fine, my son," she said, giving her short little nods. "I was just listening to his Excellency. How incredible."

"There's no reason why we can't all have a rest."

"If I am not mistaken," said the old Bishop, having overheard Gabriel, "we should soon be arriving at a wonderful little chapel. It would be a perfect place to have some refreshments."

Gabriel frowned. It seemed to him that his comment had actually made things worse for the old nun, reminding her of her fatigue. What was more, Fra had now brought his attention to her as well, and in the half light, Gabriel could see the look of concern on the old man's face. There was a great love between the Brother and the nun.

As if in answer to the Brother's prayers, the chamber the Bishop had spoken of appeared suddenly to the right. Two heavy columns rose up on either side of a dark opening, a crooked lintel holding them fast. The crumbling portal looked impressive. It was carved with what looked to be Egyptian hieroglyphs, their strange shapes shifting under the roaming beams of their flashlights. A dark chamber lurked behind, radiating the scent of pungent mildew.

"How many flares do you have left, Gabriel?" asked the Bishop over his shoulder.

"Just one."

"We had better save it then," he said, rubbing his chin. "If memory serves me correctly, this chapel has a hearth in it. Let us enter and see."

The crooked portico gave way to a large open space that appeared palatial in contrast to the tunnels behind. Under a shallow domed ceiling they could see an altar adorned with peeling frescos. It sat between two wide columns, with a life-sized wooden carving of a crucified Christ hanging at its centre. To the right and left of the altar, intricate freezes were carved into the stone walls. Natasha ran the beam of her flashlight over them, her many years studying artifacts peaking her interest.

"These carvings are obviously Christian," she said, "but they are Egyptian in style."

Gabriel came up beside Natasha as she passed her hand over one of the freezes. He could see that she was not mistaken.

Who is this girl?

"Christ is being portrayed as the Egyptian god Horus," she continued, trying to ignore Gabriel. "See the giant sun behind him? That is the traditional setting for a sun god."

Gabriel looked around, the beam of his flashlight finding a fresco depicting a scene of the Egyptian god being crucified.

"This chamber would have had to have been built in the early fourth century," he said. "Most of these frescos would have been considered heretical anytime after that."

Now it was Natasha's turn to be surprised, and she fought back an urge to look over at Gabriel. How could a man like him know so much about the early church?

"I can't believe I've never heard about this place," continued Gabriel in awe. "It clearly depicts direct parallels between Christianity and Egyptian mythology."

He looked over at the Bishop.

"Maybe that's why this level of the catacombs is off limits to the public. The church has never been able to explain how the same stories in the bible were told in Egypt, thousands of years before they ever supposedly happened."

"That is a highly contested subject, my son," said the old Bishop, his eyes wandering over the ancient paintings. "The fact of the matter remains that the early Egyptian Christians were of the most severely persecuted by the Romans. In all probability, this chapel was built as a shrine to them. If you look next to the altar, you will find a small doorway leading to a room that is filled with their bones."

It was not the first time that the old Bishop had heard mention of the disputed pagan sources of Christianity, yet even though there existed a large body of archaeological evidence in support of this claim, he did not suspect it was a matter of simple plagiarism. He felt that there was a missing piece to the puzzle; a truth that would reconcile the chronological discrepancies, without destroying the essence of what Christianity stood for.

"Truly, though," he said, thinking of Suora. "All this is of no practical concern to us at the moment."

He turned away from the frescos and looked to the back of the chapel, shining his flashlight on something there.

"What is of practical concern," he continued, "is that the inspired gentleman who ordered this chapel built, saw it fitting to equip it with a hearth. And as you can see, a long departed archaeological team has left us with plenty of material to burn in it!"

Both Gabriel and Natasha turned and focused their beams on the chapel's back wall. There, between two wooden scaffolds, was an enormous hearth under a full sized statue of the god Horus. Its falcon's head was looking straight across the chamber to the crucified Christ that hung directly opposite. Scattered around the hearth were wooden chairs and a table. To the right of the scaffold was what looked to be a crate filled with dust covered torches.

"Now that's a beautiful sight," said Gabriel, his beam focusing on the crate.

In no time at all the small party was huddling around a crackling fire, enjoying the first warmth they had experienced in many hours. Gabriel lit torches and set them around the room. In the flickering light it seemed that the chapel was suddenly brought to life, its mysterious purpose being revealed to them with utter clarity. The chamber was clearly a sanctuary, but it also held a great secret, subtly revealing clues to a mystery that Natasha had always been fascinated by. The Egyptian roots of Christianity.

While Gabriel was busy with the torches, Natasha prepared a chair for Suora and placed it directly before the hearth, lovingly covering the old nun in a blanket the moment she had sat down. Fra Bartolomeo, in all his foresight, had brought a small pot in which to heat the soup that he had also stuffed into his pack. Only one portion could be heated at a time, and against Suora's emphatic insistence to be left until last, the first bowl was given to her. The effects were nothing short of miraculous.

"Thank you, my dear ones. You are too kind to me," she said from under her blanket. "It was only these old bones and the dampness."

"Rest well, dear girl," said the old Bishop gently.

He was lowering himself into a creaking chair before a worktable, an old leather-bound book in his hands.

"We will stay here for an hour or so," he said. "After that we will have a bit of walking to do. We are very deep, but I know my way. God willing we will be out of this place in time for supper."

Natasha was next to get her soup. She thanked Fra, and drew a chair up to the old worktable, sitting down close beside the Bishop.

"What book is that, Uncle?" she asked, sipping her soup. It was warm and wholesome, and it drove away the last of her shivers.

"This is a book that belonged to Gabriel's father," said the Bishop, studying its worn cover. "I received it in the mail shortly after his death."

Gabriel was sharing some of the roast with Shackleton when he overheard the Bishop's words.

"My father?" he repeated, his mouth full. "What book is that?"

"It is a book containing all of his findings concerning the Cube of Compostela, my son," said the Bishop earnestly. "It is time that you both knew the knowledge it contains."

"The diary!" gasped Gabriel. "I went crazy looking for that thing!"

"His life's work," nodded the old Bishop, pausing for a moment and then continuing slowly.

"Out of love and an earnest desire to give you both an unburdened childhood and adolescence, much has been kept from you, but now all will be revealed. The time has come for you both to learn the truth about who you really are; a truth that we have long suspected, but one that has only recently been confirmed."

CHAPTER 20

Amsterdam, North Holland.

"Shall we get started, young man?" asked Prince Vladimir condescendingly.

He was seated directly to the left of where Christian was standing, a sharply hooked nose distinguishing him from the other old men in the room. Leaning over, the Prince stretched out a crooked finger and tapped a stack of papers on the table in front of Christian.

"It is all right there before you, boy," he said. "Right in the agenda."

Christian looked through the room's large windows, and out onto the manicured gardens.

Boy? Go to hell, you son of a bitch.

A group of men caught his eye. At first he thought that they were gardeners, but as he looked more closely he could see that this was not at all the case. The figures he saw were robed and hooded, and they appeared to be enveloped in a strange darkness, utterly out of context with the bright and sunny day. Christian frowned. Although the figures seemed to be standing still, they also appeared to be shifting from side to side. Their appearance was scratchy and difficult to discern, as though they were not entirely there.

A creeping fear was making its way up Christian's spine, spreading through his body, and making his eyes water. He tried desperately to control himself against the irrational emotion, but he found that he was powerless against it, able only to maintain the outward appearance of calm.

"Well, Christian," said his uncle, humorlessly. "Shall we begin by discussing the first item on the agenda?"

Christian turned to face him. The Prince's words had somehow broken the spell.

"Yes," he said. "Yes, of course."

Christian glanced back into the garden. The hooded figures had vanished, replaced by a decrepit old man standing in the place where they had been. He squinted at the figure, recognizing him immediately as the man who had been present at his father's deathbed; the same man who had given him his father's ring. With unmistakable purpose, the old man turned suddenly towards Christian, his cold reptilian eyes locking with his own. A current of fear shot through Christian's body like high-voltage electricity.

"Pay no heed to the Nautonnier, boy," said the Prince, his voice thick with disdain for the old man. "Father Adrianus Vanderwerken is a relic from the past. Look how his nurses come to change his diapers."

Christian watched as the old man was escorted from the lawns. His scalp was still itching from the cold sweat that had come over him when they had locked eyes. He turned to face those in the room. Why had he seen four figures where the Nautonnier had been? His mind was obviously playing tricks on him, but he would give it no further thought. He had a meeting to direct. He would consult his psychiatrist later. The dosages of his medications were most likely the cause.

"Gentlemen," he said, gathering himself. "I have been informed by the Prince that we will soon be replacing the monetary currencies in the United States, Canada, and Mexico with a new North American currency. I am told it is to be called the *Amero*, and that the current economic collapse of the United States was engineered by the Vanderhoff Group as a means of ushering in this new currency."

Christian moved closer to his chair.

"I want to know exactly what our little group is up to. If I am to lead this committee, I need to know its motives."

Christian sat down, glad of the opportunity to shake off the remnants of his disturbing hallucination. He heard an old man at the opposite end of the table clear his throat and make ready to speak.

"You will find, Christian," said the old man condescendingly, "that we have become very efficient in our work here. Over the decades we have stripped down and simplified our methods so as to arrive at the most efficient means of execution. In this way we get the most done with the least amount of effort."

Christian looked at the old man, his eyes cold as steel.

"Cut the bullshit and get to the point."

The old man looked back at him icily.

"We tear down old things so that we can build new and better things, Christian. In 1913 we instituted the Federal Reserve after engineering a major banking crisis in 1907. What most people don't know is that the Federal Reserve is not federal at all. It is privately owned and directed by us."

Christian laughed aloud.

"That's ridiculous. I won't argue that the regional Federal Reserve Banks are privately owned, that's no secret, but they are all controlled by the Board of Governors; a *federal* agency."

The man nodded patiently.

"Whose members are appointed by the President and confirmed by the Senate. In other words, by *us*, Christian. We just brought down that agency so that we could bring in the Amero."

Christian held his gaze.

"And you did this by staging last month's terrorist attack in Los Angeles."

The old man clasped his hands over the table.

"Yes," he said, smiling coldly. "We knew that a massive terrorist strike would take down the teetering U.S. Economy."

Christian smiled coldly. Fear and doubt were the two main weapons in the Vanderhoff arsenal. With them they had routinely manufactured crisis after crisis in order to implement their twisted policies.

"And why the new currency?" Christian asked. "Are you not already in control of the existing ones?"

"Our goal is to centralize power," said another man, his accent Texan, "but the things that get in our way are the political and economic systems that are currently in place. The more we centralize, the more these systems need to be revised and changed to suit our needs. This is why we created the United Nations. It provides us with a means to implement our new infrastructure. Ultimately there will be a single world currency and a central world government. It'll be split up into four unions. The American Union, the Asian Union, the African Union and the European Union,"

He rolled his eyes in frustration.

"Jesus, boy. Didn't you ever see the movie, *Zeitgeist?*"

Christian frowned in confusion.

"And exactly who will elect those in power?"

A rumble of dry laughter made its way around the table.

"The Vanderhoff Group will appoint those in power, Christian," said the old Texan. "Just like we've always done."

CHAPTER 21

Gibraltar, Europe.

Amir stood on his balcony, looking out over the sunny rooftops of Gibraltar and enjoying his favourite pastime. He tilted his head to move his dreadlocks aside, and then took a deep haul from his pipe. It was an authentic ninth century chillum, the shape and size of a carrot, and covered in ancient Vedic carvings. He had obtained the piece years ago while on an expedition in Thanjavur with Gabriel. It went everywhere with him, and just as the wandering Hindu monks had done a thousand years prior, Amir had packed it with a specially prepared mixture of hashish and kief. It was not for the novice smoker.

Amir squinted back at the flat over his shoulder. His computer had just chimed an alert. Smoke lingered around his princely features, which were offset only by a slightly protruding brow. His skin was the colour of dark honey, and he had intelligent eyes that were always bright and alert, despite his constant smoking. He held the vapours in a little while longer and then released a billowing cloud, lazily watching it float out into the open air. When his computer chimed again he groaned and turned to go inside. Someone was messaging him. He bent over the computer.

—*Amir. Something terrible has happened.*—

It was Amir's cousin Abida who wrote. He sat down and began to type.

—*Abida, you shouldn't be contacting me like this. It leaves traces. What happened?*—

Abida was the sister of Bahadur. She lived in Tangiers, and was constantly under the surveillance of Moroccan authorities, her family being directly connected to the smuggling cartel.

—*Men came late yesterday night and took Bahadur. They took the whole family along with him.*—

—*Are you absolutely sure of this?*—

—*I speak with them every day, you know that. When I had not heard from them, I went to their house, but it was empty. The neighbour told me what had happened. She said that Nasrallah's men had taken them all away.*—

—*Was anyone hurt?*—

—*No. The neighbour said she saw them get loaded into a van. Even Jadda.*—

—*Even Grandmother? Did she have her heart medicine?*—

—*I do not know. If it was the government, we could ask about them, but it was Nasrallah. The neighbour is sure of it. What should we do?*—

—*Abida, listen carefully. I'll take care of this now. Don't speak of it to anyone. You will do nothing. Do you understand?*—

—*Yes, Amir. Thank you. I know you will fix this.*—

—*OK. Get some rest. Everything will be fine.*—

Amir rose from his chair and produced his phone. He paused a moment to think, and then pushed the speed dial for Gabriel. It went directly to his voice mail.

"Boss," he said, stepping out onto the balcony. "There's trouble. Give me a call when you get this."

CHAPTER 22

Rome, Italy.

The firelight played on the old Bishop as he sat there before Natasha and Gabriel. Their eyes were glued to him as he spoke, his silvery beard and mustache picking up the hews of the fire that crackled behind them. Before him on the archaeologist's worktable lay the Professor's tattered journal. On its leathery cover could still be seen the remains of a tattered, gold embossed stamp.

The Cube of Compostela
Reality or Myth?

Fra and Suora had both fallen asleep by the fire. They had brought their chairs together so they could share the same blanket, and now sat cuddled, the nun's head resting on the Brother's shoulder. Bathed in the warmth of the firelight, the two old figures seemed to embody the objective of what the nunnery tunnel had attempted to accomplish so long ago: to unite what was always meant to be together.

Shackleton was laying in front of them, his proud head held high as he gazed almost pensively into the flames of the hearth. There was a consciousness in his eyes that seemed at odds with his species; a quiet wisdom that appeared almost divine. Within Shackleton's soul there was none of the conflict so common to the human condition, only a pristine desire to serve humbly and to protect. He turned his noble head and looked at the three who sat there at the table, focusing his amber eyes on the speaking Bishop. Entirely unconcerned with what was being said, Shackleton's satisfaction lay in seeing that everyone was safe, and getting the rest they so much needed.

"You see," said the old Bishop, "if it were not for a legend, it is very unlikely that we would ever have found you."

"I do not understand, Uncle," said Natasha, snuggling into the smoky dark wool of her jacket. "What does a legend have to do with it? I was very sick when I was a baby. Father Franco told me that he had arranged for the church to adopt me when they could not care for me at the orphanage."

"That's more or less what the Professor told me as well," said Gabriel, looking at Natasha and then back to the Bishop. "After that he ended up taking a liking to me, and decided to keep me."

"These stories are not lies, my children," said the old Bishop, "but they also leave out much truth. Before I proceed, I must repeat that it was our intention to keep all the details surrounding your early months from you until we were certain of the facts. You must try to understand things from our perspective. We had recently taken on the responsibility of raising two beautiful children, and we wanted to ensure that the life we gave them was as rich and nurturing as possible. Of what good could it be to fill your heads with uncertain stories?"

"What stories?" asked Natasha.

Her face was earnest in the firelight; her eyes almost childlike.

"You mentioned a legend. Uncle Marcus, please."

The Bishop smiled.

"I apologize," he said. "Be patient with me. There is much to convey, and I will start at the beginning. All I ask is that both of you never lose sight of who you are now, at this very moment. The things that happened in your past do not define you. They only explain how you came to be."

The Bishop looked at each of them in turn, and proceeded only after he was convinced that they were ready.

"As you know," he began, "I have, for many years now, held an office pertaining to church investigations of events that are often labeled paranormal. For me this term seems a contradiction to the truth, because things such as apparitions, demonic possessions, and other spiritual manifestations are indeed very normal, in that they have always existed, as opposed to the above-and-beyond meaning that the prefix *para* implies."

"Uncle Marcus!" cried Natasha, stamping her feet.

Gabriel was temporarily fixated despite himself. Natasha's little tantrum had displaced a lock of hair. He watched it play around her pretty lips for a moment before she absently tucked it away behind an ear.

"Yes, very well, my child," continued the old Bishop. "I will get to the point. Thirty-three years ago I received a phone call. I was at my desk, and as it so happened, Gabriel, your father was there with me. The call came from a deacon who was assisting me at the time.

'I have received two separate calls relating to suspected cases of demonic possession,' he had said. *'A girl in Argentina, and a boy in Taiwan.'*

"Now, while it was not uncommon to receive calls such as this from time to time, the remarkable thing was that in both cases, the children were newly born; something that I had never heard tell of before."

"Possessed babies?" coughed Gabriel.

A twisted scene of a demon-infested infant was playing out in his mind.

"That's pretty damn creepy."

Natasha's eyes were wide with a mixture of fear and concern.

"It was the first case I had ever encountered," continued the Bishop, clearing his throat with a barely detectable wince. "An abomination of Satan. The two children had spent their first month in a coma, only to regain consciousness in severely agitated states."

The Bishop paused, taking hold of the Professor's journal as if to open it, but refraining from doing so.

"Now if this were not already strange enough," he said, folding his hands over the weathered book, "I would soon learn from the deacon that the babies had not only been born on the same day, but also at precisely the same hour."

The Bishop sat back in his chair.

"Now although I thought it a great coincidence, I would most likely have left it at that, were it not for the fact that Professor Metrovich had overheard our conversation.

"*'Where exactly were they born?'* he asked, and I saw him take up a globe that was sitting on my desk.

"*'The boy, on an American military base in Taiwan,'* I repeated aloud, as I was given the information. *'The girl, in the village of La Quiaca, in Northern Argentina.'*

"The Professor had then juggled the globe around until he had found Taiwan, and then proceeded to locate the village, on the very opposite side of the globe.

"*'There could be more to this than mere coincidence,'* he said, and I will never forget the expression of concern that suddenly came upon him. I told the deacon I would speak with him shortly, and hung up the phone.

"*'The military base is directly on the Tropic of Cancer. Up here,'* the Professor said, pointing to the place on the globe. *'La Quiaca, is directly on the Tropic of Capricorn. Down here. And what is more, if you can see, they are exactly on opposite sides of the planet.'*

"I took the globe and looked for myself. I was amazed, for it was just as he said. The Professor clearly knew something that I did not."

"And I was the little girl in Argentina," said Natasha timidly.

"Yes, my child, that was you," said the old Bishop smiling. "And the boy on the military base was you, Gabriel."

"I pretty much figured," said Gabriel, looking at Natasha and then back to the Bishop. "So what became of us?"

"Why we went out to get you!" said the Bishop, smiling. "We brought both of you back to Rome, and Father Franco and myself laboured for fourteen months exorcizing the demons that were in you."

"Demons?" asked Natasha, aghast. "There were more than one?"

"There were fourteen in total, my child," said the Bishop rather plainly. "Seven in you, and seven in Gabriel. And as that particular ritual could only be conducted on the night of a full moon, it took us fourteen months to liberate the two of you. In the end we were successful, and miraculously, you only suffered minimal injuries."

"Injuries?" asked Natasha, leaning forward.

The old Bishop nodded.

"Burn marks at the energy centres of your body," he explained. "These were the places where the demons were extracted."

"Burn marks?" asked Gabriel and Natasha in unison, turning to look at each other.

Gabriel was the first to speak. He turned to look at the old Bishop.

"My father told me that my scars came from someone who had abused me in the orphanage before he found me."

Natasha was still looking at Gabriel.

"That is what they told me too," she said.

Natasha reached over and pushed aside some of the hair that covered Gabriel's forehead. His scar was in the exact same spot as hers. Gabriel looked into her eyes, confused, and just then Natasha pushed aside her bangs to show him. He had to bend close to see it in the firelight. The scar was barely recognizable but it was nevertheless there.

"I've got them all over my body," he said, and then he turned back to the Bishop with a frown. "Why were we lied to?"

The Bishop looked down at the table.

"I know that lying to you both was a sin, but telling you the true story would have been extremely destructive. Knowing that you were mutilated as infants has been a cross you have both had to bear all your lives, my dear, dear children, but the truth…"

The old Bishop's eyes became glassy with tears.

"We could not possibly have told you the truth."

Natasha fought back her tears.

"It is alright, Uncle," she said quietly. "You were right not to tell us. I always suspected that there was something more to the scars than I was told. When I was twelve I learned about the seven Hindu chakra points, and I saw that all my scars aligned perfectly with them. It was not long after that I found the one on the crown of my head."

"There's another one on our head?" asked Gabriel, searching through his messy hair with the tips of his fingers.

The Bishop gave a single nod.

"That was from the last demon to be extracted," he said matter-of-factly. "He was by far the most tenacious."

"Lovely," said Gabriel. "Thanks so much for letting us know all these little details about our early childhood. Very nice."

The Bishop only shrugged.

"Do not let it trouble you, my son," he said. "Let us continue with the tale."

Gabriel settled back in his chair, looking over at Natasha to find that she was already looking at him. She smiled and then turned to the Bishop as he began to speak again.

"*Is there something more that I should know about this coincidence?*' I asked the Professor. He had become very quiet since he had last spoken, as though he were lost in thought. He continued to hold the globe between his two fingers, one upon each of the locations. At length he began to speak, and I was truly amazed by what he said.

"The Professor told me of an obscure medieval artifact called the *Cube of Compostela*. Unknown to but a handful of scholars, its story had grown to become a legend among certain monasteries in Northern Spain. The Cube was believed to be the true Holy Grail; a receptacle carrying the living blood of the Christ, which to the ancients was a metaphor for knowledge, or more specifically, *Gnosis*."

"Gnosis?" asked Gabriel.

The Bishop nodded.

"The secret alchemical knowledge of liberation and transmutation," he said. "A mystical, intuitive knowledge that can only be known when it is directly experienced, as opposed to the kind of knowledge that is gained through rational thought, or theoretical conjecture. It was said that within the Cube were stored the keys to the cosmos. There was also a prophecy; one that the Professor found to be based on an ancient Egyptian creation myth."

"And what myth is that?" asked Natasha.

"A rather obscure one, my child," replied the old Bishop. "Originating from a pre-dynastic period. The myth tells the story of how the god Atum willingly sacrificed himself, and let himself fall into the underworld so as to plant the Seed Of Truth for all mankind."

"Atum was the Egyptian god of completeness," said Natasha. "He was the embodiment of the Divine Androgyne, or the Alchemical Marriage; the merging of male and female forces. He was a hermaphrodite."

The Bishop nodded.

"The myth goes on to say that from the seed that Atum planted sprung the Tree of Life. There are many such trees to be found in cultures around the world, but in our myth, the gods Osiris and Isis were said to have emerged from the tree in a state of earthly mortality."

"*Tep Zepi*," said Gabriel, remembering his Egyptology. "Also called *First Time*. The age of Osiris, when Egypt was believed to be ruled by gods in human form."

"Exactly," said the old Bishop, glancing into the flames of the fire. "According to the myth, Osiris and Isis each represented one half of what had formerly been the god Atum. In other words, his male and female aspects. They now resided in a dualistic world, where unity had been fractured into opposing states: Birth and death, high and low, light and darkness, good and evil, and so on."

"But what does the creation myth have to do with the Compostela Cube?" asked Gabriel. "And more importantly, with us?"

"Patience, my son," said the old Bishop with a smile. "I will soon get to that. According to the myth, the Tree of Life also yielded a single piece of fruit, and this was symbolic of all the Gnosis that had been lost after the fall of Atum; Gnosis that Osiris and Isis would need to re-assimilate, if ever they were to resume their former state as the god Atum. Only then would the divided become whole once again, and duality be transcended. After this, the underworld would slowly begin to be transformed into a heavenly place."

"And the fruit was an apple, right?" muttered Gabriel, pessimistically. "Just like in the bible."

"Indeed it was," said the Bishop, noting Gabriel's skepticism. "But do not forget that the apple is present in many other mythologies and cultures as well, and in almost every case, it symbolizes immortality, just as it does in this myth."

Natasha turned to Gabriel, a little annoyed by his cynicism.

"Hercules travelled to the edge of the world to steal the apple of immortality," she said flatly. "He took if from Hera, the Queen of Olympus. The apple is also identified with the Celtic god, Afallach, and his underworld home of Avalon. In folk tales and legends, the hero usually has to retrieve an apple to win the king's daughter, and fulfill his destiny to be the one to save the world from evil. The apple is everywhere in mythology."

Gabriel could not help but be impressed.

"And how is it that you know so much?"

Natasha only looked back at him.

Why is this man always so hostile to me?

Bishop Marcus answered before she could speak.

"Natasha is a very accomplished theologian, my son."

Gabriel continued his study of her.

"And from what Suora tells me, a professional ballerina too. She's just full of surprises."

Natasha looked away impetuously. The bishop made an attempt to return to the subject at hand.

"Natasha could also inform you, Gabriel, that in almost every story, discord soon arises with the appearance of the apple. Just like in the bible."

Natasha smiled in thanks.

"Please go on, Uncle."

The old Bishop nodded and looked at them both for a moment before continuing.

"Similar to the Book of Genesis," he said, "our Egyptian myth sees the appearance of the devil. This is the god *Sutekh*, or *Set*, and in our myth he comes in the form of a grotesque hermaphrodite beast; a desecration of Atum's divine, androgynous state. Set was the embodiment of doubt and fear. He was both the creator, and the ruler of the underworld. He worked against Atum, filling Osiris and Isis with a fear of the knowledge that was housed within the apple. In short, Set drove the two further and further apart from each other, until they stood alone, on opposite ends of the earth, lost in ignorance and misery."

The Bishop paused for a moment to clear his throat.

"With each passing age, and to symbolize the cycle of birth and death, Osiris and Isis would emerge on precisely the same day, on opposite sides of the earth. Due to their longing for each other, they would be reunited, and made to traverse a great labyrinth. Within they would search for a stairway to the paradise they once knew, their only possession being a single apple to give them nourishment on their journey."

Natasha leaned forward, placing her hands on the table.

"And the Professor believed that Gabriel and I are reincarnations of Osiris and Isis, and that the Cube of Compostela is the equivalent of the apple spoken of in the myth."

The Bishop looked over at her.

"To be incarnations of Isis and Osiris would be impossible," he said, "for they never existed. They are only fictitious characters in a myth. The Professor only saw an incredible similarity between your births, and the story told in the myth. The existence of a medieval prophecy surrounding the Cube of Compostela only served to further his suspicions."

"Come on, it's just a coincidence," said Gabriel, shaking his head. "Really, how can we be expected to believe any of this nonsense? It's just a myth. It has no relevance to reality."

"A myth, Gabriel, is no small thing," said the Bishop. "Housed within every myth is a wisdom incommunicable by any other means. Modern society has made the mistake of equating a myth with a lie, but nothing could be further from the truth. History, be it however well documented, will always be inaccurate, but the wisdom housed within myth will forever retain its meaning and purity. Myths are not to be taken literally. They are to be interpreted, so that the truth held within them can be understood, and assimilated on a level much deeper than rational thought."

"Like the truth that is in the story of Narcissus," said Natasha, "and how he fell in love with his own reflection. Or of Icarus, flying too close to the sun as a result of his own hubris and pride. The fact that these events never actually happened, does not change the fact that these traits can be found in every one of us."

"I suppose you have a point," said Gabriel. "You could also go as far as to say that embodied in every mythical god, is a quality that can be found in the human psyche."

"Yes!" exclaimed the Bishop. "And in its purest essence. Learn about any god, and you will only be learning about yourself, for the god is you. This was the great appeal of praying to a god whose qualities you desired. The patron saints of Christianity are no different."

"But what about the medieval prophecy you mentioned?" asked Natasha. "You have told us about the myth, but you have not explained the prophecy."

"Right you are, my child," said the Bishop with an adoring wink. "The prophecy states that during the darkest hour, the Two will come again to release the Gnosis that is locked in the Cube. In so doing, they will open a way for mankind to be awakened from its slumber of ignorance, and be initiated into the Cube's secrets."

Gabriel rolled his eyes.

"Like Isis and Osiris," continued the Bishop, once again noting Gabriel's skepticism, "these two saviours would be born on the same day, on opposite sides of the world, and under the dominion of Lucifer. In other words, they would be demonically possessed when they were born."

"But that's an impossible coincidence!" protested Gabriel.

"Yet an undeniable one!" said the Bishop firmly. "Even still, your father was not wholly convinced. It was not until he had witnessed the second half of the prophecy mirrored in reality that he finally accepted what he had always tried to explain as a freak concurrence of legend."

Natasha bit her lip.

"The hermaphrodite," she said.

The Bishop nodded.

"The prophecy spoke of its coming too. It would be born on precisely the same day, and at the same hour of the coming of the Two; a mockery of Atum, and the sexual unity embodied in the divine androgyne. Unlike the Two, however, the beast would pass its entire life in a coma vigil, only to awaken and die on the first full moon before its thirty-third birthday. During this time, he would be possessed by the devil himself. The prophecy stated that once the body of the hermaphrodite had died, the Fourteen Emissaries of Lucifer would be released upon the world. They would come to command a mighty army, and do everything in their power to prevent the Two from awakening humanity, and unlocking the mysteries of the Cube."

Natasha leaned closer.

"These emissaries, Uncle. Are they the same fourteen demons that were removed from us when we were babies?"

"Yes," said the Bishop, shuddering at the memory of them. "Yes, they are."

"Fourteen," said Natasha, thinking. "There is something about that number. In another Egyptian myth, Set kills Osiris and divides his body into fourteen parts, spreading them throughout the lands."

Gabriel turned to the Bishop.

"Who was it that made the Cube?"

"I can remember asking the very same question," replied the Bishop. "*'What is this Compostela Cube?'* I asked, *'Why have I never heard mention of it before?'*

"*'Few have,'* the Professor told me in response. *'It is believed to be a Christian relic, but I suspect that it is much more.'*

"He went on to tell me how he had first come to learn of the Cube, deep in the archives of a monastery in Toledo. Curiously enough, it was an Islamic text that he had found; a single Arabic manuscript dating back to the time of the Moorish occupation of Spain. The Cube of Knowledge, it explained, was the central subject of a treasure known to the Moors as *The Book of Khalifah,* a secret codex that had been passed from caliph to caliph over the centuries. Finding this book became an obsession for the Professor, but in all his

BOOK ONE : THE DARK RIFT

years of research, he was only able to gather a few scraps of information concerning it.

"From the manuscript he had found in Toledo, the Professor learned that the Cube of Compostela held mysterious runes, and that the Book of Khalifah contained the only record in existence of their translations. It was said that without these translations, the Cube's mysteries could never be unlocked. The manuscript stated that the Book and the Cube were linked, and that whoever possessed one, would be led to the other."

"Who was the author of this book?" asked Natasha, fascinated.

The old Bishop shook his head in bewilderment.

"It is in part an Arabic translation of an ancient Greek text that was long ago destroyed," he whispered. "One that related to an ancient Mesopotamian tablet. This tablet spoke of a Lost Cube, said to contain a wisdom capable of emancipating man from the confines of mortality and matter."

The Bishop looked at both of them in earnest.

"As well as giving detailed descriptions of the artifact," he continued, "the tablet also spoke of the Cube's possible location in the mountains of Northern Spain, and of its original resting place at the entrance of a mysterious labyrinth; a place where it would one day need to be returned in order that humanity might be made ready to receive its secret knowledge."

Gabriel was perplexed.

"Exactly how old is the Cube supposed to be?"

"The Professor could not say with any certainty," said the Bishop. "He suspected it to be pre-Egyptian, and perhaps even pre-Mesopotamian. The Book of Khalifah describes the Cube as the most prized of all treasures, and refers to it as the most ancient of artifacts. It was to the Moors, what the Holy Grail was to the Knights Templar, and the Professor believed that the two were in fact one and the same thing.

143

According to him, the Cube was the reason why the Moors invaded the Iberian Peninsula to begin with."

Gabriel pondered what the old Bishop was telling him, nodding his head as he began to understand.

"Once the Moors had crossed over the Strait of Gibraltar, they made a beeline directly for the north coast of Spain. Historians have never been able to understand the need for their urgency. They cut their way through the Visigoths in less than a year."

"Theirs was a holy quest for knowledge," said the Bishop, nodding. "Although it was not they who in the end would recover the Cube."

"So who was it that found it?" asked Natasha.

"The manuscript states that a Catholic priest found it," said the Bishop with a smile. "And that he found it while on the *Camino de Santiago de Compostela*."

"So that is where the Cube gets its name!" exclaimed Natasha. "I always thought it was named after the city. I forgot all about the Camino."

"Can somebody please fill me in?" asked Gabriel. "What Camino?"

"The *Camino* is a Christian pilgrimage," explained Natasha. "It follows an ancient Celtic footpath that makes its way through the mountains of Northern Spain. It ends at a big cathedral in the city of Santiago de Compostela, the place where the remains of St. James are said to be kept."

"Yes, of course," said Gabriel. "It begins in France. I've always heard it referred to as the *Chemin de St. Jacques*."

Natasha nodded.

"There is an old legend that tells the story of how St. James' long lost crypt was found on that trail. It says that a goat herder named *Pelaio* stumbled on it in the ninth century. They say he heard angels singing while out in the mountains at night. He walked towards the music, and saw thousands of stars raining down on the tomb. That is why they call it

Compostela. It comes from the Latin *Campus Stellae*, or *Field of Stars.*"

"Exactly," said the old Bishop. "But the Arabic manuscript told a tale far more intriguing than that popular legend."

The fire crackled in the hearth as the three huddled closer together at their table. Encased as they were, deep within that sprawling tomb, it seemed to them that the very walls were comprised of the dead. Even still, the wooden planks from the old scaffolds were thick and dry, and they burned well, shedding a much welcomed heat, and reassuring them that they were alive and well. Taking a sip from the cup before him, the old Bishop straightened his black cassock and continued.

"In the year of our Lord, eight-hundred and sixty-five, almost fifty years after the tomb of St. James was 'claimed' to have been discovered by Pelaio, the Arabic manuscript tells of a church expedition that went missing in the north of Spain. Its objective was to survey an ancient Celtic route that ran the entire length of the mountains, and to map any potential sites where strongholds might be built against the ever advancing Moors.

"The leader of the expedition was an Asturian priest and cartographer by the name of Gutierrez de la Cruz.

"Hours before dawn, while deep in the mountain wilds, Gutierrez and his expedition were said to have been overtaken by a potent demonic force; one that came upon them at the bottom of a dark valley, on the shore of a fog enshrouded lake. The party, it is said, heard the tortured cries of two children coming from out on the lake, but the evil that accompanied these cries was such that all but Gutierrez fled into the night, never to be seen again.

"Gutierrez then mounted a raft and followed the cries until he had landed on a small island. There he was overcome by a deep slumber, and witnessed the apparition of two angels in a dream. They had taken the form of a boy and a girl, and they appeared hovering over a gaping fissure at the centre of the island. From within this fissure there was said to have come great flames, and a chorus of wailing."

"A gateway to hell," said Gabriel, swallowing despite himself. "Nice dream."

The Bishop looked down at the journal, passing his hands over its worn cover, and remembering what he had read therein.

"The legend goes on to say that the angels then spoke to Gutierrez about the fissure, referring to it as *The Portal of Ahreimanius*."

"Ahreimanius was a Zurvanite god," said Natasha, frowning. "A very evil one. He originated in the Sassanid Empire of Persia, around 400 B.C."

Gabriel locked eyes with Natasha, and then turned to the Bishop.

"But what about Gutierrez?" he asked. "How did he find the Cube?"

"The angels told him where it was," replied the old Bishop with a shrug. "When Gutierrez awoke, he followed their directions, and arrived at a tomb. It was in this tomb that he found the legendary Cube, and it is here where the manuscript begins to take some unexpected turns. The tomb that Gutierrez supposedly found was said to have belonged to St. James the Just."

"The brother of Jesus Christ," said Natasha. "I can see the connection now. There were two St. James' in the bible. One was Jesus' famous apostle, but the other was James the Just. He was the biological brother of Jesus. The church has always tried to leave him in the shadows. Some historians believe that James the Just was the person Jesus chose to lead the church after his death. They claim that the Jewish high priests murdered him before he could take control."

"Alright," said Gabriel. "I get how there were two St James', but so what? What does any of that have to do with the Cube? And why would the church make up a story that would put a lost tomb of St. James in the north of Spain to begin with? It's not like it was just around the corner from Jerusalem. It doesn't make sense."

"The church legend is a fabrication," said Natasha. "It states that after Herod beheaded St. James –the apostle, not the brother of Jesus– his body was put into an unmanned boat that made its way to the north of Spain under the guidance of angels. They say that a fisherman found the body at sea, and buried it in the mountains, where it stayed lost until Pelaio found it eight centuries later."

"Definitely a fabrication," said Gabriel. "But what was the church's motive behind the fiction, and what's more, how could the Cube have been found with the body of James the Just? The Cube is medieval. I've got it right here in my pack. It's plain to see. A relic from the time of Christ could never have looked like that."

"Nevertheless," said the Bishop, "the Cube is what Gutierrez is said to have found in the tomb of James the Just. The true motives behind the church's legend of St. James, and indeed the truth behind all of this has yet to be fully revealed."

For a while the three remained silent, Gabriel and Natasha trying to digest everything they had learned thus far. There were so many questions; so many loose ends.

"Uncle Marcus," said Natasha at length. "Earlier you mentioned that the Professor had been very concerned with the similarities between the Egyptian myth, and the births of Gabriel and myself. Even if all this is true, and we are somehow connected to this artifact, why would the Professor need to be so concerned?"

The Bishop looked up at Natasha, his silvery brow furrowed.

"Because of what the prophecy relates, my child," he said slowly.

"What do you mean?" asked Gabriel, bending closer.

"It states that the coming of the Two will be marked by a great, world altering cataclysm. One that will mark the end of an aeon, and the beginning of a new one."

"A metaphorical cataclysm, is what you mean to say," said Gabriel. "A mythical, and extremely symbolic, destruction of the earth."

"The Professor believed that it would be very real, my son," said the Bishop, "and that it would take place on the winter solstice of the very year that we now find ourselves in."

"But that whole doomsday thing belonged to the Mayan calendar," said Gabriel. "That winter solstice came and went, remember? Nothing happened."

The old Bishop only shrugged.

"The myth tells of how Osiris and Isis attempted to escape from the Great Labyrinth during this cataclysm, and save the world from destruction."

"The winter solstice is less than two weeks away," said Natasha. "It is on the twenty-first of December."

"The day we both turn thirty-three," said Gabriel. "What exactly is going on here?"

"I have no idea," said Natasha, a fear coming over her, "but thirty-three seems to be an important age in this prophecy."

She turned to the Bishop.

"The hermaphrodite was one full moon away from being thirty-three when he died."

"Indeed, he was," said the Bishop slowly. "Jesus was also thirty-three when he was crucified."

Gabriel shook his head and frowned.

"Genetically speaking, thirty-three is also the age when a human being reaches its full development. After that, our DNA begins to develop errors during mitosis."

The old Bishop looked down at the tattered journal, his face growing dark.

"The prophecy admonished that if the corpse of the hermaphrodite were taken to the portal before the day of its thirty-third birthday, and buried there in a special ceremony, the Fourteen Emissaries would not be able to enter onto the earth sphere, and humanity's transition out of the fifth age would be made less catastrophic. This was what both of your fathers died trying to do. They failed."

Gabriel pushed back his messy hair and gazed into the flames of the hearth.

"So what you're saying is that their deaths were no accident."

"It would appear not," said the Bishop. "Something caused their plane to crash, and I believe that it was a supernatural force that did it; a demonic force to be more specific."

Natasha looked at the Bishop, her big eyes filled with fear. She had felt that same demonic force in her workshop. She was certain of it.

"What did the myth say would happen if Osiris and Isis failed to find their way out of the labyrinth?"

The old Bishop cringed at her question, and just then the catacombs seemed to close in around them. A frigid draft had suddenly entered into the chamber. It sent chills through them all.

"The myth spoke of perpetual night," he said solemnly. "It spoke of a *Great Dying*, and the loss of all hope."

It was at this moment that Shackleton rose from his resting place in front of the fire. He approached the door with stealth, his nose raised and sniffing and the hair on his back on end. He turned and focused an intense look at Natasha, just as Fra was opening an eye and cocking his head to listen.

"Someone is coming," whispered Natasha. "I think they have found us."

CHAPTER 23

Amsterdam, North Holland.

Christian awoke with a start, his heart racing from the remnants of a nightmare. After the Steering Committee meeting he had retired to his room to drink a bottle of wine. He had fallen asleep and dreamed of the four hooded figures. He could still hear his father's voice echoing in his mind.

"Heed the Zurvanites! Heed them! Heed them!"

Christian passed his hands over his face. He was drenched in sweat. The telephone rang, giving him a start.

"Yes?" he said dryly, picking up the receiver before the first ring had ended.

"Christian," came the Prince's brittle voice. "Proceed to the Vanderhoff suite immediately."

"Bloody Christ," groaned Christian. "I'm taking a nap."

Prince Vladimir coughed angrily.

"There is no time for your insolence!" he hissed. "The Nautonnier has summoned you!"

Christian heard the line go dead.

The Vanderhoff suite was located in the same wing as Christian's penthouse, and it was not long before he found himself stumbling there, a tumbler of wine in one hand and a lit cigarette in the other. He recalled what his uncle had told him of the Nautonnier earlier that day.

"He is a figurehead," the Prince had said, his voice tinged with hatred for the old man. "He is a remnant of old traditions and outdated superstitions. In all my life I have never seen him do anything of any importance. Your father feared him. Why, I do not know."

Christian thought back to the first time he had seen the Nautonnier. It had been at his father's deathbed, and a sinister power had radiated from the man, one that he could still feel. The Nautonnier's sudden appearance on the lawn earlier that day had only increased Christian's trepidation. The old man had been standing directly where the hooded figures had appeared; as though he and they were somehow connected.

Christian drained his glass and tossed it away. If his father had feared the Nautonnier, it must have been for a good reason. He made his way along the plush corridor, feeling the tyrannical presence of his father more poignantly than ever now. It settled around him like a cold fog; pressing down on him; suffocating him.

All power is based in fear. Fear must be maintained at all costs.

Christian arrived at a pair of towering doors, only to see them open of their own accord before him. The light from the hallway was doing nothing to illuminate the room within.

"Come in, Christian," said a brittle voice, and in that moment, Christian was filled with a deep and inexplicable dread.

"Fear me not, boy," came the voice again. "I am no stranger. Be so kind as to close the door behind you. Your eyes will soon grow accustomed to the darkness."

Christian did as he was told, shutting the door and waiting for his eyes to adjust. It was not long before an ancient man materialized before him. He was seated at a small table, the light of a dim candle illuminating his strange and unsettling features. He sat regally, his brittle white hair as thin as cobwebs, and growing from a pasty grey head that appeared to be moulting.

With the exception of his long, hooked nose, the Nautonnier's bone structure was almost reptilian. He had no eyebrows or facial hair of any kind, and his tripe coloured skin was like newly grown scar tissue, thin and brittle like old parchment. He reminded Christian of a pagan oracle; powerful and merciless, and almost skeletal. The hard line that was the Nautonnier's mouth transformed into a slit when he began to speak.

"I have summoned you here so that you might fulfill the final part of your inheritance," said the Nautonnier. "In order to do this, you must be made aware of certain facts that have been kept from you. After this, you must make a special pledge."

"A pledge?" asked Christian, arriving at the table. "What are you talking about?"

"Sit down, boy."

Christian obeyed, lowering himself slowly into a chair.

"You are of an ancient linage, Christian," said the Nautonnier, his voice like dry leaves. "Your family has always held power over others. It is no coincidence that things have been this way. Many attempts have been made to usurp your family's control, but there has always been a force that has kept it intact."

"Yes," said Christian. "It's called ruthlessness."

The old man smiled crookedly, and it seemed to Christian that his skin could be heard cracking as he did so.

"Yes," he replied. "And the driving impetus behind this ruthlessness has always been granted from below."

Christian cocked an eyebrow.

"What are you talking about?"

"I am speaking of Ahreimanius," said the Nautonnier. "The Dark Lord of Matter. The highest servant of Lucifer."

Christian stared into the Nautonnier's reptilian eyes and then began to rise from his chair.

"I'm leaving."

"Sit down!" came a sudden hiss, but it had clearly not been the Nautonnier who had uttered it.

Christian felt as though something invisible were pushing him back into his seat. His head swelled dizzily. His father was present. He denied it.

"You need not be fettered as you are, boy," continued the Nautonnier more urgently. "Forfeit your will to that of the master's, and you will be more powerful than any man alive."

"You will assume your responsibilities," hissed the voice.

Christian scanned the shadows. There was no denying it now. The voice was clearly that of his father's. His mind reeled. His father was dead. They had buried him.

"What the hell is going on here?"

The Nautonnier smiled dryly, holding up a wrinkled hand in a gesture of peace.

"I am a fair man, Christian. I will answer any questions you might have. When you are satisfied, you may proceed with the pledge, or you may choose to abstain from making it. Is this acceptable?"

Christian could feel the hold on him lessen in intensity, and he took the opportunity to reposition himself in his chair. Whatever it was that was happening, he would have to play along. The man before him was obviously his superior. His father had feared him. He was beginning to understand why.

"What kind of a title is Nautonnier?" he asked. "What makes you so important?"

The old man nodded.

"Nautonnier is the title given to the leader of our ancient society. It means, *The Great Navigator*. It is a lifetime position, and one that has been held by very important personages throughout the ages. It is a position that is held until it is taken away, for there can only be one Nautonnier."

"And who is Ahreimanius?"

The old man gazed into the flickering candle, his eyes betraying a deep fear.

"He is the greatest demon of the Luciferic Order. He is a son of Lucifer, and was first called Ahreimanius by the followers of the ancient prophet Zoroaster. He is his father's arm and fist on the earth sphere. Ahreimanius is merciless and terrible."

"And why can't Lucifer be terrible himself? Why does he need Ahreimanius?"

"Lucifer cannot access the earth sphere in his bodily form. He can exist here only in spirit. For this reason Lucifer bestows great power onto Ahreimanius, along with all the souls who are loyal to him. We are such souls, you and I."

Christian scanned the shadowy room. All the shutters and drapes had been drawn tight. Not a sliver of light could be seen anywhere.

"And what is there to gain by serving Ahreimanius?"

"By serving Ahreimanius, we serve ourselves," said the old man. "In exchange for our loyal acts we receive power over others, and great dominion over the matter that he is the master of. Everything that you have in this life, Christian, you owe to Ahreimanius."

Christian was not a spiritual person, yet he could distinctly feel a dark and sinister presence around him. He was certain he must be imagining things. The doses of his medications required altering. He would call his psychiatrist when he was done.

"Your soul is much older than you realize, Christian," continued the Nautonnier.

"What do you mean?" he asked, his fear and confusion mounting. "What are you talking about?"

"The soul of every being that inhabits this planet is ancient, to be sure, but whereas most of these souls are lowly, and of no importance, your soul has been in league with Lucifer since the time of the Great Fall. You are a Prince among the Fallen Angels, Christian. It has always been so, and just as in each of your many previous life incarnations, the time has come when you must renew your pledge to the master once again."

Christian locked eyes with the Nautonnier. As irrational and superstitious as it seemed, he sensed that this was no trivial request.

"Have you any more questions?"

Christian remained silent in his confusion.

"Very well," said the Nautonnier slowly. "There will be other opportunities for you to learn more. As I promised, I shall now permit you to decide how you wish to proceed."

"I choose to sleep on it," muttered Christian, rising slowly from his chair. "I'll get back to you after the conference."

The Nautonnier gave a dry chuckle.

"Oh no, Christian," he said. "I made no mention of giving you time to deliberate. That is not an option. You must decide now. You are free to take any decision you choose, but know this: Should you decide to abandon Ahreimanius, your special place at his table will naturally be taken from you. You are free to decide, but you must decide now and forever. Be sure not to err. Ahreimanius knows not the meaning of forgiveness."

Christian could feel the psychic tentacles of his father worming into him again.

All power is based in fear. Fear must be maintained at all costs.

"Follow your heart, Christian," whispered the Nautonnier. "What is it telling you to do? You are free to decide."

Hearing the old man speak had a great effect on Christian. He suddenly felt as though it were still not too late. A sense of urgency filled him. Around him the room had begun to warp and twist.

"What do you want me to do?" he whispered, his eyes wide.

"Merely to sign a contract," said the old man. "It is but a symbol of allegiance to Ahreimanius. A formality. It states that you align yourself with him, and offer up to him all that you possess."

The Nautonnier placed a large book on the table and opened it. It was ancient and brittle, and Christian could see that it was a ledger of sorts; a record of all who had signed their souls into the service of Ahreimanius and Lucifer. The Nautonnier took Christian's hand and pricked his thumb, filling the quill of a pen with the blood that emerged. He laid the pen next to the open book.

"You may sign it here," he said, his crooked finger pointing to a spot at the bottom of the page.

Christian took up the pen and watched his hand move the quill to the age old parchment. A mark was made, and knowing that it was done, he quickly finished the stroke.

Christian felt a dizzying surge of dark power flow into him, and then shuddered unexpectedly. Something was awakening in him; something that should never have been disturbed. He looked up to see that the Nautonnier was watching him intently now, an expression of cold malice spreading across his repugnant features.

"It is done," he hissed, blowing out the candle.

"Wait a minute," said Christian as the room plunged into darkness.

A sudden realization had flooded into him.

"What have I done? What have you made me do?"

"The way to Ahreimanius has been opened," came his father's hiss. *"Behold the newborn son of Lucifer!"*

Christian staggered through the darkness, finding the door to the suite and jerking it open. The light from the hall filled the room, but the Nautonnier was nowhere to be seen.

"What's happening to me?" he gasped, squinting into the shadows, his eyes wide with panic.

In the corner of the room he could see the shapes of four hooded figures, their bodies jerking violently from side to side, and coming in and out of existence.

"The Cube!" they hissed in unison. *"The Cube!"*

"No!" gasped Christian. "This is impossible!"

CHAPTER 24

Rome, Italy.

"We must move quickly!" whispered the Bishop.

Gabriel tiptoed to the entrance and poked his head out into the cold, dark passage. He heard footsteps, and then saw a light flash suddenly in the gloom. Within seconds, two figures had become visible. One of them was holding a lantern, but both of them were holding guns. They were clearly Nasrallah's men. He darted back into the chapel, intending to alert Fra and Suora, but finding them both awake and on their feet. He motioned Natasha and the Bishop to draw near.

"Nasrallah's men are just up the tunnel," he whispered. "I don't know how they got there. We should have seen them pass."

"They have come from above," said the Bishop.

"But that's impossible. The only way they could have found us would be through the nunnery tunnel."

The Bishop took hold of Gabriel's shoulder and passed him his father's journal. He had sealed it in an envelope. He drew Natasha nearer as well, and spoke to them both.

"There are dark forces at work here," he whispered urgently. "Their knowledge of where the Cube is at any particular moment is directly related to the amount of spiritual separation that exists between the two of you."

"What's that supposed to mean?" asked Gabriel.

"Listen carefully, my son," said the Bishop. "When you retrieved the Cube without Natasha being present, it would appear that you inadvertently directed certain dark forces to her. These forces have been with her ever since, and according to the Professor, they will continue to follow Natasha until you and she are able to fully merge."

"Merge?" whispered Gabriel urgently. "This is no time for superstitious nonsense, Marcus! The bad guys are just down the hall. What are you talking about?"

"The answers are in the book, my son. Until you resolve these problems, you will find that the enemy will always have a general idea of where you are."

Gabriel and Natasha looked at each other and then back to the Bishop. He was gazing up at the scaffolding now. In the light of the fire it could be seen rising up the frescoed wall and ending at the ceiling. There was an old ladder strapped to its side.

"If memory serves me correctly, there is a trap door up there," he said, pointing. "I believe the scaffold is hiding it. It will lead to the next upper level. Go now. You must still find your way out of the catacombs. That will be no easy task."

"But, Uncle," said Natasha, her eyes suddenly welling with tears. "The three of you could never make it up that scaffold."

The old Bishop noted her tears and dug for his handkerchief.

"We will not be going with you, my child," he said gently.

Well familiarized with the Bishop's grubby handkerchiefs, Gabriel stuffed a clean tissue into Natasha's hand before the Bishop could offer up his own. Natasha shot Gabriel a teary-eyed look of thanks. She was no stranger to her uncle's hankies either.

"The three of us will stay here and hide," said the Bishop, pocketing the handkerchief absently.

Gabriel frowned.

"They'll find you and they'll kill you!" he said, a little too loudly.

"That is not certain, my son," smiled the Bishop. "There are spirits of God here who are helping us. Have faith, and fear not for us."

"But, Uncle—" pleaded Natasha.

"Go!" said the Bishop, a rarely seen anger flaring up in his eyes. "There is more at stake than you can possibly imagine, and there is no time!"

To everyone's surprise, Shackleton took to the ladder in a single leap, making his way to the top swiftly and without pause. From below the others watched him disappear onto the top platform, only to see him poke his head out and look down at them.

"Who would believe a dog could do that," whispered Gabriel, shaking his head in amazement.

In a moment he had taken up both of their packs and was guiding Natasha to the scaffolding. She resisted at first, but Gabriel's touch seemed to reassure her.

The timbers were old but strong, and at the top they found the door the Bishop had spoken of. It was barely big enough to squeeze through, but as Gabriel shined his light into it he could see that it opened into a tunnel above. Shackleton was already through. Gabriel could see him in the shadows, sniffing the air and looking around.

"I'll go first," he said, stuffing the packs up and hoisting himself through.

He held a hand down for Natasha to take.

"Come on," he whispered. "There's no time."

Natasha was looking over the edge of the scaffolding. She could see the Bishop helping Suora into the tiny opening at the base of the altar. They would be hiding in the room that was filled with bones. Natasha saw him look up at her.

"Go!" he mouthed, motioning to her with his hand.

Natasha saw him smile reassuringly, and then disappear into the opening.

"I will see you soon, Uncle," she whispered, and just then, Nasrallah's men burst into the chapel.

Natasha saw them make for the hearth. These were not the uniformed figures she had seen earlier on in the courtyard. They were plainly dressed men, and would have appeared to be tourists were it not for the guns in their hands. Gabriel poked his head down and was going to say something, but Natasha silenced him. She gave him her hands and let him pull her up.

* * * * * *

"Radio Bahadur," said one of the mercenaries in Arabic. "Search every corner of this place. They were just here. They could not have gone far."

Bahadur arrived moments later to find most of his men in the chapel. They were all in plain clothes now, two of them emerging from behind the altar. They had found a backpack. They approached Bahadur.

"It looks as though they were sleeping in that little room, sir," said one of them, handing him the pack. "The room is full of bones, but there is a blanket spread out on the floor."

Bahadur took the pack from the mercenary and reached inside. He brought out a package, unwrapping it to find a large piece of cake, dripping with honey. He smelled it and took a huge bite.

"Has this entire space been searched?" he said, chewing.

"Yes, sir," said the soldier. "We have found nothing here but the traces they left behind. They must have been eating when they became alerted to our presence. There is still soup in the pot."

"Soup?" repeated Bahadur, raising an eyebrow in the direction of the hearth.

He had not received a single morsel of food in more than twenty-four hours now, and his tortured body was in desperate need of nourishment.

"Continue with the search as planned," he said. "They are obviously not here. Go! The sooner this is over the better."

Within moments his men had vanished, leaving Bahadur alone before the crackling hearth. He sat himself down in one of the chairs, wincing in pain as he reached for the pot. It rested on an iron grating with hot embers still burning beneath it. Beside the pot he found a slice of bread laden with what appeared to be slices of roasted pork. It had been Gabriel's, and only a single bite had been taken from it.

"Lentils," he said, blowing on a spoonful of the soup. "And roasted swine…"

He paused for a moment, thinking.

"A sin to eat, but Allah will understand."

CHAPTER 25

By the time Gabriel had lifted Natasha through the trapdoor, Shackleton was nowhere to be seen. Gabriel shone his light down the passage in one direction and Natasha in the other. There was no sign of the dog anywhere.

"Shackleton!" whispered Natasha. "Shackleton!"

Gabriel turned to face her.

"He knows what he's doing," he whispered. "We've got to keep moving. This place is crawling with Nasrallah's men."

"But which way do we go?"

Gabriel pulled out his compass.

"The main entrance is at the southern end of the necropolis."

"But we are still three levels beneath it," said Natasha.

"Good point. Let's just look for a way up then. Any preference in direction?"

Natasha pointed into the shadows.

"That way."

"West. OK. I'll always trust a woman's intuition. Let's go."

"I hope that Shackleton has the same intuition as me," said Natasha, but Gabriel had already moved off.

The tunnel they found themselves in was identical to the others. To their right and left were the countless loculi with their sepia coloured bones. Unlike the tunnels of the lower level these wound and split, bringing them to many forks and junctures along the way. They stopped at every one, each time Gabriel asking Natasha for her first intuitive direction.

"Left," she would say after a moment's pause, or, "Straight through," or, "Left," "Right,".

They walked like this for what seemed hours, feeling themselves more and more entangled in the knotted passageways. With each step, Natasha felt her hopes fading. She no longer felt the pressing danger of those who pursued them. Everything had been overshadowed by a desperate desire to escape this place; to simply get out. With every step Natasha felt as if the dead were calling to her, and with every step she feared more and more that they would never leave this place alive.

"Is it true that some people have entered these catacombs and never found their way out again?"

She could see Gabriel up ahead, his dark form silhouetted by his roaming flashlight. He stopped and turned to face her, suddenly aware of how frightened she was.

"Come here," he said grudgingly, pushing a hand through his shaggy hair. "You're lagging behind."

Natasha came closer, and Gabriel took her hands into his. In the darkness he could feel them cold and trembling. He had to make her understand.

"Everything's going to be fine," he said.

Natasha forgot all her misgivings and fell into his arms.

"I'm scared," she said amid shivers.

"Now listen to me," said Gabriel softly. "I've been in much worse places than this. Really, I have. I'm not worried. Believe me. We're going to get out of here."

Natasha bit her lip.

"But what about Uncle Marcus, and Suora and Fra?" she said quietly.

Her eyes were wide open now, staring out into the darkness that loomed behind him.

"And where is Shackleton?"

Gabriel said nothing. He could already feel her calming down as the warmth spread between them. He was feeling something he had never experienced before. With their bodies pressed together, the inner void that had plagued him for the past month felt suddenly full.

Gabriel pushed her gently away, but kept hold of her arms. Women like Natasha were incapable of accepting the kind of love he had to give. It was a lesson he had learned the hard way many times. The objective here was simply to cheer her up a little. That was all.

"Never lose sight of the facts," he said.

Her scent was intoxicating him.

"Marcus knows these catacombs well, and he's been full of surprises up to now. They will be fine. Just trust me on this one."

He moved a lock of hair out of her eyes.

"You might have all your woman's intuition," he added, frowning at an unexpected surge of affection in him, "but I've got my gut, and it's telling me they're fine. We'll be seeing them again soon. That's a promise."

Gabriel's was having a considerable effect on Natasha. In the few minutes they had been together, almost all of her fear and coldness had vanished. As surprising as it was to her, she could not recall having ever felt more safe and secure than she did at that moment, lost as they were in that dark and dreadful place. She swallowed slowly and collected herself, stepping back and wiping away her tears.

"You have a way with ladies, Gabriel Parker," she said, giving him a smile that was suspicious and timid all at the same time.

Gabriel was going to say something but Natasha reached up and put a hand over his mouth. She could see a flickering light in the darkness behind him, not fifty paces away.

"There is somebody coming," she whispered.

Gabriel took hold of her hand and pulled her back into the shadows.

"Don't even breathe," he whispered severely, poking his head out into the tunnel.

He could see the light clearly now, but was surprised to learn that it did not come from a flashlight. It appeared to be the light of a lantern, or several lanterns. It was illuminating a large area of the tunnel. Within moments the clatter of many feet were echoing around them. A voice spoke out in an Italian accent.

"Now, please, ladies and gentlemen. We will follow him, but keep together. We do not want anyone getting lost."

Gabriel turned to Natasha.

"Did you just hear that?"

Natasha had a smile from ear to ear.

"Let's stay here," said Gabriel. "We've got to be absolutely sure."

Gabriel poked his head out again to see a large group of twenty or so tourists behind their guide. Directly before the man was a handsome brown hunting dog, urging them all to follow him.

"Shackleton!" shouted Gabriel, jumping into the passage. "Come here boy!"

Natasha burst from her hiding place just in time to receive the dog into her arms. He had come bounding down the passage like a horse at play, slowing only just before arriving, and gently finding his way into Natasha's embrace.

"Oh, Shackleton!" she said. "What would we do without you?"

* * * * * *

The setting sun was blinding as they emerged from the necropolis, a relief flooding into them that could only be described as euphoric.

"What a beautiful evening," said Natasha, taking in a deep breath of the fragrant air.

Around them Rome bustled in its familiar way, oblivious to the damp graves and catacombs that lay underfoot. Shackleton let sound a deep bark.

"What is it, Shackleton?" asked Natasha, bending down.

"He's trying to tell us something," said Gabriel. "What is it, boy?"

As if in response to Gabriel's question, Shackleton raised a paw and laid it on Natasha's bent knee, nuzzling his head into her lap.

"Shackleton!" she said laughing. "What are you trying to tell us?"

The dog answered her question with a happy bark, bounding off immediately afterwards.

"Shackleton!" cried Natasha. "Come back!"

They stood up to see the dog trot past a group of tourists and disappear into the crowds. Natasha looked at Gabriel in distress.

"Now don't start worrying about him again," he said, holding out his hands. "I've got a hunch he knows more about what's going on here than we do."

"But where is he going?" she asked, pouting.

"I haven't a clue," said Gabriel. "But if I'm sure of one thing, it's that we'll be seeing him again, and probably when we need him the most."

CHAPTER 26

Amsterdam, North Holland.

"Ladies and Gentleman, I would like to introduce the president and owner of AuraChip Industries; esteemed member of the Vanderhoff group since nineteen eighty-four; Dr. John B. Middleton."

It was early evening, and the conference was now concluding its second day. The keynote speaker stepped up onto a podium in the hotel's main banquet hall, amid a full round of applause. Before him were the world's elite, more than a hundred and twenty strong. They sat at large round tables, arrayed with the finest china, and lit by the warm light of massive chandeliers.

"Thank you," he said, waiting for the applause to subside. "It seems like only yesterday that I was up here boring you all with the tiring details about Radio Frequency Identification Microchips, and their many biometric potentials. I can recall that we were just about to have dinner, and that's probably the reason why no one left the room."

Laughter spread through the hall.

"You'll be happy to know that I'm going to skip past all the technical stuff this time and go straight into what we at AuraChip have accomplished over this last year. Although our outlook is quite extensive, it can all be summed up in two words: Human Implantation."

He was forced to pause until the applause died down.

"Out of the veritable cornucopia of cutting edge biometric technology, human R.F.I.D. implantation promises to be the ultimate game changer. Over and above the many ways it will improve lifestyle, health, and security, perhaps the most powerful will be population control, and that means outlaws, terrorists, and quite simply anyone who doesn't do what we tell them to do."

Laughter and applause sounded, the group delighted with the speaker's candidness. Population control was, after all, the Vanderhoff Group's primary objective.

"The AuraChip will mean the end of organized crime and terrorism as we know it. The moment laws are broken, AuraChips will simply be deactivated, leaving deviants trackable, and without any resources. In a world where all your money is on your AuraChip, and cash does not exist, what will a criminal do if he's offline?"

"He'll clean up his act, God damn it!" exclaimed an old American man at a nearby table.

His comment was met with a healthy round of applause.

"Yes, I'm afraid he'll have no choice but to shape up," said the speaker. "Unless of course he wants to live like a caveman."

The laughter continued.

Christian took the opportunity to rise from his table and leave the hall. Over his shoulder he could still hear the speaker.

"Now, the world at large is still quite unaware of our plans for the AuraChip, and this leaves us with a tremendously exciting, and extremely lucrative opportunity to be the ones to implement this new technology across a full spectrum of applications. What I'd like to go over now is a detailed plan of action that—"

Christian closed the door behind him. Any interest he might have had in the conference had now been replaced by a cold contempt for all those attending.

"Stinking maggots," he muttered bitterly. "Putting on airs of helping humanity when all they want to do is subjugate it. If they openly admitted what they were doing I could respect them..."

Ever since the proceedings with the Nautonnier that afternoon, Christian had been consumed with anger and hatred. Although intoxicating, these nefarious emotions also frightened him. They seemed to come from a dark personality within him; a previously dormant shadow-self that had been awakened when he had signed the ledger. He began to tremble with rage the more he thought of it. The Nautonnier had tricked him into taking that pledge. Christian would make him pay for what he had done.

I'll kill that piece of shit with my own hands.

As he marched towards the main lobby, Christian could not help but flinch when he saw his reflection in a passing mirror. It jerked him back into reality, checking his wrath almost immediately. He had never been a saint, this was true, but in his eyes he had just seen a cold blooded killer. He stopped in his tracks and walked back to the mirror, looking at his reflection with deep concern. For a fraction of a second he could have sworn that his eyes were not his own, but rather those of a reptile. He produced his phone on an impulse.

"This is Christian Antov," he said. "I need to speak with Doctor Bennington immediately."

There was a pause as he listened.

"It does not concern me that he is on holiday in Paris. He will drop whatever he is doing and call me at once!"

CHAPTER 27

Rome, Italy.

Gabriel could not help but think he was staying at Buckingham Palace. The pomp of the five star suite was completely at odds with his simple tastes. Despite having managed to amass a considerable fortune retrieving lost treasures and artifacts over the years, Gabriel had never once been taken by the luxuries such wealth offered. With the exception of Italian motorcycles, German cars, and American gadgets, his tastes had remained simple and down to earth.

In almost every case, Gabriel preferred the clay goblet to the golden chalice, and if he had brought Natasha to this particular hotel, it was only because he wanted to be sure that she would be as comfortable as possible. She was currently showering in the adjoining suite, the door that linked the two rooms kept open on her insistence.

"I hope you do not mind," she had said timidly, "but Uncle Marcus said that those men will always have a general idea of where we are. And then there are those dark forces that he said were following me... I would feel much safer knowing you are close by."

Gabriel peered into her room uncomfortably. Over the running water of the shower he could hear her singing the lyrics of an Italian pop song. He shook his head incredulously.

How can a nation that spawned the likes of Puccini and Verdi possibly produce a song that cheesy?

He called the Bishop's phone again, just to get his mind on something else. When the machine came on he decided to leave a message.

"Marcus," he said. "I hope you get this. Natasha and I are out of the catacombs and checked into a hotel here in Rome."

He paced around the room as he spoke, not knowing what to do with himself.

"Something's come up. It turns out that the informant who gave us the location of the Cube was Amir's cousin: A guy named Bahadur. Nasrallah suspects that Bahadur had something to do with the robbery. He's holding their entire family hostage."

Gabriel moved to the enormous bed, looking down at its golden pillows and ornate coverings.

How is anyone supposed to get comfortable in a place like this?

He reached down and pulled away the silken cover.

"Before we do anything about the Cube, I've got to get Amir's family out of there. I'm responsible for all of this. Natasha's insisted on coming with me. We'll be flying to Gibraltar tomorrow, and then heading to Morocco from there. Call me the minute you get this. We need to know you guys are safe."

Gabriel pocketed his phone and lay back onto the bed's many cushions, his arms behind his head. He could still feel the grit from the catacombs in his hair, and felt far too dirty to be lying where he was. He got up almost immediately, looking around the suite, and feeling a growing anxiety for his three dear friends. The fact that he had intentionally left them behind was proving very difficult to bear now, especially given the luxurious surroundings.

"We had no choice," he muttered to himself. "There was no option. They'll be fine. Everything will be fine."

Gabriel paced aimlessly. He had promised Natasha that he would wait until she finished showering before doing so himself. He moved to a little wooden table by the window and pulled up a fragile chair. His old battered duffel bag was on the couch beside him. He took hold of it and noticed that it had already soiled the cream coloured upholstery with rusty catacomb dirt.

"Oh, man," he sighed, moving it onto his lap. "So much for the damage deposit."

He reached into it, carefully removing the Cube. There was something about the artifact that drove him to hold it; something that made him feel as though it needed his attention; as though it were somehow alive. Removing it from its container, Gabriel was instantly made aware of its strange characteristics, and once again found himself unable to pinpoint exactly what it was. He had seen countless artifacts over his career, but there was something very different about this one. Gabriel looked up suddenly. The shower had stopped.

"I am almost finished," chimed Natasha, and another surge of affection filled his heart.

Don't go there, buddy. She's not for you.

It was at that moment that Gabriel noticed something very peculiar. It seemed to him that a glimmer of light had caught his eye; one that appeared to have originated from the Cube itself. Gabriel looked up to the ceiling, expecting to find a recessed light that might have reflected in its gold leaf, but there was nothing there. As he looked around the room he saw that there was no lamp that could have produced such a reflection.

"Do you see how quickly I shower?" came Natasha's voice, pulling him from his thoughts as she appeared at the threshold. "I am just like a man in that way."

She was wrapped in a thick white towel and in the act of brushing her liquescent chestnut hair. Gabriel was once again captivated, despite his best efforts. It took him a few seconds to register that her happy expression had changed into one of wonder and awe.

"So that is the artifact…" whispered Natasha, stepping into the room and pointing to the Cube in his hands. "What makes it glow like that?"

Gabriel looked down at the artifact, unable to believe his eyes. Emerging from a series of cracks in its surface was an unmistakably blue light. He jumped to his feet, dropping the Cube onto a chair and instinctively moving away from it.

"What the hell is that?" he said, half shielding Natasha with his body, as though the Cube might explode. "This is impossible. Medieval artifacts don't light up."

As one, they moved closer to the relic, intrigued by the quality of its light. Gabriel was perplexed. He had examined the piece on several occasions and had been certain of its authenticity. In a split second all that had changed.

"It's some kind of a hoax," he said, squatting before it.

Natasha kneeled down next to him.

"The light seems to be leaking through cracks at the edges of the parchment," she said, picking up the artifact and moving closer to Gabriel, so that he might study it too. "Do you see what I mean? Right here, where the vellum meets the framework."

"It looks like there's another layer to the thing," said Gabriel, becoming increasingly intoxicated by the smell of soap on Natasha's skin.

"Another layer?" she asked, turning to look at him. "What do you mean?"

Gabriel looked into her beautiful, Sofia Loren eyes, suddenly oblivious of the artifact. It was taking all his willpower to stop himself from kissing her.

"It used to have a crudely painted outer shell," he said softly, moving aside the same lock of hair that had fallen over her eyes in the catacombs. "I removed it back at the monastery."

The backs of his fingers traced lightly over her ear as he tucked away the errant lock. It sent a tingling thrill through Natasha. The hint of a smile appeared around Gabriel's lips.

"I kept the pieces if you'd like to see them."

Natasha's eyes were veiled in mist now; like a doe caught in his lights.

"This artifact had an outer layer," she whispered absently. "You should have told me."

"I was going to," said Gabriel softly.

"You were?"

Gabriel nodded slowly in affirmation, his eyes taking in her pretty features.

"Yes, I was. I just forgot."

Natasha glanced down at his lips. Gabriel was such a paradox. There was no doubt that he was a nice man, but he was so self-assured, and so quietly cynical. She knew so little about him.

"Well, do not let it happen again," she whispered dizzily.

Gabriel nodded slowly, looking deeply into her eyes.

"Because if the Cube had one layer," she continued, "it could easily have another."

"I suspect it does."

"I suspect it does too."

Just then Natasha began to break from the spell, the tremendously important meaning of what was being said finally settling in. She had dedicated her life to artifact restoration, and here was the most mysterious artifact she had ever encountered, potentially ready to reveal yet another layer of itself. The realization of it filled her with a flood of excitement, and in a split second her eyes were alight with urgency.

"Gabriel!" she exclaimed, jumping to her feet and holding the Cube out before her. "Do you know what this means? Why did you not say anything? This is incredible! What did you do with the pieces you removed?"

Gabriel nodded and rose to his feet with a groan, pointing a thumb at his tattered pack.

"Go crazy," he said, half angry with himself for letting himself get caught up in her like that. "But don't get too excited. I think Nasrallah's played a little joke on us. My guess is that you're going to find a couple of nine volt batteries hidden in that thing. I've got a hunch we've been duped."

"We cannot know until we have studied it further," she said, rummaging through the leather duffel bag. "Where are you going, Gabriel?"

"To take a shower," he said, feeling almost relieved that the Cube had turned out to be a hoax. "You know, that drug lord really had me going. Apart from the silly light trick, that artifact is a brilliant forgery."

He made his way into the bathroom, leaving the door slightly ajar so that Natasha might feel safer.

"He sure went through a lot of trouble to throw us off the trail," he added, turning on the tap. "I wonder why. It just doesn't make sense."

CHAPTER 28

Bahadur finished the last of his soup, mopping up the remaining few lentils with a crust of bread held between two massive fingers. It had been the first thing he had eaten in a very long time, and although it had done him tremendous good, he was still not satisfied. He hunched over and picked through Fra Bartolomeo's pack, wondering if he might have missed something. He found a bottle of water and a flashlight.

"This is very strange," he said to himself. "Perhaps they left their food and water behind in their haste, but how far could anyone go in this darkness without light?"

Bahadur tested the switch and saw that the batteries were still good.

"Something is not right," he muttered, his voice as deep as the catacombs.

Groaning in pain, he rose from his chair and turned, leaving the warm fire behind him as he made his way to the room where the guards had found the pack. Shining his flashlight into the chamber, Bahadur passed the beam of light over the somber mounds of bones until it arrived at a small blanket that lay spread out on the floor.

"Why sleep here when you could sleep by the fire?" he said slowly.

Grunting with effort, Bahadur bent low and squeezed himself through the tiny opening, unholstering his handgun as he went. He made his way to the blanket and pulled up the edge.

"Allah be praised," he said in his deep basso.

There in the floor, directly beneath where the blanket had been, was a trap door made of heavy wooden planks. Holding his gun in one hand, he took hold of the door with the other and swung it open, his eyes opening wide at the sight before him. There, lying trembling in the cold ground, he could see three figures looking up at him, their eyes wide with fright.

"What have we here?" he said, holstering his gun. "You all look quite old, but hardly ready for the grave."

Bending down, Bahadur took hold of Suora's arm, and gentler than might have been expected, helped her out of the shallow pit.

"Sister," he said respectfully, his voice like a booming bass drum. "Please, allow me."

He shook the blanket that had been lying on the floor, and wrapped her shivering body in it.

"Thank you," said Suora, utterly surprised.

The enormous bald-headed man appeared to be a monster. His scarred face was badly cut and bruised, and there was a gruesome image of a black moth tattooed to his tortured neck. He wore a black, tight-fitting sweater and black military pants, his massive, horse-like muscles stretching the material taught. Strapped to his waist, on the opposite side of his handgun, was a massive, and very dangerous looking, military combat knife. Even still, there was a deep wisdom in his intelligent eyes. The three seniors could see that this was no monster who stood before them, but rather a tame and noble giant.

"Please," he said to the Bishop and the Brother, reaching down to help them.

They each took hold of a massive hand and rose slowly to their feet. They had only lay there for ten minutes at most, but the ground was cold and damp and their old bodies had not taken kindly to the accommodations. Bahadur helped them out of the pit, looking back over his shoulder as he did so.

BOOK ONE : THE DARK RIFT

"You need not fear me," he said, his grim and battered face at odds with his words. "I am not a murderer, and especially not of those in the holy service. I only ask that you assist me in my endeavor. Where is the Cube of Compostela?"

"I am the Bishop Marcus Di Lauro," said the old Bishop, "and I thank you for your kindness and civility. I must say it is greatly appreciated. The Cube is not in our possession, although we were close to its keeper not so long ago."

"Gabriel Parker," said Bahadur, frowning. "Where is he?"

"That I do not know," said the Bishop, "but I must confess that even if I did know, I would not tell you under any circumstances. You see, the Cube belongs to Gabriel by birth. It is his for the keeping and I will not betray him."

"Yes, of course, your Eminence," said Bahadur, nodding solemnly. "This I can understand, but you must also understand that if you will not cooperate with me, I will be forced to take you as my prisoners until the Cube is recovered. It is not I who decide it, but those to whom I am bound."

"You are a good man," said Suora Angelica suddenly. "In your heart you are true, my son. It is the wickedness of others that has led you astray."

Bahadur turned to face the little nun, his expression gentle.

"Thank you, Sister," he said in his deep voice. "You are very kind and very observant, for ugly as I am, I try to be my best under the eyes of Allah. I have taken many lives, but never those of the innocent. You are safe while under my charge, but I cannot guarantee that my master will be so kind. Please now, you must come with me."

He led them out into the tunnel.

"I will give you a choice," said Bahadur, stopping and looking very serious. "I will be taking you to our headquarters. To do this we must first leave the catacombs.

We can do this by going back to the monastery the way you have come, or we can take the much easier route up through the catacombs, and out the public entrance."

The Bishop moved to say something, but Bahadur silenced him with a gesture.

"Were we to take the way through the catacombs, and enter into the general public, any one of you could easily scream out and draw attention to us. What kind of promise can you give me that you will not do this?"

"You have shown us mercy, my son," said the old Bishop in earnest. "In exchange for your kindness, I give you my word that we will not cry out. We will go with you peaceably to your headquarters, or anywhere else you wish, and we shall trust in God, or Allah if you choose, for He is the father of us all."

"And I will honour your promise, your Excellency," said Bahadur. "Please, come this way."

The sun had already set when they approached a black van parked on the roadside, meters from the catacomb entrance. Bahadur slid open the side door, much like a chauffeur might do, inviting the three to enter with a polite bow.

"Please," he said. "Enter and sit. You will find the seats very comfortable after your long flight."

"Thank you, my son," said Fra Bartolomeo, being the last to enter. "God bless you."

Bahadur closed the door and Fra watched him through the windows as he made his way around the van. He stopped just outside the driver's door and made a phone call. Fra listened in with his sharp ears.

"He must be talking to Nasrallah," he whispered to the Bishop and nun. "Judging by his tone."

He listened intently.

"He is telling him that he has found us, and that his men are still searching for Gabriel and Natasha."

Fra looked at the Bishop in surprise.

"He has been told that they are no longer in the Catacombs."

The Bishop took hold of the Brother's arm, a combination of joy and worry engulfing his features. The old Brother held up his hand in a gesture of silence.

"They do not know exactly where they are. Somewhere in the city centre. Bahadur is agreeing to regroup at headquarters."

Just then the driver's door opened and Bahadur entered the van.

"Do you require food or drink?" he asked over his shoulder. "I am afraid I have eaten all of your provisions."

"Perhaps a cup of tea would be nice," said Suora. "If you might be so kind."

"It will be my pleasure, Sister," said Bahadur, "and a fair price for such fine lentil stew. The honey cake was also very good."

"Oh, I am so glad that you enjoyed it, my son!" said the old sister. "It is my specialty. The lentils however, were Fra's humble invention."

She timidly pointed her thumb at the old Brother, and smiled ear to ear.

"I thank you," said Bahadur. "My employer had given me a severe beating and nothing to eat for more than a day."

"Oh, my goodness," said the sister, but just then, the Bishop's phone beeped.

"Excuse me, your Excellency," said Bahadur. "It would appear you have a message waiting. Perhaps you might put the phone onto its speaker mode, so that we all might hear."

"Of course, Bahadur," said the Bishop, fumbling with the phone. "I understand."

Gabriel's message played itself out. Bahadur turned in his seat to better hear.

"-*before we do anything about the Cube, I've got to get Amir's family out of there. I'm responsible for all this. Natasha's insisted on coming with me. We'll be flying to Gibraltar tomorrow, and then heading to Morocco from there. Call me the minute you get this. We need to know you guys are safe."*

Bahadur nodded slowly.

"Amir is my cousin," he said. "His family is my family. It would appear that Nasrallah is an enemy to us all. If you will please excuse me for one moment."

With that Bahadur left the van and began pacing around outside, bent in thought. He returned within moments, speaking out immediately after he had closed the door behind him.

"I have made a decision," he said. "I will help Gabriel Parker. We will bring Nasrallah down together. He is a very bad man. I will now make a few calls. When I am done, if your Excellency will please call Gabriel and inform him that you are here with me, and that you are safe. I will arrange a private flight to Gibraltar for us all tonight. Allah willing, we shall free my family, even if we must raise a small army to do so. We must do this quickly. The moment Nasrallah learns that I have betrayed him, he will order my family killed."

Suora Angelica squeezed both the Brother's and the Bishop's hands excitedly, delighted with the new plan. Bahadur produced his phone and put it on speaker mode so that they all might hear. The connection went straight to Nasrallah's voicemail.

"Master," he said. "There has been a change in plans. I have extracted information from the hostages and killed them. A trap has been laid for Gabriel Parker at the Trevi Fountain tomorrow night at twenty-three hundred hours. I have learned that he has hidden the Cube. For this reason he must be taken alive and made to talk. I promise to have the artifact for you in thirty-six hours. Please call me if you have any questions. I am your humble servant."

Bahadur closed his phone and then opened it to dial another number.

"Stop your search," he said sharply. "Regroup all the men. We will be laying a trap at the Trevi Fountain tomorrow at twenty-three hundred hours."

He was silent while the mercenary spoke.

"No!" barked Bahadur in his deep basso. "I have other business I must attend to. I am putting you in command. You will position the men around the square. I want two snipers on the rooftops, and everyone else in plain clothes. We will be taking Parker alive."

He was silent again.

"Yes, that is correct," said Bahadur. "I will meet you in the southwest corner of the square at precisely twenty-two hundred hours. Is that clear?"

Bahadur put away his phone.

"The game is afoot," he said. "May Allah help us."

Pulling out into traffic, Bahadur accelerated up to speed.

"Now for more important matters," he said. "British tea. We must not disappoint."

CHAPTER 29

Los Picos De Europa, Northern Spain.

"To the Black Lake!" hissed a demonic voice.

The sun had already disappeared behind the mountainous peaks as Isaac battled his way down the rugged terrain. Around him the tangled branches of countless black trees seemed like threads in a spider's web. At his feet, a tarp covered sled fashioned from plane wreckage carried what was left of the rotting corpse of his son, the stench of the thing filling him with constant nausea.

Dear Father, give me strength to endure this trial.

Isaac could do nothing to escape his fear. In the end the demons had won, taking possession of his faculties, but leaving him with enough consciousness to know what it was they were making him do. He was in a waking nightmare, and it was not easy for him to formulate thoughts. His memory told him that he had at last managed to free himself from the wreckage of the plane, and that he had been dragging the corpse for days now, crossing impossible barriers, descending perilous rifts, and all the time being made victim to an icy voice that filled his mind like a swelling ocean.

"To the Black Lake," it hissed over and over again. *"To the Portal of Ahreimanius."*

It was his son who spoke, and if he knew this, it was only because he was of his own flesh and blood. Isaac had spent a lifetime at his side. Singing to him, caring for him; loving, as best he could, a child who had never once uttered a single word to him; a child who had caused the death of his beloved wife. It had been a thirty-three year long vigil of parental duty, and even now, in death, the child would still give him no peace. Isaac felt a deep hatred for his son rise up within him, and with it came an encompassing sense of guilt for feeling this way.

"To the Black Lake! To the Portal!"

It was an incessant plea; a cyclical litany; minute after minute, day and night. It came as from a hungry infant; pleading, insistent, selfish, parasitic. On occasion the corpse would throw itself into violent tantrums, its hardened bulk twisting and jerking beneath the battered tarpaulin like a great dying fish.

Isaac made his way downward into the woods. Below him he could see a tiny island; the place of his son's conception. He suddenly began to feel a great weight pressing down on him. It drove the air from his lungs, and the sight from his eyes. He brought his hands to his face as a vivid memory flooded into him.

He could see his late wife, Alina, materializing out of the blackness. She was on the edge of a circle of standing stones, the tangled trunks of the little island's interior surrounding her. They had only just docked their boat. Alina had playfully run into the woods with a picnic basket. Isaac relived the intensity of his love for her. It ached in his heart, and made any other pain he was experiencing pale in comparison.

Almost thirty-four years earlier, Alina had been introduced to him by Father Adrianus. She had been a beautiful girl, over a decade younger than himself, and deeply in need of love and support.

"It is time you took a wife, my son," the priest had told him one day. "You will take this young woman as your bride, and together you will raise a family."

As always, Isaac had done as he was told, and it was not long before he had found himself on his honeymoon, walking the pilgrimage of the *Camino de Santiago* with a wife at his side.

Now, in his delirium, he was revisiting that time and place, and he saw that he and Alina were once again making love atop the great monolithic stone. A chilling fog had settled in. Something was terribly wrong. He looked down at Alina, but to his horror and repulsion found that the corpse of his son had taken her place.

Isaac broke from his twisted reverie, his eyes finding the cadaver at his feet. Through the tarpaulin he could make out its macabre form, and a sudden desire to destroy the thing filled him to the quick.

CHAPTER 30

Rome, Italy.

Gabriel emerged from the bathroom, clean shaven and wrapped in a plush white bathrobe. He found Natasha sitting cross-legged on his bed. She was wearing a pair of hotel pajamas two sizes too big, and her chestnut hair was piled up loosely on her head, accentuating her graceful, ballerina's neck. A heavily laden tray of food sat at the foot of the oversized mattress, its contents still covered with fancy silver lids.

"I asked room service to put it here," she said casually, reading his thoughts. "I hope that is alright. I thought it would be more fun this way. Like a picnic."

She smiled shyly.

"Great idea," said Gabriel with a nod. "And that's quite the picnic. It looks like you ordered every item on the menu."

Natasha beamed and then moved away a pillow that had been in front of her. Gabriel gasped in surprise. She had been busy. The Cube had undergone a complete transformation. It lay there amid six, cross shaped sheets of parchment, and a jewel encrusted framework that was completely dismantled. All that remained was a perfectly formed cube that looked to be made of semi-translucent stone. As before it was glowing, and the colour it took on was an incredibly beautiful iridescent blue.

"Happy to see me?" flirted Natasha.

"I guess I am..." Gabriel said, coming closer.

His eyes were glued to the artifact.

"How did you know?"

"Because it got brighter when you saw me."

Gabriel sat on the bed, his attention fixed on the strange artifact.

"What the hell is this thing?" he asked. "Is this some kind of a joke?"

Natasha crawled to the foot of the bed and began to pour out the coffee. Gabriel glanced up for a moment, his stomach rumbling, but his eyes returned to the artifact like iron to a magnet.

"It is no hoax, Gabriel," she said plainly. "I am absolutely certain of it. Whatever this is, it is authentic. Look closely at those parchments."

Gabriel examined each parchment in turn. They were cross shaped; comprised of six, equally-sized, square-shaped sections. Their creases revealed how they had previously been wrapped around the Cube. The parchments were beautifully worked, each one written in tongues belonging to the six great faiths: Islamism, Hinduism, Buddhism, Judaism, Taoism, and Christianity. Gabriel could not understand. Given the tremendous detail, it would have taken a forger years to complete a work of this magnitude. The parchments simply had to be authentic.

"If you look on the back side of the one that is written in Latin," said Natasha, pouring out the coffee, "you will find that it is signed by Gutierrez de la Cruz. Do you remember him?"

"He was the priest in Marcus' story," muttered Gabriel, picking up the parchment that Natasha spoke of. "The guy who found the Cube. He appears to be representing the Christian faith in these documents."

Gabriel turned his attention back to the Cube itself, laying down the parchment and picking up the strange, semi-translucent stone. He was amazed by what he saw. Covering its glowing surface were strange and ancient runes.

"These are the runes that Marcus was telling us about," said Gabriel, looking up at Natasha. "The ones that were deciphered in the Book of Khalifah."

He returned his attention to the artifact.

"This Cube isn't Sumerian. It's Neolithic. By the structure of these runes, I'd say it was proto-Basque."

"How old do you think it is, Gabriel?"

"It's difficult to say," he said. "The origins of the Basques have always been shrouded in mystery. Many theories point to them being the first Cro-Magnon people to populate Europe, some forty-thousand years ago. By the looks of these proto-writings, they might be right. If it's genuine, this Cube could easily be that old."

"You cannot read the runes?"

"Not at all," he said, still studying them. "They're abstract symbols. Proto-writings. The Sumerians were the first to come up with an actual alphabet. Before that, people just drew pictures to tell stories. Whoever deciphered them must have been privy to some very specific knowledge. These symbols could mean absolutely anything."

Gabriel looked up at her before returning his attention to the artifact.

"At least this explains how Gutierrez could have found this in the tomb with James the Just," he continued. "This artifact would have been ancient even by their standards. It must have been Gutierrez and his contemporaries who built the framework and covered it in the illuminations. There's only one problem. How the hell can a forty-thousand year old artifact be glowing?"

Gabriel shot a baffled glance at Natasha and then returned his attention to the Cube.

"To produce this kind of light, a power source of some kind would be required," he muttered to himself. "It's too bright to simply be phosphorescent."

The more Gabriel turned it in his hands, the more confused he became. The material it was comprised of had a strange, organic quality to it. What was more; there was still the matter of its bizarre density. More than ever, it reminded Gabriel of a cube of very firm flesh, similar in density to the flank of a strong horse, but looking very much like translucent stone.

"I've never seen anything like this," he said, shaking his head.

Natasha handed him a steaming cup of coffee.

"Would you like to see something really amazing?"

"Sure," said Gabriel, taking a sip from his cup.

"Empty your mind of thoughts," said Natasha. "Just think of your coffee."

"Alright…"

No sooner had Gabriel done so than the Cube ceased to glow.

"What?" he said, looking up at Natasha, only to see it come to life once again.

Natasha clapped her hands in delight.

"It is magic, Gabriel!" she chimed. "It only glows when we are thinking of each other."

"How on earth did you figure that out?"

"Because you stopped thinking about me when you went into the bathroom."

Gabriel paused before answering.

"As a matter of fact, I did," he admitted at length. "I was feeling a little overwhelmed about everything. I decided to have a timeout."

"Interesting," said Natasha, rubbing her chin. "And how do you feel now?"

Gabriel returned his attention to the artifact, his brow furrowed.

"Overwhelmed."

Natasha leaned forward and kissed Gabriel's cheek.

"I like you very much, Gabriel Parker," she said, rolling off the bed before he could react. "And just for your information, I will be returning to my room as soon as we have eaten. So do not get any ideas."

Gabriel gave her a curious glance, his eyes following her as she made her way to the suite's balcony. Her words had sounded more like an invitation to him than anything else.

Like I said before: Don't even go there, buddy.

"You seem so familiar to me, Gabriel," she continued, gazing out over the glittering lights of Rome.

Gabriel tore his eyes from her, and brought his attention back to the Cube. She seemed incredibly familiar to him too, but he would not allow himself to be drawn into this conversation. There were more important issues at hand. Namely, a forty-thousand year old artifact that somehow glowed. He emptied his mind of her, and watched the Cube begin to grow dim as a result. After a few minutes Natasha returned to the bedside only to see that Gabriel had completely forgotten her. The Cube was like a lifeless stone.

"Hey!" she said, her hands on her hips.

Gabriel looked up at her, the Cube bursting to life the moment he had done so. He picked it up, shaking his head in amazement.

"Natasha," he said, still fixated on the thing. "This truly can read our thoughts."

"That is what I said," she muttered dejectedly.

Climbing onto the bed, Natasha busied herself with the food, occasionally glancing over at Gabriel as she prepared the plates. Gabriel seemed to reside in his own universe. He was like a planet, and she like a reluctant moon caught in his gravitational field.

I should never have let him hold me in the catacombs. It was a big mistake.

Gabriel studied the glowing artifact, oblivious of Natasha's thoughts. He was not one to believe in magical trinkets and unicorns. There was a scientific explanation for its light, and another to explain its obvious thought reading, neuro-feedback capabilities. The Cube somehow knew when they were thinking of each other, but that hardly meant it was magical.

Gabriel passed a hand over his jaw, absently looking for any stubble he might have missed. He could remember reading about BCI's, or brain-computer-interfaces, but he had never heard of wireless versions before. He could devise no hypothesis that might explain why an object of such seemingly advanced technology would be inscribed with Neolithic proto-writings, and wrapped in authentic, eleven-hundred year old manuscripts. It simply did not make sense.

At that moment, Gabriel noticed the lights in the room dim. He looked up to see Natasha standing by the light switch, the sight of her driving the enigmatic Cube from his mind. He felt as though he had been freed from one trance only to be entrapped by another. He watched her climb onto the bed, taking up the two plates she had prepared. Their delicious aroma reminded him of how hungry he was.

They ate mostly in silence, each of them lost in their thoughts. Gabriel made an effort not to think about her, but failed entirely, the glowing cube betraying his outward appearance of indifference. It amazed him that they could be so comfortable together, sitting alone in a hotel room without having to say a word.

Once they had finished, Natasha piled the dishes onto a tray and carried them back to the serving cart. When she turned to face Gabriel again she could see that he had leaned back and closed his eyes. She stood there silently for a moment and then gave a forced yawn.

"Well, I guess it is bedtime," she said.

Gabriel responded with a sleepy grunt and pushed himself back into the pillows. Natasha stood looking at him for a while longer. Every man she had ever loved had lied to her and caused her pain. As she looked down at Gabriel she could not help but wonder if he was like everyone else.

Go to bed, Natasha. You are thinking too much.

Natasha moved to the bedside and turned off Gabriel's lamp, reaching down to touch him but pulling her hand away at the last moment. Who was this man? How could he be so gentle and yet so strong, all at the same time? She smiled softly and then went back into her adjoining suite, leaving the door slightly ajar behind her.

CHAPTER 31

Amsterdam, North Holland.

Christian stood on the terrace of his penthouse suite, a lit cigarette in one hand, and a brimming glass of red wine in the other. A full moon was beginning to rise over Amsterdam, and far below he could see the last of the conference attendees boarding their limousines at the hotel's front entrance. He drained his glass of wine as if to toast their departure, ending his farewell with a grimace of disdain.

Turning back inside, Christian filled his glass again, drawing heavily from his cigarette as he poured. In his mind there was still the insistent voice of his father. It echoed only two words, over and over again:

"The Cube!" it whispered urgently. *"The Cube!"*

Having no idea what the words could mean, Christian was content to suppress their message, using the familiar tools of denial and alcohol to do so. There was no need to worry. His doctor would soon be providing him with medications that would silence the voices completely.

He fell onto the sofa and clicked on the television. It was eleven o'clock, and one of the many Vanderhoff-owned news channels was filling the screen, its famous slogan being proclaimed against a background of flashing imagery and hypnotizing graphics.

"GNN. The planet's most trusted news network."

Christian smiled wryly.

"What a joke," he said bitterly. "The only reason they are the most trusted is because they don't stop saying it."

Christian watched the introduction finish with a flourish. Within seconds the anchorman had announced the top story.

"Today, the President of the United States, along with the Canadian Prime Minister, and the President of Mexico, sign the final legislative documents ushering in a new age for North America. On the first of January, the Amero will become the newest currency in the global marketplace. Coming up, a rebroadcast of this evening's Presidential address from the White House."

Christian turned off the television. It disgusted him. He had only wanted to see that all had gone as planned, and it had. The machine he had so recently been given control of was working perfectly. He threw the remote onto the coffee table, and just then heard a knock at his door. Rising slowly, he made his way to answer it.

"Hello, Mr. Antov," said the beautiful young woman at the door.

She had an innocent, seductive smile, her hair red and curly.

"Good evening, whore," he said with hatred in his voice. "I want you naked on the bed, and I don't want to hear another word coming out of that painted mouth of yours for the rest of the night. Is that clear?"

The smile vanished from the girl's face. She nodded in affirmation, her eyes focused on the floor as a sudden fear flooded into her. Hopefully he would not hurt her. She had been warned that he was very rough, but nobody paid more than Christian Antov.

Christian watched her undress and climb into his bed. She was perfect, but he saw no beauty in her. He was engulfed in hatred. He felt it flare up within him, and once again, it was directed at himself. He despised his need to lie with women. He despised that he should require any service from any human being, least of all the demeaning act of animal satisfaction. Many had been the times that he had tried to deny his bodily needs, but he had always failed.

An unexpected knock came to the door. Christian looked over, his annoyance transforming rapidly into anger. He left the bedroom and reached the door in a series of aggressive paces, jerking it open.

"What do you want!" he said, but instantly he became silent.

Standing there on the threshold was none other than the ancient Nautonnier himself. Christian felt the room reeling around him. He hated this man more than he had ever hated anyone before, and an urgent desire to snuff out his repugnant life came flooding into him once again.

"Perhaps it is not what I want that is important," said the Nautonnier in answer to his question, "but what your master wants."

With a dismissive shove, the old man used his bony forearm to push Christian out of the way, making his way into the suite. No sooner had he entered however, than he raised his long nose into the air, taking two quick sniffs.

"You have a lovely scent, my sweet girl," he said in the direction of the bedroom. "Now put on your things and leave us. We have important business to discuss that need not trouble your pretty little ears."

Christian looked puzzled by the Nautonnier's remark. It had been his specific request that the girl wear no perfume. Within moments she had emerged from the bedroom, her clothes donned haphazardly. She made her way to the door, her head bowed in humility and fear, but as she passed, the Nautonnier's brittle hand shot out, clamping onto her upper arm with the strength of a vice. He pulled her close, running his grey lips over her perfect neck and inhaling her scent deeply.

"Ah," he said, sniffing her as a dog might do, "I can see he has not gotten to you yet, my darling."

And then shooting a glance at Christian he added:

"See the pretty little redhead saved from a ravishing! You might thank me, little one."

The girl twisted under his grip, smiling politely while trying to free herself from the stench of his breath.

"Thank you," she said meekly.

"You do not know the thrashing I have saved you from my sweet." breathed the Nautonnier, licking her neck and then looking to Christian. "Neither does our esteemed Mr. Antov. Now go! And never whore yourself again! Go to church girl, and ask Jesus for forgiveness!"

He pushed her away and she fled to the door, fumbling nervously with the latch before finally escaping.

"Get your things together," he said to Christian, walking to the door. "You will meet me in the Vanderhoff suite in fifteen minutes. Is that clear?"

"Get out of my room," said Christian, holding the door open.

His hatred and fury were merging into a barely containable wrath.

"You can expect me within the hour. If you don't like it, you can go to hell."

The Nautonnier looked up at him, smiling darkly all the while.

"I see you are feeling the power of the dark lord Ahreimanius," he said knowingly. "We will be waiting for you."

As the Nautonnier made his exit, Christian caught a fleeting glimpse of four quivering shadows being cast onto the carpeted hallway outside. He could not bring himself to look for their source. A feeling of deep foreboding was churning in his stomach.

What is this? What the hell is going on?

He closed the door, the low chime of an arriving elevator coming to his ears just as it shut. The sound seemed a kind of death knell to Christian, summoning that dark-self within him, and sending a jolt of hair raising fear through his body.

Christian retreated into his suite on faltering legs, a snakelike voice whispering its unending message into every corner of his psyche.

"The Cube," it hissed. *"The Cube!"*

CHAPTER 32

By the time Christian arrived at the Vanderhoff suite, more than an hour had already passed. He had purposely lingered at the hotel bar, wanting to make it clear that he was not one to be ordered about. He prepared to knock, but just as they had done on his first visit, the doors opened before he could do so. The dark and somber room came into view.

"You may come in, Christian," said the brittle voice of the Nautonnier from the shadows. "Your eyes will soon adjust to the darkness."

The doors closed silently behind Christian as he entered, the room plunging into blackness. He could feel a strange presence very close to him now, almost brushing his face and body. A subtle yet unmistakable stench filled the room; one that smelled of death and rot. A terror began to take hold of him, and it was only a sudden rush of anger, brought on by that dark-self within, that prevented him from collapsing to the floor.

"This is such bullshit!" said Christian aloud, his fear transforming. "I didn't come here for a spook show. Turn on a bloody light or I'm leaving and you can go to hell!"

He heard a match being struck, and saw a candle come slowly to life. It sat in the corner of the suite, illuminating a table, along with its five shadowy occupants. They wore dark, hooded robes.

"I didn't know this was a Halloween party," said Christian dryly.

He saw the Nautonnier rise to his feet and throw back his hood.

"You will have respect!" he hissed.

"Fuck you!"

The Nautonnier sat down as Christian approached, and the others remained motionless in their seats. The air seemed to crackle with energy. There was an empty chair at the table, and as Christian arrived he stood by it, looking down at the robed figures. It was the first time he had seen them up close, and their rate of vacillation seemed to have slowed, so that they almost appeared solid. Christian fought back an urge to vomit. They were repulsive to him.

"Sit down!" came his father's icy hiss.

Christian did his best to ignore it.

"Show me your faces!" he demanded.

As one, the four reached up and pushed back their hoods. Christian stepped away in shock.

What is this? How can this be?

Fluctuating between grainy ghostliness and solidity, he could see four visages before him, so ancient that their appearance defied all natural law. They stank of rot and decay. That something could be so old seemed to Christian utterly impossible. He bent forward despite his disgust. Their features were clearly reptilian.

"What the hell is going on here?" he asked, looking over at the Nautonnier.

"Our brothers are ancient by all standards. They belong to a race of beings that dwelt on the earth long ago. We are of their bloodline, Christian. Please, sit down. I beg you."

Seeing that the Nautonnier was finally assuming a respectful disposition had a calming effect on Christian. He had had enough of the old man's arrogance. He sat down and lit a cigarette, blowing the smoke directly into the Nautonnier's face.

"Start talking," he said, feeling his self-confidence eroding. "I'm a busy man."

"You are nothing without the master!" hissed the four in unison, each of them rising to their feet.

In that instant it seemed to Christian like a great weight were suddenly pressing down on him, as though he had been submerged into very deep water. The intense pressure made his head reel in pain, but he could not cry out. He watched the Nautonnier rise to his feet and disappear behind him. The pain was intensifying. He could do nothing but grasp the arms of his chair and writhe in agony.

"Can you now feel what you are up against, boy?" came the icy whisper.

Christian could hear the voice as though it were filtering up from the floor. The stench of the Nautonnier's breath curled over his neck and into his nostrils.

"Fuck you," he managed to utter.

"You will learn respect!" cried the brittle voice, and suddenly Christian felt a piercing pain burning into his lower spine.

It shot up into his ears, silencing his scream and sending all the muscles in his body into seizure. The room went black.

When Christian regained consciousness he found that he was still seated in the same chair. He looked up to see that the table before him was ablaze with candles, each one placed at the outer points of a pentagram that had been crudely drawn onto its surface. At its centre lay a dagger with a serpentine blade. Surrounding the table were the four ancient figures, and the Nautonnier. He could feel their wicked eyes on him.

"Who are you?" muttered Christian at last, looking to the four.

"We are the Zurvanites of Ahreimanius," came the cold whisper, as dry as ice. *"We are the keepers of the Eternal Temple of Set."*

Christian passed his hands over his face. His head was spinning.

"They are The Four," said the old sage, nodding. "Since ancient times they have served the Nautonnier, and given him knowledge and power. They represent the four great forces of destruction, and are the keepers of the four dimensions. They answer only to Lucifer."

"How can you expect me to believe any of this nonsense?" asked Christian weakly.

"You will believe when you witness the destruction they shall reap through you," said the Nautonnier. "You were always a disbelieving boy. It is time you opened yourself to the truth."

"How would you know what kind of boy I was?"

"Ah, but you forget, my child," whispered the Nautonnier. "We were great schoolmates."

In the depths of his heart, Christian felt a sudden pang of intense emotional pain. It seemed to come from a long way off; from another life, or from a nightmare. He squelched it immediately, denying it utterly.

"I see you choose to forget our special friendship," hinted the Nautonnier, a sly smile spreading over his face. "And after all the fun we had together..."

Christian battled with himself. Memories that he had long ago buried were coming up from his dark childhood. His loveless father, his cruel nanny, the loneliness and isolation. They had sent him far away, to a horrible place. It was an institution. There had been teachers. *Brothers* they had been called. Catholic priests. Christian squirmed in his seat, feeling the cruel eyes of The Four on him.

"Oh," said the Nautonnier in a playful tone, "I think he is starting to remember those things we did together."

Christian squirmed. The Nautonnier's voice was like a scalpel.

"How could you have forgotten? You are breaking my heart!"

Christian looked directly at the wispy haired Nautonnier. The latter was staring back at him now, an exaggerated pout distorting his repulsive features. In his cold, cruel eyes Christian could see something vaguely familiar, and in an instant, long drowned memories came flooding back to him, as though a dark gate had been lifted, or a tired dike thrown down.

"Father Adrianus," breathed Christian in horror, moving his head from side to side. "No! It can't be you!"

A darkness was enveloping Christian now. It came in from his periphery, engulfing everything in an inky blackness. Out of the shadows a scene materialized. He was remembering. He was a child. He was in a study room in the school library.

"You've been a very dirty little boy, Christian," whispered a voice, and Christian knew at once that it belonged to the Nautonnier. "What you have done to me is very wrong, and very dirty."

"No!" screamed Christian. "You made me do it! You made me!"

"Dirty boy!" scolded the voice. "Now you will do it to me again, or I will tell everyone what you have done!"

Christian jerked into the present. He focused his eyes on the Nautonnier, remembering fully what he had been made to do.

"You!" he said, trembling with fury.

A deep shame was making its way through Christian now, as though he were drowning in it. The seething hatred and anger that came in its wake threatened to consume him entirely.

"I will kill you for what you did to me!"

"He remembers!" exclaimed the Nautonnier, clapping his hands in feigned delight.

Christian attempted to rise from his chair, realizing only then that he was completely paralyzed. He could move nothing but his head.

"And, yes, Christian," said the Nautonnier wickedly. "Your father knew very well of our little games, as did you your uncle Vladimir."

Christian was in tears of frustration. Through the Nautonnier's promptings he had now regained all the memories he had so thoroughly repressed. He could recall each and every cruelty perpetrated by those who were supposed to have loved him. The walls had broken, and all the subterfuges that Christian had created to hold onto himself were gone. There was nothing but the truth, and he refused to believe it. He refused it with all his will. He would never allow himself to accept this. Never.

As the Nautonnier came closer and closer, something in Christian transformed. From the depths of his soul, riding on a swelling wave of violence, there came to him a great surge of strength. Its power was intoxicating, and he did nothing to repress it, choosing instead to observe the beast within him as a spectator might do. It felt primal and ancient; like something he had long ago once been, and only forgotten. In a fraction of a second his dark inner-self had taken up control.

Directly before him, Christian could see the Nautonnier's creased and wrinkled face. It was contorting with mock pity. He could smell his putrid breath, and the stench of it brought a pang of sheer lucidity to his memories. His childhood suffering played out before him. He was reliving every feeling; every sordid experience at the hands of the malevolent priest.

"You will pay," he said in a low, trembling voice.

His rage was on the verge of explosion.

"Oh, he is upset with me," mocked the Nautonnier. "Is this a lover's spat?"

With one concerted effort, Christian broke free from the spell that had held him paralyzed, shooting out his hand to take hold of the Nautonnier's wrinkled, brittle throat. His strength seemed unreal.

I'm going to kill you, you son of a bitch!

To his utter surprise, Christian felt his fingernails perforating cartilage with a sickening crunch. Hot blood exploded from the Nautonnier's mouth in bubbling gouts, running down Christian's arms, and drenching his face and body.

Christian rose from his chair like an angry god, lifting the dying Nautonnier into the air as though he were a limp rag doll. He could see the old man's eyes bulging from the pressure, but there was still an icy smile on his bloodied lips, as though he were somehow encouraging Christian to continue. The latter was beside himself now. Running in his mind was a movie of all the torments he had suffered at the hands of this man. The humiliation. The sheer humiliation.

Christian reached down with his free hand and took hold of the serpentine blade that lay on the table. Ever so slowly he sunk its full length into the Nautonnier's neck, sawing ineptly until he had at last severed the screaming head. He tossed it onto the table when he was done, and then watched the lifeless body crumple to the floor. The head had landed in the centre of the table, amid the pentagram of burning candles. Its eyes were still blinking. The smell of burning hair filled the room. Around the table the Zurvanites stood unmoving, shuddering and flickering in and out of being.

Christian was in a kind of ecstasy. He felt sated and free; like one who has finally rid himself of a postulant wound, or pulled an infected thorn from his flesh. His hatred rang like a bell's note. He took a long, deep breath and looked up at the Zurvanites as they stood there before him, his eyes dark and reptilian.

"It is done," they said to him, bowing in reverence. *"The prophecy is fulfilled."*

Their voice was no longer a physical one. It came like a thought from somewhere deep in his own mind. A wave of fear and repulsion passed through Christian. The Zurvanites were now inside of him. He and they were somehow fused. He gagged and bent over to vomit.

"Hail the new Nautonnier," they hissed as Christian sank to the floor, *"All power to Ahreimanius, the Lord of Darkness and Matter."*

CHAPTER 33

Rome, Italy.

Natasha stood before the balcony in Gabriel's suite, the shutters drawn aside. Eruptions of lightning where filling the horizon, spreading sheets of fleeting light over the distant clouds. Framed as they were by the starry sky above, the masses of cloud resembled mountains, black and threatening. From them there came an ominous rumbling that seemed to grow louder with every passing moment. An immense stormfront was drawing closer, and the busy streets of Rome seemed oblivious to its impending wrath.

Behind Natasha, Gabriel slept soundly in his bed. She knew that there was no reason to be frightened. She had only had a nightmare, but nevertheless something deep in her seemed persistent in its warnings. She passed her fingers through her hair.

"You're up," came Gabriel's groggy voice.

Natasha turned to find him propped on an elbow, his brow furrowing with concern the moment he saw her face.

"What's wrong?" he asked. "Did you have a bad dream?"

She stood there without moving, looking helplessly at him. Her eyes began to fill with tears.

"I am so sorry for coming into your room like this, Gabriel."

Gabriel got up and went to her. He put a hand on her shoulder, not knowing what else to do.

"You're trembling."

"We were together in hell," she said. "Then we became separated. Oh, Gabriel, I felt so lost."

Natasha threw her arms around him and began to cry. The rolling thunder boomed.

"I cannot understand," she sobbed. "Why is all this happening?"

"It was just a dream," Gabriel heard himself say. "Just a nightmare, that's all."

Natasha pulled her head back and looked into his eyes.

"Something happened to us when we were babies," she whispered, pushing aside his hair and tracing the tips of her fingers over the scar on his forehead. "Something horrible."

Gabriel felt a cold shiver run down his back. An instinctive urge to deny what she was saying took hold of him, but he dismissed it at once. The idea that they could have spent the first fourteen months of their lives infested by demons was horrific, but it had to be accepted. He reminded himself that it was only through this paranormal event that the Bishop had found them, and if they were who they were today, it was only because those events had taken place.

Something horrible happened to us when we were babies.

He moved away from Natasha and stepped out onto the stone balcony. It was past midnight but the streets of Rome were still bustling below.

"I've had dreams too," he said slowly, facing out into the night. "All my life. I've always pretended that I didn't have them, but when they came, I always knew something was wrong."

"Then we are not in this alone, Gabriel," came Natasha's voice, but this time there was a renewed strength in it. "That makes everything different."

Gabriel turned to find that Natasha had gone over to his bed. She lay there on her stomach, propped on her elbows and gazing into the glowing Cube. Once again Gabriel was captivated. The Cube's blue light was washing over her face as though it were moonlight. He could see that she was no longer frightened, and her resilience surprised him, helping him to douse his own fears.

Gabriel shook his head in wonder. Just like the Cube, it seemed to him that deeper levels of Natasha were being revealed to him with every passing moment. This being said, it was getting easier for him to keep his distance from her. The more virtues he saw in her, the more unworthy he felt. She was intelligent, genuine, and compassionate, without ever coming off as prudish or self-satisfied, and he was, after all, a whore monger and a thief; a tomb robber. He felt more empty than ever.

"Do you remember what Uncle Marcus said about the spiritual separation between us?" asked Natasha, her attention still fixed on the glowing Cube.

Gabriel gathered himself before answering.

"He said there'd be dark forces attracted to you as long as we were not spiritually merged. Whatever that was supposed to mean."

Natasha looked over at him through dark, curling locks.

"Two days ago I felt a supernatural presence in my workshop," she said, tucking her hair away behind an ear. "It was evil, Gabriel. That is why I went to stay with Uncle Marcus. It really frightened me. I thought I was going crazy."

"Two days ago," said Gabriel, letting himself fall into an ornate chair next to the bed. "The same day I recovered the Cube."

"That would make sense," she said, sitting up and facing him. "Uncle Marcus said that dark forces were alerted to my presence when you retrieved the Cube without me being there."

Gabriel thought for a moment.

"Do you think the dark forces could be in tune with our separation, in the same way that the Cube is in tune with our togetherness?"

Natasha shrugged.

"Considering that all positive spirituality is based on unity, and that all negative spirituality is based on separation, it could be so."

"By negative spirituality, do you mean Satanism?"

"Among other things," she said. "There are two opposing belief systems. The right hand path, and the left hand path. Followers of the right look for integration with the godhead. They want to achieve divine creative power by achieving union with all. That is what *'All Is One'* means."

Gabriel nodded.

"And followers of the left?"

"They seek the glorification of the individual self," said Natasha. "They want power over others, and fragmentation. That is what *'divide and conquer'* means. Throughout history the left hand has always been synonymous with evil because of these two different paths. As a matter of fact, in Latin, the word left *means* sinister."

"Dextra et sinistra," said Gabriel in Latin. "Right, and left."

They both fell silent, each one caught up in their own thoughts. Natasha continued to examine the Cube.

"You know," she said at length, "I am thinking we might find something if we could scan this with a biris."

"What's a biris?"

"It is a portable imagining scanner. I have one in my shop. It is on loan from the National Research Council of Canada. I am using it to capture all the Vatican pieces I have been restoring."

"How does it work?"

"It uses three twin-aperture lasers to scan an object," she said, "and then it triangulates the data to generate a three-dimensional image. With translucent objects like this one, you can scan them inside too. A biris is like an x-ray machine and an MRI, all in one."

Gabriel's face lit up.

"We've got to get that gizmo, Natasha," he said, a roll of thunder filling the room as he spoke. "It might give us a clue as to what makes that artifact tick."

Just then Gabriel's phone rang, the name on the display filling their hearts with hope. Gabriel hit the speaker setting.

"Marcus?" they said together. "Is that you?"

"It certainly is!" came the familiar voice. "And I must say that I am delighted to be speaking with you both!"

"And Suora and Fra? Are you all safe?" asked Natasha.

"We are all fine," came the humble voice of the old nun. "The good Father sent a noble giant to save us."

Gabriel and Natasha looked at each other.

"Bahadur?" asked Gabriel.

"That is correct!" said the old Bishop. "He will be coming to Gibraltar to help us organize the rescue."

"I don't understand," said Gabriel. "I thought he was being held prisoner by Nasrallah."

"Bahadur was the leader of the men who invaded the rectory, my son. Nasrallah forced him to do his dirty work by threatening to kill his family, but Bahadur has happily decided to join our side instead."

"You've got to tell him how sorry I am, Marcus," said Gabriel, frowning. "This is all my fault. By stealing the Cube I put his entire family in danger. I had no idea this would happen."

"It was not entirely your fault, Dr. Parker," came the deep voice of Bahadur. "Had I thought twice before giving you and my cousin Amir the information, all this might have been avoided. Nonetheless we will free them all. Everything will be fine. Of this I am certain."

"What will happen now?" asked Natasha.

"I have chartered a plane that will take us all to Gibraltar," continued the giant. "We will leave Rome immediately. There is a storm approaching. You must come quickly."

"Is there any way we can meet you in Gibraltar?" asked Gabriel. "We have to gather some important equipment in Florence first."

"That will not be a problem," said Bahadur. "I can arrange to have a plane waiting for you there. How much time will you require?"

Gabriel looked at Natasha.

"How tired are you?" he whispered, covering the microphone.

"I feel like I have been sleeping for an entire month," she said, smiling.

"Let's see," said Gabriel into the phone. "It's about a three-hour drive from here to Florence, but in a fast car I could do it in less than two. We'll need an hour to gather the equipment. How about three hours from now? That would put us there at around three-thirty in the morning."

"Consider it done, my friend," said Bahadur. "I will text you the particulars."

"If you don't mind me asking," said Gabriel. "How can you be so sure you'll find a plane on such short notice?"

"Dr. Parker," said Bahadur. "My position has its advantages."

"I'm sure it does," said Gabriel with a dry laugh.

"Very well then," chimed in the old Bishop. "Off you go! At the *Pillars of Hercules* shall we meet!"

The elevator doors opened, revealing the hotel's pompous lobby. They had not taken two steps forward before they were approached by the concierge.

"Dr. Parker," he said formally. "The car you have requested is waiting in the courtyard."

"Thanks," said Gabriel, stuffing a hundred Euro note into the man's jacket pocket. "It mustn't have been easy to arrange at this hour."

"It was my pleasure, Doctor," he said cordially.

A peal of thunder shook the air as Natasha led the way outside. There was a black Audi R8 parked in the courtyard, its sleek curves reflecting the silent flashes of lightning that lit up the night sky.

"Wow," she said to Gabriel. "I am impressed."

"We needed something fast," he said with a shrug.

Gabriel lead Natasha to the passenger door and held it open long enough for her to fall in. A moment later she felt a dense thud as the door sealed itself shut, the car's interior reminding her more of a fighter-jet cockpit than anything else. In a moment Gabriel had entered as well, quickly firing the engine to life. He slipped the car into gear and Natasha felt herself being sucked back into her seat as they sped out of the hotel and into traffic. Following Gabriel's example, she clicked her seatbelt home, delighting in the car's sexy interior.

"Here's where she really sings," said Gabriel, entering the autostrada's onramp and gunning it.

The car lurched instantly into dizzying acceleration, but just then heavy drops of rain began to strike the windshield, smacking into it with the force of small stones. They were headed right into the storm. Gabriel gripped the hand-stitched leather steering wheel and settled back into his seat.

"Good thing we've got the quattro-drive."

CHAPTER 34

Rome, Italy.

The rain was pummeling the tarmac, sending water shooting upwards in great splashing torrents. In all of his years in Rome, the Bishop had never seen a time when it had rained with such profuse density. It seemed an almost tropical storm, an anomaly in keeping with the strange, and often catastrophic, weather conditions that had been battering the planet of late. On this particular night there was not a breath of wind to be had, only a slight breeze being stirred up by the rain itself.

"How can we possibly fly in this?" muttered the old Bishop to no one in particular.

They were making their way out onto a runway that looked more like a fast moving river. Up ahead, the Bishop could vaguely discern the shape of a parked plane materializing through the downpour. It looked to be an old twin prop, its engines already running.

"Please, come along!"

It was the deep boom of Bahadur that called out to them. He was guiding them forward through the downpour, their umbrellas heavy under the falling water.

"We are almost there!"

Through a wall of rain the Bishop saw a staircase appear. He moved aside to allow Suora to pass first. Bahadur stepped up to help her, taking her umbrella and making sure she did not slip on the wet steel.

"Thank you, my son," she said as they made their way up. "God bless you."

Fra Bartolomeo followed, with the old Bishop slogging his way up last. The aircraft looked to be a relic of the early seventies; a silver cargo plane built like a tank. The interior was no different. Single rows of seats lined a wide cabin, leaving a broad cargo area running down the centre of the fuselage. It was hardly luxurious, but it offered a welcome shelter from the rain. The Bishop took a seat behind Fra, strapping on his seat belt and settling back into his chair.

Bahadur had just finished assisting Suora on the other side of the fuselage when the plane began to move. The Bishop watched him swing his massive body into the seat behind her, strapping on his belt and turning to look out the window with bruised eyes. The pounding rain, combined with the roaring engines, was making for a very noisy take off, but in the matter of a minute they were airborne, the plane rising sharply and banking to the right.

Outside the night was black under the dense rain, only to ignite into a flashing landscape of cloud when the lightning struck. The frequent claps of thunder sent shuddering quakes through the fuselage. Crossing himself, the old Bishop joined his friends in their well earned slumber. He had long ago given his life to God, and he feared death no more than one might fear a future dentist's appointment. That is to say, without looking forward to it, but accepting that the time would come when he would find himself sitting in that chair with a bib tied around his neck.

* * * * * *

Gibraltar

Amir hung up the phone and then picked it up again, dialing a new number. He had just arranged hotel accommodations for the Bishop and Brother, and had also, at the nun's request, phoned ahead to the convent to let them know to expect her. He was now in the process of calling an old friend; one of Gibraltar's most infamous smugglers. He could hear the phone ringing but there appeared to be no one home. He was about to hang up when a voice sounded on the other end of the line.

"Yeah, yeah! Alright for Christ's sake!"

It was gruff from too much smoking, and aggressive; the voice of a Gibraltarian pirate, its British accent rounded by its marriage with the Andalusian dialect.

"I'll get the bloody phone, don't you move a leg darling! Hello!"

"Scotty," said Amir in his steady tenor. "Sorry to be calling so late."

"Amir!" came the reply. "Late? The night's just beginning, mate! Bloody hell! The wife's had me locked up in here with her all day, and it's bloody tiring! I'm bloody well knackered from it!"

Amir smiled.

"Your wife keeps you out of trouble."

Robert's reply was being directed at someone other than Amir.

"Well if she don't shut up, I'm gonna lock her fat ass in the closet again, the bloody WITCH!" and then in a friendly tone, "What can I do for you, mate?"

Amir's dreadlocks shifted as he shook his head in disapproval, smiling despite himself.

"We're in trouble, Scotty. Could you help us?"

"Of course, mate. What's the problem?"

"Nasrallah's putting the screws to Bahadur. He's taken our family hostage. He's even got granny."

"That bloody bastard," said Roberts, genuinely shocked. "That's heavy shit, man. How can I help?"

"Bahadur is flying in from Rome tonight. He's talking about taking Nasrallah down, and busting our family out. They're being held in Nasrallah's digs."

"Bloody hell, mate," said Roberts, a little shaky. "That's a bloody fortress. I'd love to see it happen, but that's a bleeding war you're talking about."

"Listen, Scotty," said Amir, frowning with concern. "A few of us are getting together at Dickey's shop down in the marina; sometime around sunrise. I know it's early but do you think you could make it?"

Amir could hear the smuggler screaming at his wife in the background, the rubbing sound of his hand on the phone's mouth piece doing little to mute the dialogue.

"Shut up, you bloody whore!" he bellowed. "Can't you see I'm on the bleeding phone! …What's that? Well I don't give a bloody shit what you think, so you can shut your bloody mouth is what you can do!"

"Amir, my mate," said Roberts returning to his good natured self again. "For you, anything. I'll be there. And don't you worry. We'll find a way to get them out."

Amir nodded.

"Thanks, Scotty."

Amir could hear the screaming continue for a few seconds until the line went dead. He shook his head and smiled. Some people never changed.

CHAPTER 35

Los Picos de Europa, Northern Spain.

Isaac dragged the bloated corpse of his son onto the rocks of the island, the air entering and leaving his lungs in great gasps. His feet slipped in the soft clay, his bleeding toes curling into the yielding earth in an attempt to find traction. Over the course of the crossing, the cadaver's weight had almost doubled, the water having found its way in through the decomposing rib cage, leaving it waterlogged, and wretched beyond belief. Isaac strained to heave it onto the rocks.

Above him a thick tangle of trunks and boughs were dissolving into the grainy depths of the island. Somewhere outside of that cursed mountain range the sun would be rising, but it was invisible to him. He was in a low valley, the sky above dimmed by a somber mass of cloud that churned and boiled forebodingly.

"To the Portal of Ahreimanius!" came the icy hiss yet again, but this time with an insistence that was almost crippling.

"To the Portal!"

A muffled cry escaped Isaac's tightened lips. The demons within him were frantic, and the corpse of his son had begun to lurch and contort again, its limbs thrashing violently in great uncoordinated jerks. The stench of it was outlandish. Clotted masses of maggots, excrement, and vitriol were being pumped from the broken carcass with every freakish contortion.

"To the Portal!" it hissed voicelessly, the fiendish words stabbing like needles into his brain.

With a desperate and frantic tug, Isaac dislodged the corpse from the rocky depression where it lay, and proceeded in haste to drag it to the place of its incestuous conception. The rocks were slippery with the blood that left his feet, the incline steep and treacherous. Nevertheless, Isaac did as he was compelled to do, so that after an agonizing trial, he had arrived at the clearing, the skin on his hands and knees broken and torn, and his breath coming to him in choking grunts.

The circle of standing stones was better lit than the tangled path he had followed. Whereas the dense trunks had blotted out almost all of the predawn light, the clearing itself offered a dead glow of filtered illumination. It fell over the place like a pall. The central monolith seemed to call out to him. It lay there heavy and massive, its weathered top flat, and ready to accept what had burdened him for so long.

With his last ounce of strength, Isaac heaved the corpse onto its surface, a chorus of icy whispers driving away the last remnants of sanity from his mind. Around him, spread out in a perfect circle, were the fourteen standing stones, as tall as men, and disfigured as though they had been subjected to tremendous heat.

Isaac produced a shard of metal and proceeded to disrobe the jerking body. Black shadows had appeared on its skin, showing him where to cut. Without a word he began to butcher the undead flesh, all the while gagging and vomiting from the stench of it. No sooner had the corpse come into contact with the central stone than it had begun to tremble. It was as if each piece of the grisly carnage were somehow alive; quivering and contracting as the crude blade divided it up; the fingers gripping; the toes curling and uncurling. A tortured voice in Isaac's soul cried out helplessly.

Dear Father in heaven. Deliver me from this hell.

With the corpse now divided, Isaac proceeded to take up the fourteen butchered sections, placing each one at the base of a different standing stone. Overhead, a mass of heavy black cloud rolled in under the boiling sky, and a great clap of thunder shook the island.

With the grisly sections at last distributed, Isaac stood motionlessly at the centre of the ring, looking down at the top of the stone where he had done his butchering. It was crawling with the maggots that had been left behind, and beneath them he could see the image of a labyrinth carved into its surface; the crude figure of a man standing at its entrance.

"What horrors have you been forced to commit, Isaac," came a voice of such cunningness that he was instantly lured into its spell. *"Where is your loving God? How could he have allowed this to befall you?"*

Isaac teetered as though on the edge of an abyss. He was suddenly back in the hospital room, the demonically possessed body of his son in the bed before him. To his right and left he could see the stiffened corpses of the two priests, hanging by their necks in the cold blue light.

"I am Ahreimanius," hissed his son from the bed suddenly, and Isaac looked down to find a pair of wicked eyes looking up at him. *"Your blessed Father has deserted you, Isaac, but I can give you powers beyond your comprehension. Come with me, and I will make you more powerful than God."*

Isaac's soul groaned in agony. Ahreimanius was right. Throughout his tribulations, Isaac had never once felt the presence of God. On the contrary, he had felt as though God had abandoned him when he needed him the most. A great temptation to accept the offer arose in Isaac, and as he considered it, a vision of himself on high appeared before him. No sooner had he contemplated these things, however, than a voice within him cried out against the insidious offer.

"Never!" he exclaimed with all his will, and just then he was back on the island, released from the demons who had forced him to butcher the body of his son.

"You and your stupid little Cube!" hissed the voice of Ahreimanius in fury. *"Did you really think that I would ever allow you to do anything but serve my purposes? You will never assist the Two in their endeavors! You will die here tonight, and your pathetic life will have served no purpose but mine!"*

Isaac staggered backwards, looking around in shock. He could suddenly think clearly. He struggled to understand.

"What have I done?" he gasped, bringing his bleeding hands to his face. "Lord Jesus, what treacherous sin have I committed?"

Like the world returning to one who has awoken from a long slumber, so was the unholy scene revealed to Isaac. Forgotten now by the demons that had possessed him, he found himself stumbling to the edge of the circle, cowering in the dense undergrowth but unable to look away from the centre of the clearing.

Whereas each of the standing stones had begun to sink into the ground, the central monolith appeared to be rising ever so slightly into the air, its bulking mass levitating until it hung there weightlessly. Countless worms and other lightless insects scurried around beneath it.

Quite suddenly, in the depression where the monolith had rested, there appeared a rapidly growing pit of fire and ice, and the surrounding circle of stones were sucked into it, along with their grisly charges. A great chorus of wicked cries was issuing forth now, and from the black pit there arose fourteen great demons, like dense clouds of earth and dust. These were the Fourteen Emissaries of Ahreimanius, and their forms were horrendous. One by one they rose, churning in the air like blackened masses of cinder smoke; one by one screaming in hatred before shooting upwards into the boiling sky.

Only then did the floating stone fall, its ancient bulk fracturing suddenly into countless shards before being swallowed by the gaping portal as well. Isaac trembled with fear. Deafening claps of thunder were assaulting him from above now; an incessant barrage of lightning crackling down around him and setting the island alight. The demonic chorus grew louder and louder until it seemed to Isaac that the entire world would be consumed by it.

"What have I done?" he moaned, his hands covering his ears. "What have I caused to happen?"

Before him he could see that a conflagration had begun, and that the twisted trunks around the clearing were fully ablaze. Stunned and exhausted, Isaac stumbled wearily through the thickets to the water's edge, throwing himself into the black lake so that his death might come by drowning, rather than by fire.

"Forgive me for what I have done, Father," he said, his somber face lit by the flames of the burning island. "Save my soul."

CHAPTER 36

Florence, Italy.

The black sports car rolled slowly over the cobblestones, its headlights cutting through the heavy downpour. Natasha was looking intently through her window, scanning the shadows as they proceeded. They were driving along a narrow alleyway in the city centre, the heavy rain blanketing them.

Given the weather, the drive from Rome had taken more than twice what it should have. It was almost sunrise, and they were only approaching Natasha's workshop now. They had decided to take the back entrance as a precaution.

"So far so good," said Gabriel, easing the car forward along the constricting laneway.

He pushed a button and Natasha watched as the side view mirrors collapsed inwardly.

"You are like a little boy with your new car, Gabriel," she said, laughing.

Gabriel was tired from the long drive.

"Just keep an eye out for the opening," he said. "If you're good I'll let you play with the mirrors later."

Natasha guffawed in surprise.

"Don't you tell me what to do," she said. "I will look where I please!"

Gabriel pretended to ignore her, looking through the windshield to scan the peeling plaster walls that passed outside.

"Did you hear what I have said?" she asked, frowning.

"Did you hear what I have said?" he mimicked inaudibly.

"You are a *testa di cazzo*…" said Natasha.

On an impulse, Gabriel turned to Natasha and began to sing. It was a romantic piece of music from a famous opera by Puccini; his voice mimicking that of a tenor's.

O soave fanciulla, o dolce viso
Di mite circonfuso alba lunar,
In te ravviso il sogno
Ch'io vorrei sempre sognar!

Gabriel finished proudly. He was an avid opera fan, but hardly a tenor. He had tried his best to sing the part as correctly as possible, and Natasha had at first been wooed by its melody, her peevishness dissolving instantly. But as the passion had gained in intensity, Gabriel's voice had become more and more abrasive, until Natasha was at last able to regain her perspective. She looked over at Gabriel as though he were crazy, still laughing at his botched crescendo.

"You think you are really a good opera singer, don't you?" she said, shaking her head in disbelief.

"Oh, yes," said Gabriel, nodding emphatically.

He continued his scanning.

"Hey," he said. "There's an opening in the wall here."

Natasha rolled her eyes and looked out the window.

"You can park your fancy car now, Pavarotti," she said. "We are here."

By positioning the car next to the opening, Gabriel allowed Natasha to open her door directly into it. He climbed over to her side and followed her out. They made their way through a narrow passageway and into a drenched inner courtyard, arriving at a pair of old wooden doors. Natasha produced a large iron key from her bag in the pouring rain.

"I really hate this storeroom," she said, inserting it into the lock.

In a moment the smell of raw earth and ancient mildew had wafted out of the darkness to greet them. With the increased humidity, the musty air could almost be tasted on the tongue, and Gabriel breathed it in deeply, savouring the antiquity like a connoisseur.

"Got a flashlight?" he asked, squinting into the darkness.

Natasha produced one from her bag.

"Follow me," she said.

They made their way through the maze of shelves until they had reached the front room. It was not as dark here as in the storeroom. The bluish light from the street lamps was filtering in through the watery panes, casting shifting patterns of light on the floor.

"Please, make yourself at home," she said, beginning to pack a field case with equipment.

Just then Gabriel's phone rang.

Gabriel remained on the phone the entire time that Natasha packed the equipment. She could see that he was doing more listening than talking, but it was not until she had finished, that it looked as though his conversation might end.

"Alright then, Amir," said Gabriel. "If all goes well we'll be seeing you later this afternoon then. Stay in touch."

He pocketed the phone, turning to Natasha.

"What is it?" she asked.

"Natasha," he said, "we've got some driving to do."

* * * * * *

Gibraltar

The old Bishop awoke to find the plane in a sharp bank. It was no longer raining. Looking out his window he could see the Rock of Gibraltar turning below him, its small cosmopolitan centre twinkling with a thousand lights. Stretching out into the distance, the shimmering waters of the Bay of Algeciras could also be seen, dotted with freighters and ships of all kinds.

To the starboard side towered Gibraltar's majestic peak, silhouetted against a predawn sky. It was a time sculpted rock formation, topped with the famous single white cloud that had come to be known as *El Levante*, named after the easterly wind that was responsible for its formation. In minutes they had circled the small peninsula, leveling off to make their landing approach on the short strip of runway that separated the British colony from the Spanish mainland. The Bishop smiled in delight.

"Gibraltar!" he exclaimed. "One of the two great pillars of Hercules! The fortified bastion of the British Royal Navy, and home to the largest per capita density of pubs in all of Christendom! Aye, but a pint of stout would be nice. That and a breakfast of steak and kidney pie!"

CHAPTER 37

Amsterdam, North Holland.

It was just past six in the morning when Prince Vladimir Rodchenko arrived at the Vanderhoff suite. The front desk had awoken him with orders from the Nautonnier to go there immediately. Christian met him at the door and led him into the room, locking the door behind them.

The old Prince gasped in horror. Resting on a table at the back of the suite could be seen the severed head of the Nautonnier, propped in a pool of coagulated blood. In a facing chair, Christian had placed the headless corpse. It sat there stiff and macabre, like a gruesome figure in a wax museum.

"As you can see," said Christian, positioning himself behind his mortified uncle, "there has been a change in command. The Nautonnier has ceded his position to me."

The Prince seemed only then to come out of his shock, and would have fled the room had Christian not placed a heavy hand on his shoulder.

"Do you remember when you used to drop me off, and pick me up from school, Uncle?"

"Before and after every holiday," stammered the Prince.

"Was it ever difficult for you?" asked Christian. "Knowing that you were taking an innocent boy to be buggered by the man who is now dead before you?"

The Prince froze, unable to respond. The psychologists had assured them that Christian's memories would remain suppressed for the entirety of his life.

"I had nothing to do with it!" he stammered. "It was something between your father and the Nautonnier."

"You had everything to do with it! You knowingly allowed it to happen!"

"I will not be held accountable for your father's actions!" said the Prince with rekindling authority. "I am leaving!"

He attempted to move, but found that an invisible force was holding him fast. He struggled to free himself from it, his eyes bulging from the effort. Christian looked on. In the space of a few seconds, the Prince's face had gone from a pasty, ashen white to a vivid purple.

"Sit down!" barked Christian with icy hatred. "I am the Nautonnier now. You will leave when I am finished with you!"

"Please, Christian. I am your family," said the Prince, giving up his struggle and sinking into a chair.

It was on hearing this reference to his family that yet another deep, childhood wound surfaced in Christian. Impossible as it might seem, it had been the cause of more pain than all the abuses suffered at the hands of Father Adrianus. Christian had once had an older brother named Isaac. He had been the only source of love and support in his deprived life.

It was not long after the birth of their sister Alina, and the death of their mother, that Isaac had been sent off to study at Vatican City. From that point onward, everything in Christian's life had changed. Christian lost all contact with his brother, and two years later would himself be shipped off to school, returning home on his first holiday to find that his baby sister had also been displaced.

"What happened to my brother and sister?" said Christian, trembling with a strange combination of fear and rage. "Tell me about my brother and sister!"

The Prince remained silent until he felt the force of a vicious slap to the back of his head.

"Your father sent Isaac to be manipulated by Father Adrianus. He was persuaded to disown himself from the Antov family. Your sister Alina was sent to be raised in another household."

The Prince held up a hand to ward off another blow. Christian obviously wanted the full story. He proceeded with trepidation. He could well imagine the effect that the truth would have on Christian, and he feared for his life.

"Your father repeatedly raped your sister in Satanic rituals, Christian. He drove her to madness, and then disowned her at sixteen. She became a prostitute. Years later, in accordance with their plan, she was recovered and brought to Father Adrianus at the Vatican. She and Isaac were then made to marry. Of course, they did not know that they were brother and sister, but through their union a hermaphrodite child was conceived. Alina died giving birth to it."

Christian looked down in silence, unable to comprehend what he was being told. It made no sense.

"The child was created to fulfill a Satanic prophecy," said the Prince slowly. "Your father and the Nautonnier were obsessed with the occult. They used our science facility in Jerusalem to genetically mutate the child while it was still in Alina's womb. They used the genes in our bloodline to create a monster."

Christian broke from his stupor and turned to face the Prince, his eyes smoldering with deadly rage.

"And you knew all this?" he said, coming slowly out of shock.

The Prince shook his head from side to side as Christian bent down over him.

"No," gasped the old Prince, his eyes wide with fear. "You do not understand."

Christian's face was contorting with the pain of betrayal now. This was his uncle. His family. How could he have allowed this to happen to innocent children? He reached out a hand, as if to caress the Prince's face, but instead took him by the throat and began to shake him violently.

"You did nothing to stop it," he snarled. "You didn't give a shit."

Christian was beside himself with fury. How could such a thing be possible? It was too repugnant to even imagine. He stopped shaking the Prince and released him suddenly in disgust. The same dark-self that had possessed him when he had killed the Nautonnier was paying him another visit. All he could do was watch as it took control.

"You're responsible!" he bellowed suddenly, the veins exploding from his neck. "You stinking SON OF A BITCH!"

The force of Christian's violence and hatred caused the old Prince to recoil in his chair, his head jerking backwards in fear. He brought one of his hands to his chest, and the other he thrust outward, beseeching his nephew to desist. Christian positioned himself directly over the old man, smiling cruelly.

Under the candlelight, the Prince's unfocused eyes were blinking erratically now, his facial features contracting with pain. He was clearly having a heart attack. In his cold eyes there could almost be seen a cry for mercy, but it seemed wooden and insincere. Christian drew closer until his lips were physically touching the old man's ear. He smiled coldly, his wickedness ringing like an icy bell.

"Dear, Uncle Vladimir," he said with mocking innocence, his words twisting into the Prince's head like a carving knife. "Now you will DIE!"

The Prince's pupils contracted with fear, a look of surprised desperation contorting his features. He struggled to breathe, trying frantically to ward off the icy hand of death. Christian moved away from him in disgust. He could see the life force slowly leaving the body. He smiled wickedly, watching with great satisfaction as his uncle executed a long, drawn out death rattle. When all was over, he spat on the corpse, and then bent immediately afterwards to tenderly kiss the forehead, a tendril of saliva stretching and breaking as his lips pulled away.

* * * * * *

The morning was still young when the chief inspector left the Vanderhoff suite with Christian. Behind them, in a shaft of sunlight, the dead Prince could be seen sitting opposite the decapitated corpse, the Nautonnier's waxy head still on the table.

"A tragic incident, Mr. Antov," said the inspector solemnly, closing his notebook. "It is clear that your uncle died of a heart attack after murdering Father Adrianus. No investigation will be needed."

"Very good, Inspector," said Christian darkly. "Thank you for your diligence, and please have this mess cleaned up. I will have my assistant make the funeral arrangements."

"Very good, Mr. Antov," he said. "And a peaceful day to you, sir. You have my most sincere condolences."

Christian watched the inspector leave.

The matters of the Permanent Secretary are above the law.

Suddenly Christian felt himself being pulled back into the room, as though by an invisible hand. He made his way to the Nautonnier's body, and acting on an impulse, removed a bejeweled ring from the corpse. He placed it on his finger, directly next to his father's ring, and moved to look at himself in the mirror. A chorus of whispers sounded at once in his mind.

"Hail the new Nautonnier. And all power to Ahreimanius, the Lord of Darkness and Matter."

Christian shuddered as an icy chill rushed up his spine. In the mirror's reflection he could see the repugnant Zurvanites standing behind him now. They were positioned around the

Nautonnier's severed head; their grainy forms jerking violently from side to side, untouched by the sunlight that streamed into the room. Christian spun around suddenly with boiling wrath.

"Get away from me!" he bellowed, but they had already vanished.

In that moment Christian knew that he had indeed become the new Nautonnier, and he recalled what his wicked predecessor had told him of the Zurvanites only days before.

"They are the Four. Since ancient times they have served the Nautonnier, and given him knowledge and power."

Like a floodgate opening, Christian was at that moment made privy to many strange and mysterious things, and he was certain that the Zurvanites had imparted this knowledge on him. As though through churning mists, there came to him strange and formless recollections. In the blink of an eye he had been taken back through time; past the days of Herod, past the rule of the Zoroastrians, and further back still to when the world was watery, and men were like reptiles, and they were murderous and cruel. This was his ancestry; the lineage of all the Nautonniers who had gone before him. With it came a knowledge of the things that needed to be done at present, so that the dark plans of Lucifer might come to pass. He picked up a handset from its place on a table below the mirror.

"This is Christian Antov," he said. "Get me Cynthia."

"Hello, Mr. Antov," came her silky voice. "How can I help you?"

"We will be checking out tonight."

"Of course, Mr. Antov," she said. "I will arrange to have your things packed immediately. Will you be needing anything else?"

"Dr. Bennington will be getting here shortly. Call me the moment he arrives."

"Yes, sir," she said seductively. "Anything else?"

Christian turned to study his reflection in the mirror again. For a split second he saw himself shift and transform in much the same way that the Zurvanites did. He bent closer to the glass. For that fraction of a moment he could have sworn that his features had become reptilian. Christian ran his hands over his face. He was beginning to understand.

"Connect me with the head secretary of our Jerusalem office," he said.

Cynthia was silent for a moment, surprised by Christian's odd request.

"Right away, Mr. Antov."

Christian waited impatiently.

"Yes, Mr. Antov," came the voice of a man, his accent Israeli. "How can I help you?"

"We will be moving all operations to the Jerusalem complex this afternoon. Coordinate with Cynthia. I want our pilots ready for takeoff at thirteen-hundred hours, and I want everyone in the Steering Committee on that plane. I will accept no excuses. Set up a group meeting for tomorrow morning. Have my private jet fueled and ready for immediate takeoff. Is that clear?"

"Yes, sir, Mr. Antov. Immediately, sir."

CHAPTER 38

Gibraltar.

The Bishop could see the traffic barriers on either side of the runway finally rising into the morning air. They had been lowered to stop the flow of pedestrians and traffic across the tarmac while their plane had made its landing. Now, as they taxied toward the small terminal, the traffic had begun to flow again, a mad rush headed by a smoky cloud of buzzing scooters.

"Your Excellency will be glad to know that Amir has arranged accommodations for you and your friends."

It was the deep voice of Bahadur that spoke. He was out of his seat now, and on his way to open the hatch.

"It would appear that you read my mind, dear Bahadur," said the old Bishop happily. "You must thank Amir for us."

"You can thank him yourself, your Excellency," said Bahadur, pulling open the hatch.

In an instant Amir was inside, embracing Bahadur heartily.

"Good cousin!" said Bahadur, rubbing Amir's back with his massive hands. "Have faith in Allah. We will get them out safely."

"I'm not worried," said Amir, his groomed dreadlocks shifting as he shook his head. "We've got a small army to help us do it."

Amir pointed to the cockpit with his thumb.

"You were lucky to make it to Gibraltar. They shut down all air traffic across Europe."

"Why have they done this?" asked Bahadur, frowning.

"Terrorist attacks," said Amir, looking over at the Bishop. "All in the last hour. Bombings. One in Madrid, two in London, two in New York City, one in Atlanta, and only ten minutes ago a massive explosion in Rome. They say it's all been coordinated by Al-Qaeda. Thousands are dead. They've declared Martial law in the U.S.."

The Bishop stood up in alarm, as did Suora and Fra.

"We must contact Gabriel and Natasha!"

"Your Excellency," said Amir with a slight bow. "I just got off the phone with them. They're fine. They're on their way here."

CHAPTER 39

The French Riviera.

The black sports car screamed through a curving tunnel west of Monaco, its tuned exhaust reverberating off the chiseled walls of the mountain pass. To the left, flickering through a series of gallery openings, the Mediterranean was shimmering under a rising sun. At long last the rain had stopped, and they were finally getting a chance to make up for lost time. Gabriel looked down at the speedometer and shook his head in amazement.

Two-hundred and forty kilometers an hour and I'm barely pressing the accelerator.

With all air traffic having been suspended after the terrorist strikes, they had been forced to drive to Gibraltar. It was now seven in the morning, with very little traffic on the autoroute. If they could maintain an average speed of two-hundred, they would be crossing into Gibraltar seven hours from now.

"Maybe we can look at this now," said Natasha, producing the envelope containing Professor Metrovich's journal.

"Do the honours," said Gabriel.

Natasha opened the envelope and removed the tattered book. It was thick and worn and smelled of old leather.

"Gabriel," she whispered, opening it carefully. "This journal is filled with illuminations."

She held it up and Gabriel shot over a quick glance. In the second he had looked, he had seen intricate medieval illustrations, glowing gold leaf, and precise calligraphy.

"I had no idea," said Gabriel, shaking his head.

Many times he had seen his father working in the journal, but he had never been permitted to know what was within. When he had asked, his father had always given the same response.

"When it is time, Gabriel, and only then."

Somehow the journal had always disappeared, and as a boy, no matter how thoroughly Gabriel had searched for it, he had never once found it.

"So what's in it besides pretty pictures?"

Natasha was studying the book as she spoke.

"Eighth and ninth century texts. Perfect copies, Gabriel. Letters, scrolls, papyri, ancient maps. Some are in Greek, others in Coptic, Aramaic, Arabic… Here is a Latin manuscript. Guess who it is by."

Gabriel shrugged.

"Gutierrez de la Cruz," she said.

"That guy's everywhere."

Natasha turned another page. It was covered in gold leaf.

"This book is a masterpiece," she whispered. "I cannot believe that your father made this. It is even hand-bound."

Gabriel only nodded. He missed the old man terribly.

"Listen to what he writes on the very first page," she said. "It is an excerpt from the Pistis Sophia.

"And the spirit of the Saviour was moved in him, and he cried, 'How long shall I suffer you? Do ye still not know? Do ye still not understand that ye are all Angels, and Archangels; all Lords, and Rulers? That ye are from all; of yourselves and in yourselves in turn; from one mass, and one matter, and one essence?

"It refers to humanity's divine nature," said Natasha, "and the high places we held before the Fall. The page next to it only has a single line on it."

Gabriel looked over at her.

"What does it say?"

Natasha read it aloud.

"To transcend the Cube is to see it in all things."

Gabriel raised an eyebrow but was soon lost in his thoughts. He was thinking of his father. Natasha continued to study the book.

"This journal is divided into sections," she said at length. "The first treats with a medieval author named Chrétien de Troyes, and his book *The Quest For The Holy Grail.*"

Gabriel paused to think.

"That was a fusion of Celtic folklore and Orthodox Christianity, wasn't it?"

Natasha nodded.

"Yes, and Jewish mystical symbolism too. It can be interpreted on many different levels. Some say it is an allegory of the secret teachings of the Alchemists."

"The ones who could turn lead into gold," said Gabriel.

Natasha nodded again.

"The Alchemists were Gnostic priests," she said. "The Church burned them all and destroyed their knowledge. It was called Gnosis, and your father was obsessed with finding out what it was."

Gabriel smiled and shook his head.

"That sounds like Dad."

Natasha pulled an iPad out of her backpack, her eyes wide with excitement.

"What are you doing?" asked Gabriel.

"I am researching," she said, tapping at the screen.

Gabriel gave a nod.

"According to this," she said after a few minutes of surfing, "the person who possesses the Gnosis becomes an immortal creator of heavenly worlds. His every desire is fulfilled, and life takes on a perpetual state of excitement and bliss."

Gabriel raised his eyebrows.

"Sounds like Las Vegas."

Natasha shot him a sidelong glance.

"The only problem," she continued, "is that there are practically no traces of the Gnosis left. The little that remains is veiled in legend and myth."

"So basically it's a lost knowledge."

Natasha continued scanning the document she had downloaded.

"Learning the Gnosis was an initiatory path," she said. "Pieces of the knowledge were given to the student as he advanced. The alchemists believed that acquiring the Gnosis was the meaning of life. It was all about remembering to be something that we already are, instead of trying to become something we are not."

"So what are we?" asked Gabriel.

Natasha looked over at Gabriel as he drove.

"It says we are all gods."

"Gnosticism," said Gabriel, thinking. "The ultimate heresy. Christianity as myth."

Natasha nodded.

"The alchemists combined Judeo-Christian mythology with other ancient mythologies. To them, the story of the Garden of Eden was not so much the cause of the Fall, but the result of it. In their version, the serpent is not even the devil. She is the benevolent Mother, and the knowledge contained in the apple is the Gnosis that reminds Adam and Eve of the Virtue they lost as a result of the Fall."

Gabriel scanned the road ahead.

"Just like in the myth that Marcus told us about."

Natasha put away the tablet and returned her attention to the journal, reading silently for a while longer before looking up at Gabriel. Her eyes were wide with the wonder that only a theologian could feel about such things.

"The next section is about Gutierrez de la Cruz," she said. "According to this, he was not only the one who found the lost Cube; he was also a member of an organization called the *Council of Six.*"

Gabriel glanced over.

"The Council of Six?"

"It was comprised of representatives from each of the six world religions," said Natasha. "All summoned by the Moorish Caliph of Toledo in 866, to translate the proto-writings inscribed on the Cube."

Gabriel recalled the parchments that had previously covered the Cube. They had been written in six different languages. He had only skimmed over them at the time, but it now occurred to him what they must have spoken of.

"Of course," he said. "That's what's written on each of the six parchments: Discourses on the translations they made. But why? Why gather scribes from the four corners of the earth to translate crude symbols that could have meant absolutely anything? Could there really be some kind of secret knowledge locked up in the Cube?"

Natasha shrugged.

"Your father suspected that everything would be explained in The Book of Khalifah."

"And that's why he was so obsessed with finding it," said Gabriel. "That book must be pretty damn special."

Natasha looked over at him.

"We must find it, Gabriel."

"I agree," he said, his eyes glued to the road. "Keep reading. I want to know everything my father knew."

CHAPTER 40

Los Picos de Europa, Northern Spain.

Isaac awoke to find a brown hunting dog licking his face. The sun was up now, and the terrible storm had passed. His mind worked to remember where he was, and how he had arrived there.

Where did this dog come from? What is happening?

Isaac saw that he was on the shore of a mountain lake. At its centre he could see a small island burning steadily. In an instant all his memories came flooding back. He reached up and patted the dog's head.

"I remember," he said. "It is thanks to you that I am alive."

Isaac shuddered as he recalled the horrific events that had only just transpired, and how he had swam out into the waters to escape the hellfire. He had been certain he would drown, and was on the verge of letting the lake take him, when a dog had swam up to him unexpectedly. He had lost consciousness shortly after.

As Isaac lay there, his mind went over all the things that had happened since his plane had gone down. He was perplexed by his clarity of mind. It was as though he had regained his judgment; something his doctor had told him would never happen. He looked at the dog, puzzled by the deep intelligence in its amber eyes.

"Where did you come from, my friend?" he asked. "There can be no explanation for your appearance here other than divine intervention."

The dog gave a round nod and barked. He put a paw on Isaac's chest as he lay there, and it seemed to Isaac that the animal was trying to communicate something to him. He examined the dog's collar. It was made of rough twine, and had the lid of what looked to be an olive jar tied to it. Isaac saw that there was a name written on its underside.

"*Sir Shackleton,*" he read, smiling. "A fitting title."

He sat up, groaning with pain, and took a deep breath of the fresh mountain air.

"I cannot recall when my head was ever this clear," he said to the dog. "Perhaps it was when I was a boy. Everything is so vibrant; so beautiful…"

Isaac looked around in wonderment, only then remembering his medication. He had not taken it for many days now. He searched his pockets, a panic beginning to take him. In over forty years he had never missed a dose.

"I must find my pills…"

Just then he felt Shackleton's muzzle poke him in the side, and he turned to see that the dog's eyes were focused on him. There could be no mistake as to what the dog was trying to communicate. His failure to take his medication was the reason for his recovery. He looked at the dog, his brow furrowed with confusion.

"But Father Adrianus always insisted that I never miss a dose," he muttered. "He said that my sanity depended on it."

Shackleton gave him another poke.

"Very well," he said, frowning. "I will get up."

Isaac rose unsteadily to his feet, noticing only then that Shackleton had returned him to the very place where he had first embarked onto the lake. Not a few paces away was the makeshift sled he had used to drag the corpse from the crash site, as well as the pack of supplies he had taken from the dead Father Franco. Isaac looked down at the dog.

"Who are you, my friend?"

Shackleton let out a resounding bark in response. He trotted over to Father Franco's pack, picking it up in his maw and dragging it to Isaac's feet. Within it Isaac found cured sausages and biscuits. It was not long before he had sat himself down and was sharing a meal with his new friend.

"Something of great importance has happened, Shackleton," he said, looking out over the water. "I must try to understand."

The flames on the island were beginning to subside now, replaced by a thick plume of rising smoke. Even though the sight of it served to affirm the reality of the demonic horrors he had experienced, the smoke was also strengthening his faith in God. That such a powerful evil could exist only confirmed the existence of an even greater force of good.

As he looked out over the lake, it seemed to Isaac that all the events of his life had lead him to the place where he now found himself. He took a deep breath and rose to his feet, scanning the mountainous peaks that encased him.

"I do not understand, Father," he prayed quietly. "Lucifer used me, and then discarded me. He left me for dead. I am an abomination. I dismembered the corpse of my own son. I released an unspeakable evil onto the world. Why do you spare my life, Father? Why do you send this noble animal to help me? Should I not be despised and cursed by you?"

Isaac returned his gaze to the island, his eyes filling with tears.

"My life is yours, Father," he whispered. "Help me and guide me so that I might put right the terrible wrongs I have done."

CHAPTER 41

Gibraltar.

Bahadur stood on the edge of a rusty dock in the shadows of the lower port. Around him loomed the clutter of Gibraltar's industrial marina, the smell of stale diesel fuel and brine filling the morning air. A dusty sun had already risen behind the rocky peak, but the sky in the west was still holding on to a few scattered stars. The dawn had come up blood red. There would be hard weather today.

"A good day to storm a castle," said Amir, emerging from a dilapidated workshop and looking up at the sky.

He struck a match and stoked his chillum until they were engulfed in its fragrant smoke. Amir took a deep haul and offered the pipe to Bahadur, but the giant shook his head absently and turned to look out to sea, his face bearing an expression of deep concern and fatigue.

"They'll be fine, Bahadur," said Amir, seeing the worry on his cousin's face. "Nasrallah knows you. He'd never hurt them. He's a coward."

"Where is Gabriel?" said Bahadur deeply, glancing over at Amir.

"They're on their way. They're planning to arrive at around two or three."

"Your friend knows how to drive."

Amir released a billowing cloud.

"He's been averaging two-forty all the way from Florence."

Bahadur nodded and then looked off to sea again, frowning.

"I am concerned about the men," he said in his deep basso.

"They'll all be here soon," said Amir.

The brown giant shook his heavy head darkly.

"It is not our men I am concerned for, cousin. It is Nasrallah's men that I am thinking of. They are good men. They have wives and children. They work hard. They do not deserve to die."

"They know Nasrallah," said Amir, pushing aside a wayward dreadlock. "If they choose to work for a murderer they—"

"They do not choose!" said Bahadur, turning to grasp Amir's shoulder before proceeding more gently. "They have families to feed. It is that simple."

"Cousin," said Amir with consternation. "Maybe there's another way. Once Nasrallah's been taken out, our new coalition will be in control. There'll be work for everyone. If we could somehow let Nasrallah's men know about our plan. They'd rather work for you."

"We cannot take that risk," said Bahadur gloomily. "It could easily go the other way. Men take what is real. They do not risk their lives on promises. Nasrallah pays them at the end of every month. That is all they are concerned with, and I cannot blame them for that."

"Then men will die," said Amir, spitting into the oily water. "Men will die."

CHAPTER 42

Costa Brava, Spain.

The rocky cliffs were racing past in a blur, and Gabriel was enjoying the drive tremendously. The purring Audi was finding no difficulty in maintaining a cruising speed of two-hundred and forty kilometers an hour. It felt like the car was on rails. Natasha looked up from the book.

"There is an Arabic document here that your father has transcribed," she said, bending closer to the book. "It is dated 661 A.D., and addressed to the Umayyad Caliph of Cordoba. It is from one of his clerics."

"What does it say?"

Natasha scanned it for a moment before answering. She wanted to make sure she was translating it correctly.

"It says that Arab forces took Alexandria and found the Urn of Theophilus."

"I've heard of that artifact before," said Gabriel, scratching his head, "Theophilus found the Urn in the Great Library of Alexandria, just before he ordered it burnt to the ground."

"Theophilus was the Bishop of Alexandria," said Natasha.

Gabriel nodded.

"At the end of the fourth century. Theophilus was leading a Catholic movement to destroy everything heretical. Sacred temples, priceless art, ancient writings."

He paused to remember.

"Legend has it that there were some very old tablets in that urn. They were supposedly written by the first Mesopotamian kings."

"According to this letter," said Natasha, "those tablets spoke of a Cube of Knowledge, Gabriel. It is there where the Arabs first learned of the artifact. Listen to this. I will do my best to translate it as I go.

Know, Prince of the Faithful, that at the time of the Emperor Theodosius, the Bishop Theophilus issued forth an order for the demolition of the great heathen library of Alexandria. From therein he was brought a golden urn of such beauty and richness, that he could not bring himself to destroy it, but instead took it secretly as his own.

Within this urn were ancient tablets belonging to Alulim, who was the First King of Sumer, and who reigned for 28,800 years in the kingdom of Eridu, in Mesopotamia. The tablets spoke of a Cube of Knowledge, and of the Nephilim, who took the Cube from its resting place at the entrance of a great labyrinth, and gave it to Alulim, to whom they taught many wondrous things.

At the End Of The World this Cube is said to reside, oh Prince, in the land of the warrior-priests. It was recovered by the Kristos of Judea, and laid within the tomb of his brother, who guards it until the day of reckoning.

"Kristos is Greek for Christ," said Gabriel.

Natasha was still studying the text.

"It comes from *Krishna* in Sanskrit," she said.

Gabriel thought for a moment.

"If the tomb belongs to the brother of Jesus, that would mean that this document is referring to the same tomb that Gutierrez found. Do you think there's a connection between the labyrinth it mentions and the one in the Egyptian myth that Marcus told us about?"

"Yes I do," said Natasha, tucking her hair behind an ear.

"That would mean that the entrance to this labyrinth is on the same island where Gutierrez found the tomb," said Gabriel, turning to look at her.

Natasha looked back at him and nodded excitedly.

"You said that the markings on the Cube were Basque?"

"Yes," said Gabriel, squinting into the distance as he drove. "Proto-Basque."

"Are not the Basques and the Celts of Ireland related?"

"That's what the DNA implies."

"Gabriel," said Natasha. "There is evidence that suggests that Christian evangelists landed in Ireland four years after the crucifixion of Jesus; that they were led by James the Just, and that they succeeded in converting the Druids to Christianity."

Gabriel frowned.

"The Vatican deemed the Celtic Church heretical," he said. "They called it Insular Christianity. How could it be heretical if it was created by Jesus' own brother? I see what you're getting at though. The Druids must have known about the Labyrinth. That's why the runes on the Cube are Proto-Basque, and that's why Jesus delivered the Cube back to them. The Druids must have been its original keepers."

"It is just speculation," said Natasha, looking down at the journal, "but your father seemed to think the same. He was convinced that the end of the world was not so much a time, but a place; a Celtic place…"

"Finisterre, right?" asked Gabriel.

"Yes," said Natasha, looking up from the book in surprise. "How did you know?"

"Because it's not far from Santiago de Compostela. It's a small village on the west coast of Galicia, but it's also been called *The End Of The World* since the time of the Druids."

Gabriel sped past a grouping of trucks.

"So the Labyrinth is in Finisterre…"

"Not exactly," said Natasha, "but your father believed that it was somewhere close. According to him, that whole area was considered to be the end of the world."

Natasha turned to a different part of the journal.

"Here is a section entirely dedicated to the Labyrinth. Your father refers to it as *The Great Labyrinth of Sarras*."

Gabriel scratched his head.

"Sarras was the heavenly city in *The Quest For The Holy Grail*."

She looked up from the book and nodded.

"The place where Galahad saw the Grail and healed the Fisher King."

"Thus satisfying the legend, and restoring life to the kingdom…"

Natasha nodded again.

"Some historians believe that the original Grail romances were written by members of *Rex Angelus*, and that they carried secret messages that contradicted the Church's doctrine."

"Rex Angelus?"

Natasha bit her lip.

"A society that claimed to be the direct descendants of Jesus Christ, and the keepers of his original teachings."

"A bloodline of Christ?" asked Gabriel, rolling his eyes.

"It is a well known hypothesis," said Natasha with a shrug. "Gutierrez de la Cruz claimed to be Rex Angelus himself. Your father believed that he only became a priest to infiltrate the Church."

Gabriel had to break hard and wait for a car to get out of the passing lane.

Natasha read one of the Professor's annotations aloud.

"To all Rex Angelus, the Holy Grail is a symbol of the Original Gnosis. It is the receptacle of the wisdom that Jesus himself taught, before it was distorted by the Vatican in order to control the masses. In the story, when the Christ-like Galahad is pure enough to behold the

Grail, he restores the Fisher King to full health, and in this way the wasted kingdom is restored. If we follow the allegory, this is another way of saying that when humanity is ready, the true teachings of Jesus Christ will triumph over the greed and hypocrisy of the Vatican, and result in a kind of heaven on earth."

Gabriel shook his head in astonishment.

"So it's exactly as Marcus was saying back in the catacombs. The Cube and the Holy Grail are the same thing."

"It seems so, Gabriel," said Natasha, her big eyes alight with excitement. "Your father makes the point that throughout history, the Grail has not only been described as a cup, or a chalice, but also as *A Stone Within A Cup.*"

She read from the journal again.

"A stone which fell from heaven, and symbolizes the wisdom that is imbibed when one drinks from the metaphorical cup of the Kristos."

Natasha looked up from the book.

"According to Rex Angelus, there is only one primordial source of wisdom. It is a doctrine that became fragmented over the ages, with different parts being adopted by each of the six world religions. It would appear that the ancient Druids were the guardians of that original knowledge. They were the warrior-priests that the letter spoke of; the Keepers of the Cube. Your father believed that if the fragmented parts could be unified again, then there would be harmony between all the religions, and humanity would at last have access to the entire truth, instead of just small fragments of it."

"What exactly have we stumbled onto here?"

"Your father's life work," said Natasha in awe.

Gabriel rubbed his eyes in an attempt to stave off the sleepiness. There was so much to consider, but his faculties were losing their edge. He needed to shut his eyes for a while. Natasha continued to carefully turn the pages.

"What are you reading now?" he asked at length.

"You are not going to believe me."

Gabriel looked over to see her flipping back to earlier sections of the journal, her head shaking from side to side.

"This is impossible," she muttered, "but you can see it everywhere in the diary."

"Try me."

She looked over at Gabriel through a curly lock of chestnut hair.

"Your father claims that Gutierrez speaks of you and I in his writings; that he refers to us as *The Two,* but that there is an ambiguity in the translation."

"What kind of ambiguity?"

"In certain Coptic dialects, The Two, also means *The Primal King and Queen.* Your father was not sure why this particular word would have been used, when a more specific numerical terminology existed."

"But how could Gutierrez know of us?"

"Uncle Marcus said that we were a part of this, Gabriel."

"It's a product of my father's overactive imagination. He was just making assumptions."

"Gutierrez refers to you as *Gabriel, Hero of God,* and to me as *Natalia, The day of the Saviour's Birth.* Your father writes that you I are spoken of in the ancient prophecies as well, the same ones that speak of our heroic mission."

"Our mission?" asked Gabriel, turning to face her. "What mission?"

Natasha held up the journal to show Gabriel an illustration when a loose page fell from the book.

"What is this?"

She was silent while she read it.

"Well?" asked Gabriel. "What is it?"

"It is a note from your father, Gabriel. It is addressed to both of us."

"What does it say?"

Natasha read it aloud.

Gabriel and Natasha.
Once you have retrieved the Cube, you must proceed immediately to
the "Bodega del Pi" in Toledo. You must go there as quickly as you
can. DO NOT DELAY. Ask for Yuri. He will explain everything.
You can trust him with your lives. MAKE HASTE!

Natasha felt herself suddenly pushed forward against her seatbelt. Gabriel was braking hard.

"What are you doing?" she asked, surprised by the sudden change in speed.

"We're taking this exit to Toledo," said Gabriel. "If we cut through the middle of Spain this *Bodega del Pi* won't even be out of our way. Besides, it's your turn to drive. I can hardly keep my eyes open anymore."

CHAPTER 43

Somewhere over the Mediterranean Sea.

"This is Galaxy Network News, the most trusted news network in the world. Spain is reeling this morning after a string of seventeen car bombs ravage Bilbao, Barcelona, Madrid and Zaragoza. Hundreds are dead, and many more injured. As well, violent riots spreading throughout the Muslim communities of the United States and Europe. Is the war spreading into our homes? Stay tuned for a special GNN report: *The Fist of Islam. Christendom is Burning.*"

Dr. Bennington looked at the monitor mounted on the cabin wall. He was in a private jet en route to Israel, being taken there against his will. He was an older man; lean, clean-shaven, and almost entirely bald. He wore rimless spectacles and a light beige suit with a golden cravat. His demeanor was exceedingly gentle, and consistently calm, even in his current situation.

Three hours earlier he had arrived at Christian's hotel only to be stuffed into a limousine and driven to a private airfield. Under the care of three armed security guards, Bennington had then been escorted onto Christian's private jet, and made to wait there for an hour. No sooner had Christian arrived than the jet had taken off. As it was, Christian had disappeared into the plane's cockpit, leaving Dr. Bennington alone in the luxurious cabin. He could not believe what he was seeing on television.

"Well, Steve," said the expert being interviewed, "this kind of fighting is nothing new. Taking shelter in populated urban sectors allows the terrorists to use civilians as shields. For the most part, these Muslim communities are made up of wonderful, peace loving people, but like any other community of any other faith, they've got some bad apples in the bunch, and it's these guys who have banded together to fight this war."

"This war you are referring to, Mr. Peterson. Who exactly are the fundamentalists waging it against?"

"Against whoever opposes them, Steve."

"Now isn't that the most lovely circus you've ever seen, Doctor?" said Christian, returning from the cockpit.

He muted the monitor and threw himself onto a leather sofa across from where Bennington sat, reaching lazily for his glass of wine. Much to Christian's relief, his father's whispers had subsided after the last appearance of the Zurvanites, and he was enjoying the reprieve tremendously.

"There is nothing lovely about war and chaos, Christian," said Dr. Bennington.

"They are a means to an end," said Christian offhand. "The lovely thing I was referring to is the instability."

"I do not understand."

"Can't you see that we're all in great danger?" asked Christian sarcastically. "The terrorists are very terrifying, and the population needs the government to protect them. *The Enforcer of Laws* has become the new hero. He will protect us, but we have to do exactly what he tells us to do. This is war after all."

"And what will we be told to do, Christian?"

"We will be told to comply, Doctor. The masses will soon surrender the majority of their civil rights."

Christian lit a cigarette and returned his attention to the television. They were showing footage of a Muslim uprising taking place in Washington D.C..

"It's all just propaganda," said Christian, yawning. "It's nowhere near as big as it looks. "The Muslims are as docile as lambs."

"And how can you be so sure this is just propaganda, Christian?"

Christian gave a dry chuckle.

"Because my organization is producing these stories. We own the mainstream media, Doctor. We decide how people perceive things."

"How can you possibly expect me to believe that?"

Christian rolled his eyes.

"I hope you're not one of those people who refuses to believe in conspiracy theories."

Bennington held his gaze but remained silent.

"Well, it's time you revisited your opinions and considered the validity of at least one of them."

"And which one might that be?" asked the doctor.

"Do you know the one about the group of cigar smoking men in the dark boardroom who are secretly running the world?"

"Yes," said Bennington. "That theory is familiar to me."

"Well, the theory is true, Doctor, with the exception that all the men in that room only answer to one man, and I don't smoke cigars, I smoke cigarettes."

Christian took a long draw from his cigarette and smiled with self-satisfaction. Bennington shifted in his seat, crossing his legs. He had garnered very little from Christian up to this point, and he wanted nothing more than to keep his patient talking. Christian was showing every sign of megalomania, and Bennington's professional instincts could sense tremendous turmoil behind the confident facade.

"Christian, you must forgive me if I find it difficult to believe that you are the leader of a shadow government that is secretly directing every nation in the world."

"I direct most of them, Doctor, but not all of them. Not yet. With regards to your doubt, consider that we're the only civilians flying over European airspace right now."

"I am aware that there have been restrictions made on flights," said the doctor. "But I am also aware that given your new position, you must have certain privileges."

"Yes, Doctor, I do," said Christian, gesturing toward the window. "Perhaps these privileges would explain our military escort."

Bennington rose from his seat, sliding up the blind as he bent forward. There, not fifty feet from their plane, and staggered in perfect formation, were three RAF fighter jets.

"Are you beginning to understand, Doctor?" said Christian, enjoying his new companion tremendously. "There are another three on our starboard side as well."

"Understanding would imply knowing, Christian," said Bennington, returning to his seat, "and I'm sure I know very little."

"Not to worry, Doctor, because I'm going to tell you everything. I feel like I have found a very good friend in you."

"Friends do not force their friends to accompany them to Israel by taking their wife hostage."

Christian sat up suddenly, an anger alighting in him.

"Your wife is staying in a three-thousand-euro-a-night suite in the Paris Ritz. You would think that would be good enough for anyone. Perhaps you might show some gratitude, Doctor. I am your patient. I am in need of your services."

"You threatened to kill her, Christian."

"Nobody's going to kill anybody if you do your job."

"And what might that be?" asked Bennington. "Altering your doses to prevent hallucinations? That will not be sufficient to treat what ails you, Christian. You must talk to me. You must tell me what is wrong."

Christian rose from the sofa and moved to the bar to refill his glass. He lit a cigarette and focused his eyes on the doctor.

"Strange things have been happening... Unnatural things."

"Perhaps you could be more specific?"

Christian continued to stare intently at the doctor.

"I was tricked into making a pact with the devil," he said. "I savagely murdered the man responsible. I also murdered my uncle. After I did all this, four demons appeared to me and told me that I was the son of Lucifer, destined to rule the world, but that's not the worst of it."

Bennington nodded slowly. It was important that Christian did not feel judged.

"What is the worst of it, then?"

Christian took a heavy draw from his cigarette and then placed it carefully in the ashtray. He took a sip of wine.

"The worst of it, Doctor, is that I believe them."

CHAPTER 44

Toledo, Spain.

An ancient hand emerged from the shadows, unlatching the heavy gate and pushing it outward towards them.

"This is the place," whispered Natasha into Gabriel's ear.

She motioned towards the battered sign that hung above them.

La Bodega Del Pi

Gabriel studied the pale hand and saw that it belonged to an old woman.

"Buenos dias, Señora," he said. "I am Gabriel; Agardi Metrovich's son."

"Indeed, you are," came the old woman's voice. "And an angel of hope you are as well. Come in, my child. I have been expecting you."

Gabriel shot a puzzled glance at Natasha and entered first. Everything was draped in shadow, but the darkness was soon vanquished when a shutter squeaked open to his left. In the dusty light of the window he could see an ancient woman dressed as a gypsy might be. Her silver hair was covered in a crimson shawl, and her eyes were big and green, shimmering with mystical power.

"Come in, come in," she said in her thick accent. "You too, Natasha. Come in. You are even more beautiful than I imagined."

Natasha smiled politely and entered timidly, looking around her as she did so. They were in a small tavern, its walls and ceiling comprised of ancient stone masonry. Centred under a massive arch was a dark wooden bar, behind which sat dozens of open wine bottles, lined up on oaken shelves, with their corks stopped into their necks. There was a large roast on the bar, covered in a glass dome. The old woman took up a knife that was lying next to it and used it to point out two stools. Gabriel and Natasha obeyed her silent order and sat themselves down.

"You have driven a great distance," divined the old gypsy woman, turning to face an antique espresso machine, "and at great speeds, I might add."

She worked the machine, the smell of coffee filling the air.

"There is confusion in your minds, and your bellies are empty. This combination is not conducive to learning. I will make you breakfast."

The old woman sliced some of the peppery pork roast and stuffed the meat into crusty rolls, pressing them in an old panini grill. She watched in silence as Gabriel and Natasha ate, speaking only when Gabriel had finished the last dram of his latte. He nodded to her in thanks.

"I sense that your father has crossed over," said the gypsy soberly.

"Yes he has," said Gabriel, looking down into his empty glass and turning it pensively. "He died earlier this month in a plane crash."

"Only his body is dead, my child," said the gypsy woman tenderly. "Now if you please. Come with me."

They followed her to a wrought iron staircase in the corner. It spiraled up into the stone ceiling and down into the wooden floor. As the old woman approached it, she came to a stop, her ancient hand clasping and unclasping the handrail as she thought.

"My husband's body is also dead," she said, studying the stone wall before her. "His name was Yuri Blavatsky, and he was a procurer of ancient texts and writings. For fifty-nine years he assisted your father in his research, Gabriel. Many were the secrets that they unearthed together; secrets of wisdom and power."

Gabriel looked over at Natasha, feeling the same curiosity he saw in her eyes. What secrets was the old gypsy referring to? Why had the Professor seemed so urgent in his note? Why had he never told Gabriel about Yuri Blavatsky?

The air was becoming increasingly cold and damp as they descended the stairs. They arrived at an old wine cellar and were soon surrounded by rack upon rack of vintage bottles, each one blanketed in thick cobwebs, and caked in dust.

"Toledo is an old woman," said their guide over her shoulder, lighting a battered lantern as she spoke, "but as you will soon see, her womb still bears fruit."

They had descended well into the depths of the cellar when they came upon a heavy, time-blackened rack, laden with bottles. It was built against a wall of living stone.

The old woman hung her lantern on a nearby hook and reached slowly into one of the racks, pulling on a lever hidden within it. In an instant the sound of scrapping stone gave way to a mechanical rumble of gears and counter weights. The massive rack slid aside.

"For reasons of secrecy," she said, retrieving the lantern from where she had hung it, "no electricity has ever been installed in this room. Follow me."

She led them through a low tunnel that opened into a perfectly rounded chamber, about thirty feet in diameter. In the darkness they could make out a few cluttered shapes, but it was not until the old woman had lit a large candelabra that they could truly see the wonders the room had to offer.

Circling the entire chamber was an unbroken line of shoulder high oaken shelves, crammed with ancient books, codices, scrolls of papyrus and vellum, and treasures of every kind. Covering its stone floor were luxurious Persian rugs, on which could be seen several leather wingchairs, and sturdy desks laden with still more books and scrolls. The room looked to be a library of sorts, but it was the stone ceiling that gave the chamber its unique character. Masterfully built, it formed a perfect semi-spherical dome above them.

"This is *The Chamber of the Sphere*," said the old gypsy. "It was built by Toledo's first Caliph. Here we have stored our great treasures."

Natasha swallowed slowly and followed Gabriel into the space, her eyes wide.

"What is that?" she whispered, pointing to a strange spherical apparatus that lay glimmering at the centre of the room.

Gabriel turned to look, and saw that the device was mounted on a low wooden pedestal. Its diameter was about the size of a beach ball.

"From here it looks like some kind of optical instrument," he said, squinting through the dim light. "I've never seen anything like it before."

He made his way slowly forward, his eyes never leaving the strange form. Even in the half light, it shone in all the spectral colours of a prism, reflecting and magnifying the rays from the old woman's candelabra into a million sparkling points of refracted light. He drew up to the sphere, circling it.

"It is beautiful," whispered Natasha, approaching behind him. "Look at how it shimmers."

"Hand ground salt crystal lenses," whispered Gabriel, amazed. "Hundreds of them. And just look at the work in this brass armature. By the looks of these linkages, I'd guess that the position of each lens could be calibrated to within a thousandth of an inch."

He looked over at Natasha and then back to the sphere, his eyes straining to take in as much information as possible.

"We're looking at a technological wonder of Islam," he said. "The likes of which few have ever seen. They were masters in optics and mathematics, but I had no idea they were capable of building an astrolabe this precise."

Natasha moved to Gabriel's side, looking deeply into the crystalline sphere.

"This is an astrolabe?"

Gabriel nodded, his eyes fixed on it.

"An ancient astronomical instrument," he said, still in awe. "They had many uses, including locating and predicting the positions of celestial bodies, navigation, astrology, surveying, timekeeping, and let's not forget *Qibla*."

"Finding the direction of Mecca," said Natasha. "That was the main reason why the Muslim astronomers built them. People needed to know which direction to pray in. But this does not look like an astrolabe to me, Gabriel."

"I know," he agreed. "Astrolabes were normally flat instruments, but the more advanced ones became spherical in shape. I've never seen one like this before. It would appear to be an optical astrolabe. I had no idea they even existed."

"This astrolabe was built by Al-Sufi," said the old gypsy from where she stood at the chamber's entrance.

"*Abd al-Rahman al Sufi?*" asked Gabriel, turning to face her, "The famous Persian astronomer?"

The old woman nodded slowly.

"If anyone knew astrolabes," continued Gabriel, looking at Natasha, "it was that guy. He outlined more than one-thousand uses for them back in the tenth century."

"He built it for the Caliph of Toledo," said the woman, approaching. "Following instructions found on a Babylonian tablet dated to 5000 B.C."

Both Gabriel and Natasha turned to face the old woman.

"But I thought Hipparchus was the first to invent the astrolabe in 200 B.C." said Gabriel, already doubting himself.

He was rapidly learning not to believe everything the history books had taught him.

The old gypsy woman said nothing in return, but came directly towards them with the candelabra, her time worn features shifting in the flickering candle light. Reaching over she depressed a linkage in the astrolabe's armature, and they watched as a section of the contraption swung aside to reveal a cubical orifice directly at its centre. It too was lined with crystal lenses.

"I believe you are in possession of an artifact that will fit within this space?"

Gabriel looked over to find Natasha staring at him, her eyes wide with wonder. The niche looked to be precisely the same size as the Cube. Without a moment's delay, Gabriel produced the artifact from his pack, holding it aloft before him so that the old woman could see.

"The Cube of Compostela," she whispered in awe, her voice trembling. "If only my husband were here to see it."

"And my father along with him," said Gabriel solemnly, handing the old woman the glowing cube. "Please, do the honours, Señora. Do it for both of them."

The old woman handed Natasha the candelabra.

"Your lungs are stronger than mine, child."

Natasha blew out the candles and the Cube's blue light took centre stage.

"It casts a wonderful hue, to be sure," said the old woman, taking hold of it. "I have never seen its like."

With a remarkably steady hand she inserted the Cube into its slot, carefully closing the armature door over it. The effect was instantaneous. With the Cube now installed in the centre of the astrolabe, its dim light had magnified itself tenfold, creating a spectacular cloud of glowing light that surrounded the contraption like an atmosphere around a planet.

"It is beautiful," whispered Natasha. "It is as though I could touch it."

"It looks like some kind of hologram," said Gabriel, "but what's the purpose of it?"

"The Cube's light is not sufficiently bright," said the old gypsy. "This is not the effect that the ancient scribes spoke of."

"I think we can make it brighter, Señora," said Natasha, smiling naughtily.

Gabriel turned to Natasha with a questioning glance, only to feel her arms wrapping around his neck. An instant later she had stretched up on her tiptoes and kissed him fully on the lips. The nature of the kiss took them both completely off guard. It was indescribably thrilling; a chemical reaction so encompassing that it was only the gypsy's cry of surprise that broke them from its spell. When they opened their eyes they saw what their kiss had done to the Cube.

Hair-lined streams of blazing blue light were shooting through the artifact like tendrils of plasma. They were pulsing and building in intensity with every passing second, magnified and refracted by the astrolabe's innumerable lenses. An instant later their light reached a critical point, exploding through the crystalline instrument in a blinding detonation, and causing them all to cry out in surprise.

A glittering atmosphere of shimmering light was being emitted from the sphere now, reflecting off what looked to be tiny polished stones that had been concealed within the dome's structure. The result of this optical interaction was a brilliant hologram that filled the entire space, surrounding the three awestruck observers, so that it appeared that they themselves were a part of the projection.

"Is it a galaxy?" whispered Natasha, moving her hands through the illusion.

"It's *our* galaxy, by the looks of it," said Gabriel, his eyes wide with wonder.

The projection was a perfectly scaled replica; an exact shimmering recreation of the Milky Way in all its entirety. What was more, it appeared to be in motion, its bright core and many arms orbiting a fist-sized, black sphere at its centre. It was being projected directly above the astrolabe itself. Natasha was the first to notice it.

"What is that?" she asked, pointing to it.

"It's what astronomers would call a super-massive black hole," said Gabriel, pushing back his messy hair as he studied the thing. "It sits at the centre of our galaxy, and has the density of about a trillion stars."

The old gypsy woman stared into the black hole.

"The ancient astronomers of Sumer knew more of this black hole than all our scientists combined," she said. "Watch and see all their fears confirmed."

"What do you mean, Senora?" asked Natasha. "What fears?"

In answer to her question, the old woman pointed to an arm of the galaxy. There was a magnified section there, glowing within its own shimmering sphere.

"That is our solar system," said the gypsy. "Draw closer to it so that you can better see its precarious position."

Gabriel and Natasha did as they were told, wading past countless stars and nebulas to arrive at an inconspicuous location within one of the galaxy's many arms.

"I see nothing unusual about its position," said Gabriel. "Are you sure you got your information right?"

"You must lower your line of vision until it aligns with the galactic plane," said the gypsy.

"Galactic plane?" asked Natasha.

Gabriel looked back at the old woman before answering Natasha's question.

"The galactic plane lies along the galaxy's equator," he explained. "As a result of their overwhelming mass, super-massive black holes spin at unbelievably high rates. Because of this, their projected gravitational field isn't spherical anymore. Instead, it gets flattened out and forms a massive spinning disc; kind of like a pancake. Ours is a hundred-thousand light years in diameter, but only a few centimeters thick."

Gabriel bent his knees until his line of vision had aligned with the galaxy's equator. Natasha followed his example. To their utter surprise, the hologram's light vanished completely as their eyes passed through the thin disc of the galactic plane, only to return to its original splendor as their line of vision emerged from its underside.

"Why is this happening?" asked Natasha, lowering and raising her line of vision above and below the galactic plane.

"The gravitational field is just like the black hole," said Gabriel, doing the same. "It sucks up all the light that comes into contact with it."

"To the ancients it was known as the *Dark Rift*," said the old gypsy. "Our solar system will soon pass into it."

Gabriel and Natasha could see that the old woman was not mistaken. In the holographic projection, the magnified section that contained the earth's solar system was clearly moving closer and closer to the galactic plane.

"But what does this mean?" asked Natasha, looking at the old woman.

"It means the end of an age, my child," she said, walking towards them.

"You said that the ancients feared this," asked Natasha, "Why?"

Gabriel was the first to answer.

"Because every time our solar system passes through the galactic plane, the sun and the planets are exposed to massive magnetic and gravitational fields. Getting close to it would be devastating. Crossing it would be catastrophic."

Natasha considered the implications.

"So all the strange weather we have been experiencing for the last decade; all the earthquakes and tsunamis and tornados and hurricanes, they are all being caused by our proximity to this gravitational field?"

"Yes," said Gabriel with a shrug. "If this hologram is accurate. According to astronomers, our solar system travels in a kind of wave pattern as it moves along its orbit. It dips up and down through the galactic plane every fifty-million years or so. Every time this happens, our north and south poles shift in position."

"And how do they know this?"

"Core samples, mostly," said Gabriel. "They take them in Antarctica, and use them to study the magnetic alignment of the molecules frozen into the ice. Every fifty-million years they see massive and sudden changes recorded there. But that's not the only evidence. They also know that many of the places that are now arctic were once tropical, and vice versa. It would appear that the earth has not always spun on the same poles that it spins on now."

"The end of each age is marked by a great cataclysm," said the old woman, nodding in acceptance.

"But why all the destruction?" asked Natasha in horror. "What causes it?"

"The earth isn't a hard ball of rock like everybody thinks," said Gabriel. "It's a ball of liquefied magma covered in a thin crust of stone. It's so malleable that when it spins, it actually bulges at the equator. Shift the locations of the poles and it'll bulge in different places."

"And the oceans and tectonic plates will shift to fill in the gaps," whispered Natasha.

"A natural occurrence for the planet," said Gabriel, "but one that's pretty devastating for all us insects living on its surface."

Gabriel and Natasha watched as the old gypsy removed the Cube from the astrolabe, the hologram vanishing as suddenly as it had appeared.

"We pass through the Dark Rift on the twenty-first day of this month," she said, relighting the candelabra. "The cataclysm is unavoidable, but its catastrophic effects on both the earth and humanity can be mitigated, if you fulfill your purpose."

"What purpose do we have to fulfill?" asked Gabriel, drawing closer to the old woman.

"You must awaken humanity to a true knowledge of itself."

"How are we supposed to do that?" snapped Gabriel, frustrated.

The gypsy woman scowled back at him.

"You must return the Cube to the great *Labyrinth of Sarras*."

Gabriel moved to say something, but the old gypsy silenced him with an upraised hand.

"You must pass through the *Seven Portals*, and open the *Seven Seals of Gnosis* to the world. In doing these things, you will save us from perpetual darkness."

Gabriel exchanged a look with Natasha. If it were not for what they had just seen, they would have thought this old woman a lunatic, but given the oddity of everything that was coming to pass around them, her words seemed impossibly valid.

"But how can you expect us to accomplish any of this?" asked Gabriel. "The labyrinth could be anywhere in those mountains, and besides, what possible difference could our efforts make? This is a geological phenomenon. It's unstoppable."

"The passing of our planet through the Dark Rift will affect changes on both physical and metaphysical levels. It will affect matter, but it will also affect consciousness."

"How so?" asked Gabriel.

"Every mind will be cast into darkness and confusion," said the gypsy with a frown. "Humanity's collective consciousness will come under great duress. We are in dire circumstances, my children. Over countless millennia we have unwittingly allowed the forces of darkness to penetrate into our souls. These forces have twisted and distorted the truth about life and death. They have isolated us from one another, and more importantly, from ourselves."

The old gypsy woman looked into the flames of the candelabra.

"This coming age will mark the passing of yet another galactic year. It will be the first anniversary of the complete annihilation of our distant ancestors. If you fail in your mission, humanity will follow in their footsteps. Our souls will be drawn into the lower spheres of Hades, and reside there for aeons to come."

"Wait a minute," said Gabriel, turning to face the old woman. "It takes two-hundred and fifty-million years to complete a galactic year. Are you suggesting that there were people on the earth back then?"

"The beings that existed then were not like us," she said, "but their society was as fully developed as our own."

"And what happened to them?" asked Natasha.

"They passed through the Rift in a state of spiritual darkness, and the Great Cataclysm ensued."

Natasha looked at Gabriel to find that he was shaking his head incredulously.

"What is wrong?" she asked. "What are you thinking?"

"Only that two-hundred and fifty-million years ago was when the Permian–Triassic extinction event occurred. It's also referred to by geologists as P-Tr, or *The Great Dying*."

Gabriel began to pace back and forth.

"P-Tr was the mother of all extinction events," he continued. "It makes the one that wiped out the dinosaurs sixty-five million years ago look like a terrestrial hiccup. When P-Tr occurred, ninety-six percent of all marine life was completely decimated, along with eighty percent of all the terrestrial vertebrate species. Even most of the insects were wiped out, and that never happens. It never occurred to me before, but P-Tr occurred around the time of our galaxy's nineteenth birthday."

Natasha frowned and bit her lip.

"And this galactic year we turn twenty?"

"Astrophysicists would say, yes, give or take a few thousand years," said Gabriel. "But if what Señora Blavatsky says is true, we'll turn twenty when we pass through the galactic plane, five days from now."

"This is our last chance to turn the direction of the spiritual spheres," said the old gypsy. "The Great Cataclysm is once again upon us. Succeed in returning the Cube to its original resting place before the crossing is made, and humanity will be preserved. Pass through the *Seals of Gnosis*, and the knowledge held within them will be released unto mankind. Only then will the balance of our universe be tipped in favour of the Light. Our collective mind will then manifest itself in a new world of peace and societal evolution. If you fail, all will be lost."

"Release the Gnosis from the Seals?" asked Gabriel, perplexed. "How are we supposed to do that? You must forgive us, Señora, but we don't know anything about this artifact."

"And even if we did know," said Natasha, "how could it be done? The world cannot change in less than one week."

The gypsy sat down in one the leather wingchairs.

"To transcend the Cube is to see it in all things."

Gabriel and Natasha looked down at her, their eyes filled with confusion.

"You must be in Truth," she explained, nodding slowly, "but you must also be in Love. Once you have fully merged, the exact location of the lost Book of Khalifah will be revealed to you. It is imperative that you find this codex. Within it are the six translations needed to unlock the Cube's mysteries."

"You said *fully merged*, Señora," said Gabriel, looking over at Natasha. "What does that mean?"

"You were both demonically possessed when you were infants. Did you know this?"

Gabriel and Natasha nodded slowly.

"And do you know the origin of your scars?"

"Yes, we do," said Gabriel uncomfortably.

The gypsy woman smiled darkly and continued.

"Before they were exorcised, the fourteen Emissaries infected both of you with demonic parasites," she said. "They infect you still. They work to keep you apart. Find these entities. Bring them into the light of awareness. They will dissolve, and you will merge."

"How do we find them?" asked Natasha, her eyes glassy with concern.

"You must look within, my child," she said with a smile. "They will be hiding where you least want to look. They will be shrouded in your fear."

The gypsy rose to her feet.

"You must begin your search for the Book of Khalifah at once. You must find the Labyrinth and complete your mission."

Natasha sat down in a chair next to where the old woman had been sitting. Gabriel remained standing. He had packed away the Cube and was examining the astrolabe again.

"We will do this," he said solemnly. "But not before I fix the damage I've done."

"What are you saying, child?" said the old woman, turning to face him. "Of what damage do you speak?"

"Because of my efforts to retrieve the Cube, innocent people are being held prisoner by a very bad man. Their lives are in danger. I'm not doing anything until they're safe."

The old gypsy came up to him, a sense of urgency filling her.

"Gabriel Parker," she said firmly. "You will leave all else aside and fulfill your destiny! You know very well there is not enough time!"

Gabriel turned to look at the old woman just in time to feel her grasp his wrist. Her green eyes seemed to him like churning waters, and he was instantly drawn into their emerald depths. The room around him was suddenly transforming, a cataclysmic wasteland of oblivion and destruction materializing before his eyes. Stumbling amongst the devastation could be seen throngs of twisted, corpse-like figures. Their eyes were lifeless, their mutilated bodies riddled with festering wounds. By some unknown power the gypsy woman had filled his mind with a vision of the despair that would befall humanity should he and Natasha fail. Gabriel tried desperately to break from the enchantment. He had somehow been carried into the depths of hell.

"There will be time for everything, Señora," came Natasha's voice, and Gabriel was immediately released from the vision, opening his eyes to see Natasha smiling up at him.

She had gently taken hold of the old woman's hands.

"But the Dark Rift approaches..." pleaded the gypsy, only to grow suddenly calm.

She took a deep breath and smiled, seating herself next to Natasha.

"Of course, my child," she said, patting her hand. "Your wisdom is true."

Gabriel looked gratefully at Natasha. She had pulled him from a horrible place, but it had nonetheless left its mark on him. The gypsy's dark future would need to be avoided at all costs, and an almost desperate sense of urgency filled him now. Perhaps there would be time for everything, but they certainly had no time to waste. Gibraltar was still hours away, and they had yet to make their way to Nasrallah's castle, and free the prisoners.

"Come on," he said to Natasha, shouldering his pack. "We're leaving right now."

CHAPTER 45

Somewhere over the Mediterranean Sea.

Christian opened his eyes to find the doctor looking down at him. He was lying on the sofa, the luxurious interior of the jet's passenger compartment reminding him of where he was.

"What happened?" he asked.

"I had you in a hypnotic trance, Christian," said Dr. Bennington, his gentle smile doing nothing to mask the concern in his eyes.

Christian's memory came flooding back to him. He rubbed his face and sat up.

"What did you learn about the Cube?"

Bennington sat down opposite Christian and scribbled some notes onto a pad of paper. Before the induction, Christian had told him everything that had transpired up to that point; beginning with the death of his father, and culminating with the murder of the Nautonnier. Bennington had asked many questions, and Christian had answered them all, insisting finally that he be put under a hypnotic trance. He wanted to uncover the meaning behind his father's incessant whispers, and to clarify his own role in the events that were transpiring. He had warned Bennington to conceal nothing, reminding him that the entire induction would be recorded on the jet's security system.

"Well?" asked Christian.

Bennington looked up from his notepad.

"It is important that we deal with this calmly and methodically," he said. "You are a very troubled individual."

Christian rose to his feet, snatching the notebook from the doctor's hands.

"I'd say that's pretty bloody obvious, Doctor. Why don't you tell me something I don't know?"

Christian flipped through the pages, trying to decipher Bennington's illegible script.

"What did you learn about the Cube?" he asked, flinging the book back at the doctor.

"You told me a lot, Christian. But we must be careful. You are not ready to know many of these things yet."

Christian's face grew dark and menacing.

"What did you learn?"

Bennington sat back in his chair, thinking of his wife. There was nothing he could do but comply. He would have to tell Christian everything. He could not afford to take any risks.

"You repeatedly referred to an ongoing battle between good and evil. You spoke of Jesus Christ and Lucifer as being the personifications of the two opposing sides."

"And I'm on Lucifer's side."

"Yes," said Bennington. "Your task, as you described it to me, is to lay waste to the world. When this is done, you are to rebuild it in a way that removes all civil liberties and spiritual pursuits. In essence, you believe that your purpose here is to make the earth as much like hell as possible."

"And why am I supposed to do this?"

Bennington paused before answering.

"You believe that Lucifer demands it of you, Christian. That you are to do whatever is needed to prevent humanity from rising to its next level of societal evolution."

"Why?"

"You claim that it is the only way that our souls can be stopped from escaping into the higher realms."

Christian frowned in confusion.

"And why doesn't Lucifer just let the souls go? What does he care?"

"Because if he lets them go, he loses power," said Bennington. "An overlord is only as powerful as those he holds beneath him. Take away his subjects, and a tyrant becomes nothing. This, you said, is why kings and emperors live in constant fear. Lucifer is no exception."

Christian's eyes seemed to light up with understanding.

"I see," he said, crossing his arms over his chest. "Please, continue."

"You told me that many souls had already ascended since Jesus Christ opened the way two-thousand years ago," said Bennington, raising an eyebrow. "Despite Lucifer's continuous attempts to stop them from doing so. You said that these ascended souls no longer require to be incarnated again and again; that they have used Earth for the purpose it was created, and have purified themselves enough that they can now live in the higher realms. From there, you said, they will assist other souls incarnating on earth, and help them to ascend as well."

"Is that so?" said Christian quietly.

A deep understanding was slowly penetrating him now, and it seemed to him that it came from those same churning mists that the Zurvanites had shown to him the previous day.

Bennington studied his patient's face with concern. It was as though a hollow darkness had come over it. Something in Christian was transforming before his eyes.

"You claimed that humanity is still very much bound to Lucifer," he continued, "but that there is something that threatens to change this relationship."

Christian looked intently at the doctor.

"Yes," he said. "What is it?"

"A mysterious, cube-shaped artifact," said Bennington, holding Christian's gaze.

"Finally!" he exclaimed, beginning to pace excitedly. "The Cube! What is it? Who made it?"

"By some it is called the *Cube of Knowledge*," said the doctor, "by others, the *Cube of Compostela*. You said that it is an artifact that is ancient beyond reckoning. You asserted that humanity only requires a consolidated push in order to move up to the next level of societal evolution, and that the Cube is capable of giving us this push."

"I don't understand," said Christian, looking intently at the doctor. "How will the Cube do that?"

Bennington held his gaze.

"You were not sure, Christian," he said. "You claimed that it is not so much a question of what the Cube does, but what humanity does with it. You explained that the Cube is a tool of sorts; a key, or a map, if you will. You admitted that you know very little about this artifact."

Bennington stood up and put a hand on Christian's shoulder.

"Do not lose sight of the metaphorical meanings behind your delusions, Christian. The Cube would appear to be a container of knowledge, and knowledge is always symbolic of freedom."

"I see," said Christian, nodding. "And this is why the Cube must be destroyed."

"The Cube does not exist, Christian," said Bennington. "It is a creation of your subconscious mind. What is important to note is that you have endowed your creation with the capacity to dissolve all fear, and to liberate humanity. This is a very positive construct."

"First of all, Doctor," said Christian, turning away, "the Cube does exist. It's very real, and so are the stories I've told you. Secondly, I have no interest in dissolving fear. Fear is what we use to control people; to make them do what we want them to do. I have no interest in liberating the masses. That would be pointless and stupid. How could any wealth be generated without the masses to do the work?"

A blank expression filled Christian's face.

"All power is based in fear," he uttered by rote. "If fear in the masses were ever lost, everything we have worked so hard to build would be destroyed. Fear must be maintained at all costs."

"But can you not see that those are not your own words, Christian?" pleaded the doctor. "Can you not see that you were programmed to say them? I know that this all seems very real to you, but you must believe me when I tell you that it is all in your mind. It is myth. If you make the effort to understand the stories, you will be able to make sense of them, and find peace."

"What else did you learn, Doctor," said Christian, turning to face Bennington. "You will tell me everything."

Bennington let himself fall into his armchair, defeated.

"You told me that your brother and sister conceived a hermaphrodite child so that an ancient prophecy might be fulfilled. You said that this child was born so that a portal to hell might be opened, and a great host of demons be unleashed onto the world. You told me that your brother would accomplish this by returning the corpse of his son to the place of its conception, where he would divide it into fourteen pieces, just as the Egyptian god Set had done to his brother Horus."

"I see," said Christian, squinting ever so slightly. "I remember now. There is a tremendous symbolic meaning behind this division, Doctor."

He looked down at Bennington, his arms hanging limply at his sides.

"Fragmentation is Lucifer's way."

As Christian spoke these words, a dark roll of thunder sounded ominously outside the plane. With this last piece of information, it was as if a curtain had been drawn aside for Christian, and all the knowledge of which he had only previously glimpsed, was at last made fully available to him. The jet banked and began its descent into Jerusalem.

"What are you going to do, Christian?" asked Bennington, his voice fearful and unsteady. "Surly you will not act on these mythical constructs."

"I will do what I was born to do, Doctor," said Christian, already becoming lost in his thoughts. "I feel I am finally ready to begin."

Here ends
Book I - The Dark Rift.
The Last Artifact Trilogy continues with:
Book II - The Lost Labyrinth.

Gilliam Ness is a writer and visual artist.
For information on existing and upcoming works please visit
www.gilliamness.com

Milton Keynes UK
Ingram Content Group UK Ltd.
UKHW010853040923
428018UK00004B/499